Town End Farm
Croughton.

THE CONSUL AT SUNSET

THE CONSUL AT SUNSET

GERALD HANLEY

THE REPRINT SOCIETY LONDON

FIRST PUBLISHED 1951
THIS EDITION PUBLISHED BY THE REPRINT SOCIETY LTD.
BY ARRANGEMENT WITH WM. COLLINS SONS & CO. LTD.
1952

PRINTED IN GREAT BRITAIN BY
WILLIAM CLOWES AND SONS, LIMITED, LONDON AND BECCLES

To my wife, Asha

CHAPTER ONE

"IT'S not that there is anything wrong with Turnbull," said Colonel Casey. "It's just—how can I describe it—well, he's not quite one of *us*, if you know what I mean. Too long in the ranks, too long in Palestine and places like that. Everybody knows that a commission these days is anybody's present. It's unfortunate, though, that such easily won commissions are not presented only to officers who are definitely going into an active theatre, where it doesn't matter these days whether an officer is one of us or not. He just leads men, gets killed, decorated, wounded and so on. But in a job like this, it really requires gentlemen. It takes gentlemen to deal with savages, or natives anywhere for that matter. And a gentleman is becoming a rare thing."

It was a world which now had no time for gentlemen and gentlemen had little time for the world they were now living in. Buggins was in power in many places to-day. But to get back to Turnbull. He was not a bad chap, mind you. Take him carefully and he'd eat out of your hand. Like all these regular rankers, he admired a gentleman, and it came out when the time arrived.

"You have no need to worry there, Sole, I can assure you. You've been frank with me and I appreciate it. So I am being frank with you. You are a junior officer and I am discussing an officer of your own rank with you, which normally would be wrong. But you are not just a soldier now, you are an administrative officer lent from the army. You have had Colonial experience as I have. Turnbull is only a soldier and his job is to assist the civil power. Do not forget that—

7

assist the civil power—and *we* are the civil power. His troops are there for your use."

Turnbull was a bit difficult, a bit hidebound by regulations and too much knowledge of duties and rights. But firm handling by a gentleman of experience could always get the best out of these chaps. Friendliness? Yes. There was no harm in being friendly, but it had to be made clear that he, Sole, was in charge of the area to which he was now going. Sole would be in charge of all the transport. He would be responsible for the signal station. The radio would be his. If Turnbull wanted to listen to the radio he could always go to Sole's house. True, the transport and the radio were bones of contention between the army and the political officer, but that was the way it was, and that was all about it.

As for the tribal chiefs, there would be no nonsense. They came under Sole. Turnbull's duties were to supply guards and patrols. In the event of trouble, he would act under the orders of Captain Sole. That was quite clear and anyway Turnbull would know it. Turnbull, it could be relied upon, knew where his duties began and ended, and it was important that Sole should be quite certain of his too, for if you gave these fellows an inch they took the lot. Firmness and friendliness. Tact and goodwill. There was, as we all know, some feeling between the army and the political officers. It was the same on the Indian North-west Frontier and all over Africa. Well, one had been a soldier, too, for a time anyway, but if an officer had brains he went into the political service. In war-time it was different. Any Tom, Dick or Harry could carry a rank on his shoulders and lead a platoon. But it took a gentleman to administer savages and that was being forgotten in Whitehall and Downing Street.

"Some of the temporary officers now giving orders to the savages in some of the occupied enemy territories would not in peace-time have been allowed to join the bloody army as privates," said the Colonel. He knew he had said that many times before, and he must plead to be forgiven if he repeated himself, but by God it was true. "I've seen wogs who are better than some of the so-called officers we have to put up with nowadays," said the Colonel, and he pressed Captain Sole to have another drink.

Outside the wind was lonely again. It moaned, seizing swirls of sand and spraying it against the latticed windows of the fort. Sole thought of the thousands of miles of desolation outside, the cold desert which to-morrow would turn again into a shudder of blinding sunglare, the stars which would wink out one by one in the damp grey dawn. He shivered and poured some filtered water into the cheap brandy in his glass. It was the best the Colonel could do. Drink was getting scarcer. They both knew the agony of a night without drink. It was like an ache somewhere within the body, like an aching tooth. You took what you could get. The brandy brought the familiar glow to the solar plexus, or was it to the soul? It was as though the soul warmed up, like a silent engine. Drink, reflected Captain Sole, was necessary in certain conditions of life, especially in this lost desert where one got to know too much about one's self. In the streets of the city, or the clubs of the Colonies, on ships and in hotels, it was as though much or most of the trash and dross within himself was absorbed and lost in the endless conversations, chats, pursuits of women, worries over bills or in the procession of meals, half-registered sensations, games of golf. But here, hundreds of nights alone, or with one other officer, gave one the terrible knowledge of self. Not wisdom. For Sole, it was a slight nausea, the sick realisation that there was no point in being alive. It was the distractions of the busy life, he was certain, that sustained the belief that life was a boon, was good, and had a point. Curious that he had to come here in order to learn it. To sit for hours at night with a forgotten book on your knee, a glass of brandy in your hand, watching the ants swarm on to a piece of biscuit and laboriously convey it to their nest. Not really seeing this, but knowing of it, while the film in the mind raced through the store-room of memory, wonder, speculation on the mystery.

He could hear the Colonel's voice and he nodded and looked wise while not listening, after the fashion of those who have done this many times, who have lived too long with a talker.

He had never met Turnbull : only knew of him, or perhaps had seen him vaguely for a moment in the Officers' Club at Korma, a thousand miles to the south-east with its growing files, its starched uniforms and its conquered, bored, almost demoralised Italians. God, the Italians, they smoked their misery away in cigarettes, drank it away in endless small cups of coffee, sitting in their worn white suits, watching the British crumble from an army into a uniformed club.

" *E cosi la vita*," they said and smiled. " The British will drink even more the longer they stay here in this sand, among these mongrel savages, the accursed." For the Italians hated the *indigeni* who had seen them conquered after a time of power ; who were arrogant, cruel, avaricious and vain. Given to everlasting quarrels among themselves, they were highly strung and treacherous, though stoic in suffering or pain. But the Italians would never forgive them for the mutinies in the native regiments when the British began their advance. They murdered their officers and turned, armed with modern weapons, to slay their own people, nomads who lived on the milk of camels and the flesh of goats. The Italians, good-natured and cynical, waited for the day when they would wield power here again. Power and a whip.

Sole had many Italian friends with whom he had argued for hours. He wanted them to be reasonable about this matter ; to see the two sides. There were three kind of savages in the world. These natives, the peoples of Europe, and the Americans. It was only a question of how you savaged your neighbour. The Italians would not agree that the Italian people were savages. And this seeing of reason, these two sides of the question : it was an English disease, no, *signor*, it was an English luxury. " When you have seen what these natives can do, you cannot flog them with a whip of reason, *signor*." The English had no natives like them in their colonies. These were savages, fanatical Moslems who did not even read, let alone understand the Quran. Let the English think as they wished, but let them not meddle too much with these savages who would one day, unbalanced by the English weakness and lack of disciplinary control, turn on them all, Italian and British, and really show what savages could do.

" *Signor*, I have seen things——" said a grey-headed ex-officer, " things you have not seen. Here. In this country."

Everybody had seen too much. The continual competition of suffering between men and men. Always there was someone who could claim to have seen more suffering than others or to have done more great things, had more opportunities, known more women, held more drink. But the older one got, Sole reflected, the more one could forgive, the more doubt grew in one's heart about what was right and wrong, about what was unforgivable. Or was it that this doubt was growing in all men in this terrible and merciless century ? The century that looked after your teeth and liver, gave the germs no rest, stole pain from the body, but which gnawed like a rat at the mind and heart. A big, clean, sterile, silent rat, he thought, with pink antiseptic nostrils and large quiet vacant eyes, mad, with the madness of reason.

The Colonel was talking about when he was a young man. He was a man who had been accustomed to taking orders all his life until the war elevated him to a position of authority, yet he had that gift of expecting service and efficiency from all his subordinates and getting it, while doing little himself save reading books about China, a country he had never visited but of which he had dreamed since boyhood.

" We never get what we want," was his favourite phrase before refusing a request for leave, transfer, petrol or promotion from one of his underlings. Though indolent, he had a live and active mind and the stupid courage of convictions which had caused him to insult his friends and lose many of them. He knew his faults, but had given up trying to correct them. He had once accused a great friend of stealing two books from his house, and was surprised when his friend was angered. " But, my dear chap, I know you wanted the books. You once asked me to sell them to you. Why shouldn't you steal them ? Everybody steals. I've stolen many books in my time "—he had laughed then—" but never was caught, of course."

" So you think I stole them, after my denial ? " his friend had said.

In the silence of midnight they had faced each other over the two hurricane lamps and the nearly empty brandy bottle, the trays of crushed cigarette ends, the grubby limp copies of the *Tatler*.

" I don't know," the Colonel had said at last. " And I don't care either." And he did not. But his friend had walked straight to his own quarters and they had never spoken again. The Colonel, then a lieutenant of thirty, had never missed him, had gone on with his own life, aching for China and trying to write reasonably affectionate letters to his father, who had forced him into the army. He had wanted to enter a business house in China, but his father had refused this. Often the Colonel quoted his father, after the fashion of many men who have disliked or hated their fathers, but have grown to admire them as time dims the memory of obstacles cast into the fierce, youthful path. The sense of failure which is in most men was in the Colonel's heart too, but he had hated the army and the organisational machine since first he had seen the officers' mess as a new subaltern. The chasm between that mess and China had never narrowed. Of his dislike of the service he had told no one, not even when drunk, not even his wife, whom he had left after six months. When he was alone with a glass of brandy in his hand, he knew he was with the real self. The one who had not done very well for himself, who was considered to be somewhat erratic, but courageous. He seldom drank before sundown, and then he would drink until satisfied. Satisfaction was when he felt warmer inside, when his mind worked faster, when he could argue without failure, when he felt that failure did not matter anyway. There was a private illumination that took place in his mind and heart then, when he saw things as he wished them to be. He was well liked, but was seldom asked for advice, for he was always ready to give it, in floods of words, remembrances, examples. One thing, though, the junior officers would say, and it was saying a lot, he would always back you up. A lazy old devil, crafty, but he'd back you up if anything went wrong.

He did not mind, for instance, if his officers kept native women, providing that they were never seen. He knew that men were, after all, only human beings. To expect a man to do without women, for a year in the desert, was asking too much, if you asked the Colonel. But they must never be seen.

Now, at fifty-nine, he imagined that he had grown more tranquil, wanted fewer things, was more resigned to the failure he saw within himself. He could never quite believe in this failure, but it was a fact that he had not done well. Anyway, he would ask himself after the fourth brandy, what the hell is failure, anyway? And what is success? A good and loving wife and children? The directorship of a company, a yacht and a costly woman? To be a Chinese scholar? Or to be a fifty-nine-year-old colonel whom nobody hated, sitting in a desert with a good collection of books and a case of brandy? And after the fifth brandy who the hell would care anyway? God? Now there was something to think about, but better to push that thought out of sight. The thought about God was like the white scut of a rabbit disappearing into dusk.

"Now," he said to Sole, "it's a matter of files. Once the filing system is working, no chief, no fortune-seeker, no holy man, no tribal lawyer can come into your office when you're new on the station and spin you a cock-and-bull story about what the last officer promised them. It's all in the files. Every agreement about camel grazing, every dispute over a water-hole, every reported killing, every case of cheating by chiefs, by mullahs : they're all in the files. It is the filing system which runs the country—indeed, the Empire. The Empire is a filing system. Every agreement ever made should be in the files, with signatures—or thumb-prints. They can't get past it. They are defeated. I tell you it's agony for them to see you reach for the file. For they know it is all in there and that their lies will avail them nothing."

The Colonel was now drunk after his fashion. He knew when he was drunk by the sensation of not caring whether he was fifty-nine or twenty. Life appeared endless and he was filled with a power, an enthusiasm, not for life, but for the things one hated in it. Like these natives. They looked effeminate, but they were demons. They were wolves. They sometimes seemed happy and childish, but they were full of schemes. They said *Hamdul'illah*, but they watched you for that small chink, that crack in the armour, that gap in the filing system, or that slight lack of knowledge concerning some tribal custom. And when they found it, they were in, through the crack, like thirsting bugs. They would argue all day and intrigue all night. Cruel and undisciplined, for they lived as nomads do, ready to die of thirst or spears at twelve or fifty, they had no mercy, for their God showed them little; though Allah, the beneficent, the most merciful, they worshipped through the Quran, which they did not understand. No, the Colonel hated them, though he never showed them this. They liked to be cunning, and so was the Colonel. Let them wait. They could wait outside his office for days, were they too impatient. Chiefs could stand before his desk and not sit, had they not shown their willingness to co-operate. You had to prevent these people from killing each other. "That is why we are here," said the Colonel to the bemused Sole. "To stop them killing each other. They love to kill each other, to mutilate, to destroy. Progress, education, agriculture, it can, it must, all wait. These people are murderous religious maniacs and kindness to them is a matter of finding and hurting the men who would lead them on a killing raid." The Italians were queer. They seemed to have been frightened of these natives, yet they had done good things with them in many cases. But sometimes they fell into panic and did stupid things. But the Italians were always liable to panic when human beings were not like Italians. "You see, Sole," the Colonel continued, "we, the British, have still a message to deliver to all these people, whether they are these savage bastards who are out there "—he pointed towards the desert—" or the Malays, the Indians, the Africans, and the millions of others who live under our flag. But we are becoming afraid to rule, and when that happens the natives can smell it, as a horse smells a man's fear. And what does the horse do? He chucks you off. He kicks you and goes his own way."

The Colonel's voice was sad, yet there was anger in it. He clenched his thin, brown fist. Sole saw the long fair hairs on it glinting in the yellow light of the hurricane lamp.

"Buggins did it. It was Buggins who, once he got some power, thought he understood things which his dim little mind was never meant to even consider. The bloody little Labour M.P.s, Bill this and Sam that, with their mouthings about the exploitation of the native peoples. What do they know about the work we've done. About the five years it might take to win over an African chief to the idea of giving up some barbarous and revolting custom, or about the other things in India. About roads, railways, hospitals, schools, hygiene. But Buggins has no use for that. It was done by gentlemen so it is no good. Buggins hates the gentlemen because the gentlemen know the value of good things. Buggins is trying to destroy the good things we have done." Through his clenched teeth, he said, "God, how I loathe and detest Buggins when he's out of his place."

He poured out some more brandy, offered the bottle to Sole, who said, "Thanks, sir," and splashed more than usual into his glass. Let the old boy talk on and on. An occasional yes and no would do to keep it going. Sole was thinking about women and he knew he was becoming drunk. As the alcohol seeped through the walls of the will, an aching began in him. No, it was not exactly an ache. It was a sort of hunger-sickness, a blending of desire to be loved with tenderness and a sexual anger which disgusted him. He no longer trusted his wife. He believed that she had not been faithful to him during the three years he had been overseas and separated from her. He really did not know why he required her to be faithful to him, he told himself, for he was tired of the eternal boring worm of love, sex, possession and jealousy. He had grown tired of it during his last leave with his wife. The voice in the night from the next bed saying, " Are you *sure* you *really* love me ? I can't seem to get *hold* of you. You seem to be escaping from me in some way. Yet you do all the things that a man in love with his wife should do. But there seems to be something missing. Like a stranger inside your face who has moved what I knew away."

On and on—the voice, a sweet voice coming from a body which had captivated him, but the words " I can't seem to get *hold* of you " were the key. She wanted to own him and to be loved day and night, to have this love explained to her. What it felt like, what it did to his mind and body, what it would be like if she died. She began to strangle his mind in 1939. He imagined that he did not really require a woman to live with and sleep with. He would have preferred a seasonal love, like the animals of the field and forest, and that the rest of his life could be free for living, unhazed by the smoke of desire, for Sole hated the body. He resented the voices of its appetites, its insistence on doing this or having that until the eyes saw the object described by this appetite as something desirable. If the object was a woman and he unleashed the hound of the body, then it all ended with ash in the heart, for the woman wanted things to last. The monkey in him could not argue with the bird of love in the woman's heart. Woman complicated things. What was an act of terrible necessity for a man was a spiritual communion for the woman. Her body was to be a prison for the man whose appetite never really rested, but lurked unseen on the edge of the mind's forests, waiting. Sometimes it whimpered. Sometimes it roared, but Sole, who had thought on these things for so long during his desert wanderings, never ceased to resent the goad of this disgusting necessity. This disgusting necessity—that was what it was. Though one could deny it, there was no escaping from that fact. It was as though the personality, the body and the soul, all the twisted skeins of goodness and badness that made a man, shouted for reproduction, and when denied, moaned with sadness inside. Then again it would leap angrily into the forefront of the mind. Perhaps it was because Elizabeth would have no children that this desire was so persistent, for Sole had wanted children.

But Elizabeth was afraid of children and the ugliness and pain which she imagined brought them into the world. She had begged him with tears in her eyes not to ask her to have a child, to wait and see if she could get over it. Sole had recoiled from her, feeling as though he were some dangerous and menacing beast. He remembered shuddering and the terrible loneliness he had felt in that moment. Then the anger, like a wave of fire, so that he wished to strike her. It was as if she had given him deadly insult. So she was a coward. Or secretly she was revolted by him and by all men, but was part conquered by the love she felt for him. Or she was in love with her body, as he was. And he resented his slavery to this body.

Now he gripped his glass and the Colonel's voice was saying " That was when I was twenty, though "—through the mist—" I wouldn't do it again." The long slim legs, brown and strong in the summer, the breasts which melted his heart when he saw them, the large eyes which sometimes had lit like soft lamps of greyish fire. In his mind he saw her, and pain came, a queer pain behind the ribs which he had felt in certain moments with her, watching her eat. Or when she turned to speak to him and laugh, or to see her stroke a cat and whisper to him. These things had torn him with the strange pain which only a woman could bring, and they hurt him now so that had she appeared before him he would have run to her and pressed his head against her body, and she would have held it tightly against her, murmuring the wonderful, tragic gibberish of love. He was lost in it for some moments, saying things to her.

His eyes widened and his lips were drawn back slightly from his large teeth, as if he were hurt. Then he drained the glass, feeling the brandy pour like a warm comforting stream into him. He remembered her cat-heart. He had loved her so much that the feeling of hatred and despair had come easily to him. You can never have anybody, he thought. No, never, never, never can you have anybody inside you, possessed, safe, secure. The demon always comes. He believed it now.

The Colonel banged the table. " You know as well as I do, Sole, that there may be trouble up in the Ashang country. Those savages are getting plenty of arms, God knows where from. We have a few bits of information but not enough. The Italian native non-commissioned officers who went back to their tribes after the Italian retreat will lead them if there is trouble. Camels and women and adventure. The tribesmen will follow their leaders for these things." The Colonel took a gulp of brandy. " You'll have to watch them carefully, Sole," he continued. " Turnbull knows a few things, perhaps, but don't rely much on his intelligence. He's a ranker and like all rankers he's more likely to recommend the whip, or perhaps can advise on the finer points of a native woman, but not much more. He's there to help you in an emergency and you must impress that on him. Do you *know* Turnbull, by the way ? "

Sole looked at the Colonel across the lamp. He was a

handsome man, long-faced, with close-cropped white hair and hard grey eyes which now watched Sole's face with the intensity of near-intoxication. His face was very brown. He looked like a British colonel from an American film, thought Sole. Handsome and arrogant, yet humorous and reliable. How would it really be to serve under him ? He was friendly now. Would the next meeting in Sole's office, hundreds of miles to the north, be embarrassing because of this friendliness ? Sole detested confidences, lest the confider regret it later and become awkward on meeting, embarrassed or curt. His heart, like a castle, was full of guards against all these awkwardnesses which spoiled so much of life.

" No, sir," said Sole. " I don't know him. I have heard a good deal of him. He got the D.C.M. at Dunkirk. They say he did rather a good show."

" Possibly," said the Colonel. " But Dunkirk itself wasn't a good show from all accounts." He felt he had been unfair. " Turnbull's probably a very courageous but unimaginative chap. Commissioned in 1940. He was a sergeant-major with the—I forget what regiment. Probably a damn' good sergeant-major, but a little out of his depth now."

He paused and stared into his glass. " Now, I want to talk to you about Milton. You should be able to relieve him in three days from now, that's Saturday. That will give you Sunday, Monday and Tuesday to take over the station. He doesn't like Turnbull much. Says Turnbull interferes a little too much with politics and administration. From what Milton has told me, some of the chiefs like Turnbull. Apparently he speaks some Arabic. He served in Palestine for a long time. Turnbull is one of those chaps who knows all the rules, all his rights and so on. He shows a tendency to treat native troops as one would treat British soldiers—you know, always fighting for their rights ; jumps straight into Milton's office if any of Milton's irregulars and levies interfere, as he calls it, in the slightest way with his troops. He checks all the rations and kicks up a shine if Milton's men have made the slightest mistake in weighing them. He can be a bloody nuisance, from all accounts. But one thing Milton did say was that Turnbull's troops are almost model soldiers. He's a strict disciplinarian, though he goes too far in many ways in being friendly with them. Runs with them half-naked, plays football every evening with them, and so on. His troops seem to have been taught that they take orders only from him. They seem to resent political officers, and probably Turnbull has told them that Milton is not empowered to give them direct orders. You know Milton, don't you?" Sole nodded. There was something revolting about Milton. He was always trying to please everybody, always smiling and rubbing his hands, always agreeing with you until you had gone.

"Well, Milton," said the Colonel, "has had one or two difficulties lately, you know. You may have heard."

Now Sole became angry. One or two difficulties. Why not name them? Sole wished to say, "Oh, don't be so bloody mealy-mouthed," but the other was a colonel and a colonel cannot be mealy-mouthed to a captain. Sole could see the Colonel was becoming drunk and was in a good mood.

"I know, sir," he said, "that Milton's native tart has caused a lot of trouble in the station and that he is in debt because of her."

"You don't like Milton?" said the Colonel keenly.

But Sole was not to be drawn out. "I don't feel anything about him," he said.

Then the Colonel moved back to the other subject. "So you know about the woman, eh? Do they all know down in Korma?" His voice was anxious.

"They know, sir," said Sole, "as far as the Mufid river. Every tribe knows about her. Her name is Aurella. She was the mistress of an Italian general for years, and of a couple of other Italians as well. She has lived in Italy too. She is said to be one of the most troublesome bitches in the country."

Bitches. How would the Colonel take that? He watched him cautiously. But the Colonel leaped to the subject. Women.

Always the talk came round to women. Wives, tarts, bitches, old hags—call them what you like, the Colonel knew you couldn't do without them, and if you had none, then you talked about them.

" She's very attractive and quite highly trained, I'm told," said the Colonel. " Trained in every way." He leered.

The Colonel liked women in their place. He was not sure where their place was, but it was not with men, only with one man. Bars, clubs, messes were for men only. Women spoiled the atmosphere. A chap was standing at a bar with a group of men and they were talking. They could use blasphemy, foul language if they wished, for this was the atmosphere of men. But let one woman come into the group and what happened ? Well, for a start, several of the men would turn into peacocks. Their eyes sharpened as they watched the woman. Was she free, was there any hope ? And the atmosphere changed—a kind of electricity, human energy and the great power of the wanting, came into it. The men did not swear any more. Before they knew it they vied with each other for the honour, the honour of buying her a drink, of amusing her, of wanting her. The evening was ruined. Perhaps she was the kind of woman who wishes to be one of the chaps. To be treated like a man. None of this nonsense about being a lady. But to be treated like a man, sensibly, pay your way and all that. Well, these were the worst bitches of all, for they made a chap want to curse them, to tell them to get to hell out of here, which would be treating them like men. But you couldn't curse them, for you were still a gentle-man, and anyway you wouldn't give them the satisfaction of treating them like men. This accursed emancipation. How could it work when a woman was a victim of the moon and tides ? Each of them had a moon in her blood, under the hard face, the paint and the lipstick, the small veins in the neck and the other things which once would have made you desire them. But they were a bloody nuisance. No matter where you went, they were trying to get in. If you were in a club the women were fretting in the lounge. They wanted to get into the bar—or at least the room near the bar. They hated the men to be together, without women, for the bar was one place where women could not use their power. The power of the terrible tenderness. In the bar men thought clearly, their minds undisturbed by the agony which in the end destroyed the agonised. Better to be out here in the desert with brandy and a bit of power, and a handful of books and only the memory of women, only the memory. You could deal with the memory.

Sole yawned and dropped his head. The yearning had gone and he could feel the curious dying of his mind which meant exhaustion. He had been four and a half days on the journey from Korma. Burst tyres, heat, sand, bad water. Then a bath in the Colonel's house, and after that, fourteen hours of conversation, dreams and drink.

Suddenly the Colonel fell back into his canvas chair, as though someone had switched off his mind and muscles. His head fell to one side. Sole looked at him and felt pathos. Always a drunken man in an out-station, consumed with God knows what hunger or memories, looked sad when he fell back into his drunken sleep. That was the time when a woman could hold him and feel the quiet, stupefying tenderness which women feel for men they love.

Damp grey light was seeping through the lattices, and in the brief misery of this light Sole could see the grey, lumpy, and scabrous walls.

On the wall over the doorway leading to the Colonel's bedroom was a painting of a naked Italian soldier. He wore only a sun-helmet, and in his right hand he carried a rifle with fixed bayonet; in his left hand was a wine bottle, tilted so that the red wine was spilling like blood on to the yellow sand. The soldier had a shaggy, black beard, and he was laughing, showing good teeth. Printed underneath in large letters were the words, "Il Taverno degli Insabbiati," and "Qui Rido Io." Sole puzzled over the right translation of

" Insabbiati." " The Tavern of the Besanded." The Tavern of those Stuck in the Sand and—Here laugh I.

It must have been the bar of the garrison officers or non-commissioned officers. Stuck in the sand. Here laugh I. Most of the Italians had been frightened of these deserts and their fanatical peoples.

" Ah to hell with it," said Sole aloud. He got to his feet, scattering his thoughts. He took off his khaki shirt and felt the chill, grey light fall on his body. He was tired and sickly. The heavy smell of camels and their trodden dung came to his nostrils. Already there were people at the nearby well, drawing water, chanting and crying to their camels. For a hundred yards round the well, the top layer of ground would be composed of pounded camel droppings. When the sun came up, the bitter, smoky smell would penetrate the fort. The Colonel had talked about it last night. He said it was like living inside a camel.

The misery of these nomads' lives now overwhelmed him. All day, the great sun in a cloudless sky. Sand and rock for thousands of miles. Bitter water at scarce water-holes. Milk and a little meat, or failing this a handful of coarse grain, meal-paste and a mouthful of brackish water. Killing, stealing and litigation. Praying, and a callousness about all life. A contempt for pain and death, which shocked the European stranger, and a simplicity, a round-eyed, sometimes sharp-eyed simplicity, which could be terrifying, like that of a wicked, handsome child who is thoughtfully cruel to his pet animal, or to his sister. These people drew the dagger before they were insulted. They killed as other men eat, of necessity. A man's life was worth one hundred camels. A woman's life, even though she was only a woman, was worth fifty camels. A woman was just a woman, no more. Circumcised barbarically, she produced children, but in their conception could feel little. The horizon of pleasure, the anguish of physical love, was unknown territory for her. She could never discover these places. Her man beautiful to look at, but with the heart of a disappointed animal, held the dagger and the spear. He was near God. At thirty a woman was withered, sun-dried, beaten down by the desolation which surrounded her, but armed with the tongue of a shrew.

The misery of these people. Sole sat on the edge of his camp-bed. Good old Yassin. He forgot nothing. He had even laid out all the shaving material, the tin cup, a bottle of filtered water. The folded mosquito net. The slippers. Sole rasped his dark chin with unknowing fingers. He would bathe. He would shave. He lay back on the bed, only for a minute, he was so tired. Then sleep came up like a fast mist and enveloped him. His mouth opened and he sighed.

Outside the camels grumbled and the sun was climbing from the rim of the desert, evaporating the sparse dew along with the cold of dawn. The light, golden and soft, with that deceptive freshness of morning in lands where the sun is master by midday, was hardening. It soon became a fierce, white light, clinical and sterile, like the dazed desert on which it shone.

CHAPTER TWO

ABDI came in at half-past seven. He absorbed the scene quickly. Both officers had drunk all night and they would feel ill and irritable when he woke them. He moved quietly towards the table and extinguished the two hurricane lamps. Their soft yellow glow gone, the untidy, littered table took on a new ugliness. Spent matches littered the cement floor. Bottles, one on its side, mirrored the misery which Abdi felt on these mornings. When a strange or a new officer visited the fort, then the Colonel would talk all night and he would drink and drink. The Colonel's head was thrown right back, his mouth open, showing his small, yellowish teeth. One of the two bars of medal ribbons had come undone from its pin and it hung down across the now dulled brass button. Tenderly, Abdi fastened the ribbons. The Colonel did not stir. Abdi was proud of the Colonel's ribbons, for he had a lot of them. These young officers had none, though Turnbull *Effendi* at El Ashang had ribbons. He was an experienced soldier, stiff and hard and sometimes kind. Abdi knew, though, that Turnbull *Effendi* was not a gentleman like the Colonel. The Colonel had told him that Captain Turnbull had been an *askari*, an ordinary soldier, for years, but now was an officer because there was a war. A gentleman was like the Colonel, kind but hard, yet with a manner which showed that he was used to servants, used to things being done for him, and when he was angry with a servant, he was quiet and reasonable, only a touch of hardness in the voice, irritable, as a man would be with a machine which was not working properly.

Abdi went into the bathroom and took a bottle of tablets from the rusting shaving cabinet which stood over the wash-basin. He dropped two tablets into a tumbler and then crushed them with the end of the Colonel's toothbrush. He poured water over the tablets, measuring the amount with the out-stretched first two fingers of his left hand just as the Colonel had taught him over ten years before. The occasions for this mixture were far more rare than when Abdi had served with the Colonel in far Sierra Leone. In those days the Colonel had drunk with other officers every night, had fallen asleep in his chair. As he had risen in rank so had the night-long parties diminished in frequency. Now the Colonel was getting old. Abdi could see it in many ways. It took longer for the Colonel to recover nowadays, and he suffered from pains and twinges in the hips and back. He complained, and when Abdi told him, " *Effendi*, we are both growing old," the Colonel had worked himself into a rage.

" So you think I am old, do you ? " His eyes had widened in hurt surprise. " How am I old ? " Then he had cursed in English—the curses familiar to Abdi. " Christ damn it, explain yourself."

"We are old, *Effendi*," said Abdi gravely. "All men grow old. It is a time that comes to us all. I am much slower in my walk. I sit and think more. I am old. You too are old. You are now wise and grey-haired. All men listen to you for you have eaten many years."

Then the Colonel had dropped his head and stared out of the window at the glaring white sand. They were alone. "Yes, I know," the Colonel had said, "I am growing old. I am just an old man. I know you would sooner be with a young man. Why don't you say it and go? Why don't you go and leave me alone?" Hurting Abdi was one of the Colonel's favourite pastimes.

Abdi had clapped his hands. He remembered now the sorrow which had borne down upon his heart when the Colonel had spoken those words. "Oh, no, *Effendi*," he cried, "I never meant that. I do not wish to leave you. I only said we were both old." Then the Colonel sat up and crashed his fist on to the bamboo table before him so that bottles and glasses had fallen to the floor.

"Then don't say it again," he shouted. "Never say it to me again. You are deliberately trying to make me unhappy. You creep about here like a wounded cow, trying to show me how old you are, trying to wring my heart." His voice rose. "But you'll never do it. Nobody ever wrung my heart and *you'll* not do it now. I am not old. I may be grey. I may be wise, but I am *not* old. Do you hear? *You* are old because you spent your nights in the brothels of too many villages. You squandered your manhood. But did *I*? Did *I*?" He stared into Abdi's shrewd dark eyes.

"No, *Effendi*, you did not," said Abdi humbly.

"No, I did not, and I am still young and fit, and don't you forget it. Remember that those two young lieutenants had to sit down and rest last moon when we marched to Sadakh. I went on. And how many times did I use my water-bottle on that march?"

"Twice, *Effendi*," said Abdi, his eyes averted.

" And what did Captain Turnbull's troops say about it ? "

" They said that you were as strong and hard as a warrior."

" Right ! " said the Colonel. " Now you get out and get my bath ready." And Abdi had gone, but through the screen he had watched the Colonel press his hands to his hips and sigh, looking old and tired.

Gently now he woke the Colonel, shaking his right shoulder slowly. It was persuasive and guaranteed not to shock the sleeper, who might wake in an evil temper. The Colonel stirred and opened his eyes and the intelligence rushed swiftly into them. The grip on one's self, the self-possession, the face-saving, the coolness for every situation. He reached out and took the glass from Abdi, drained it, his mind working, piecing together the memories of the last talkative hours. Sole lay far away in the corner on his back, mouth open, one trousered leg wrapped in the mosquito net. The sun had turned the black hairs on his chest into a gold froth of light.

" Tea," the Colonel snapped. " Tea, quickly. Call the Sergeant and my clerk. Tell the Captain's escort that his truck is to be ready in one hour. Tell the Captain's servant to make his bath ready. Breakfast in half an hour." Abdi took the glass and hurried away.

With the pleasure of an elderly man who has drunk much in his time, and who now imagines that he has drunk a much younger man under the table, the Colonel walked stiffly over to Sole's bed and shook him.

" Sole." His voice was thick and hard. " Sole."

Sole sat up at once and saw the Colonel smile, saw the triumph in his eyes, and knew what to do at once.

" Quite a night, sir ! " he said pleasantly. " You don't show a sign of it."

" Not me," the Colonel's voice could not hide his pleasure. " You do. I know how much I can take. Perhaps you took rather a lot."

By God, you smug old bloody hypocrite, thought Sole. But all these old boys were the same. So he was silent when

he reached for his slippers, and the Colonel, satisfied, said,
" I've given orders to your chaps, if you don't mind, to be
ready to move in an hour. Does that suit you ? "

Of course I mind, Sole thought. He thanked the Colonel,
saying it suited him admirably. Why should the Colonel not
have his way ? He was a Colonel, but still they were Sole's
men, and oh, to hell with it anyway. His head ached, and his
throat was burned and dry from the countless cigarettes and
the cheap brandy. He would not be able to clean his teeth
properly this morning. He knew the nausea that would come.
Remorse, the familiar remorse, flooded his heart. If only he
could live a normal decent life, without drink, without
cigarettes, or even ration himself. Discipline, control, the
satisfaction that would come from that. It was not that he
was a drunkard, or even a heavy drinker. No, he could go
without it for days, weeks. For the first two or three drinkless
days there was always a pang of longing for a drink about
sundown. Then it wore off. But it was talk and a bottle and
two men, a desert, and some private misery, or a homesick-
ness that drove one to finish the bottle. By then nobody cared
much. They opened another bottle if it was there, and the
talk flowed and life could be fascinating. One cast gems of
wit haphazardly. All argument was easy. But now, in the
morning, one was full of death and repentance. He sat up
and licked his dry lips. The Colonel had gone into the bathroom. Why didn't one's cursed mind rest ? Why, these days,
was it no longer neat and tidy ? Once it had recognised all
dross at once and had rejected it. The discipline, the free
happy discipline of a classical education, seemed to have gone.
Now the mind was like a vacuum-cleaner. It sucked up all
the cigarette ends of life, the used tickets of trivial information,
the digested magnifications of the well-known tit-bits of
knowledge, read against the will at the bottom of magazine
pages. A man's body contains enough lime to whitewash a
rabbit-hutch six feet by four, and enough iron to make a nail
measuring . . .

He thought of his last leave in England. The last despair with Elizabeth, and the incommunicable thing that stood between them. Sometimes it seemed to be his inability to reach out to her and admit his failures. His silences. His occasional fits of hatred for her because he wanted to own, to possess her completely, and resented this. There was that part of him which hated to surrender himself completely to a woman. His brother had gone down in a burning Spitfire over Dunkirk. A queer chap ! Religious and honest, a member of the Oxford Group and given to tears. He had written to Sole about salvaging civilisation from the ruins of the devil. For the dead brother, Michael, had firmly believed that the devil was at the bottom of the world's sickness. It was the devil which drove man to sin and death. Now he was dead, and there was still the devil and sin and pain in the world. What difference had Michael's presence made on earth to the sum-total of the world's living ? What difference did anyone's presence make ? And what difference had his death made to the war ? He had shot down two German planes before somebody faster moved into his life and destroyed him over Dunkirk. Sole had been in action himself for three months in the Western Desert, and he had been surprised that it was life, and not death, which frightened him. The fear of life and its consequences had grown in him during the last two years. Sometimes he thought it might be the effect of the war, the fleeting friendships, the misery of damp messes on rainy nights in the bush. The tin cups, and the soap which was never dry in the tray in that certain mess in which he had nearly gone mad with boredom. The transit camp and the strange officers moving into your room in the night in wet battle-dress. The heaps of kit, the anger in the mornings when the strangers had gone, taking one of your shirts with them. For a time it had been better than living with Elizabeth, for there was no need for the constant examination of the conscience, the probing of the heart. One ate and slept and trained for death, victory, or defeat. One could not be sure what it was that one was preparing for. But one day your heavily-booted feet would crush the rubble in some enemy building and there would be fear. Or fear in some desert before the attack, or perhaps one would never go anywhere, just stay here, eating and sleeping and training. The three months with the battalion in the Middle East had gone swiftly. A fast process of bombings, shell-fire, snatched hours under trucks in the sand, then the incredibly exciting and frightening attack on a German position in which his platoon was practically wiped out. He would never forget the sudden massed fire of the German machine-guns and the fear and hate in his mind as they rushed the first positions. One was unable to forget the slaughtered platoon. Had there been any need for it ? If that attack had never been made, would it have altered the war very much ? Poor, foul-mouthed, good-humoured Sergeant Pellick, a red glittering fountain spurting from his chest while he gasped and strangled like a slain sheep. And young Andover, broken with a lash of fire, screaming because he did not know what was the matter with him. It was very like the books about the first world war, sometimes, but there was not much poetry being written about it. Nobody was bitter or inspired in this war. The world accepted the war as it had accepted the brilliant cruelty and violence of the last thirty years. In the war people would have to die, and the less said about that part of it the better. After all, it had all been said between the wars.

Yassin came into the room. He was tall, very lean, and bluish-black with a grave handsome face. Now he was angry, because Abdi, the Colonel's personal servant, had shouted at him. " Why do you not look after your Captain ? " he had scolded. " He should have had his tea half an hour ago. But *I* gave it to him. And *I* polished his boots. Where were you ? "

Yassin was sullen. " Close your great mouth, old man," he said. " This world is tired of old men."

Abdi had just given him a look. A long, fierce look, almost

frightening, and had walked out of the kitchen. Yassin was now subdued, anxious to please. Abdi was a well-known figure to all the officers' servants throughout the territory in which the military government ruled. He had power, being a colonel's servant, and he did not let you forget it, though he would never remind you unless something was so amiss as to merit the reminder. He loved the British, the men anyway, with whom he had been associated all his life, since a tall, thin English officer had taken him away from his occupation of diving for coins in Aden harbour over forty years before. Abdi was half Arab and half Abyssinian. He had been told that he was a Moslem and sometimes he went to the mosque. But he ate pork when he could get it, and drank a little of the master's brandy when he was tired. But he was fair about this. He would only drink a very little of the brandy and only when the Colonel had plenty. Sometimes he felt tired on a hot night after a day of ironing, washing, watching the young thieving boys who worked in the kitchen. The Colonel had never known that Abdi liked an occasional brandy, and Abdi was determined that he should never know. It might break the Colonel's heart to know that his oldest and most trusted servant was a thief. Abdi would sigh when he thought of it and would press the charcoal-heated iron harder on to the Colonel's damp khaki drill.

Sole watched Yassin trying to please. The smirk and the creepy touchings up of the folded clothes on the empty wooden packing-case which served as a table.

"Yassin, go away for Christ's sake and do some work," said Sole quietly in English. "There's nothing to do here. Go and help load my truck and *don't* forget to fill the water-bottles. If you forget this time, I'll leave you in the desert, half-way to El Ashang."

Yassin smiled and said in his strange Lascar-English: "Good, master. To doing just that." The Captain was always threatening to do something to somebody who annoyed him, but he did nothing. He liked peace and was only really annoyed when he suspected a man of trying to start trouble. The Captain detested trouble. He would control himself when he knew that a man had cheated him or was charging too high a price for grain or sheep which were brought weekly for the troops' rations. He would pay, casting the money contemptuously on to the table in front of the contractor, his dark eyes fixed on those of the cheater, who though he might look uncomfortable, nevertheless could bear with this treatment in order to obtain the extra money. One of the chiefs, a clever, scheming old man, had told the elders during a discussion about Sole that the Captain liked to make gestures with the Government's money. But would he do it with his own? All the elders thought about it and one said, "By God, it would be good to see." There were no interesting quarrels or lawsuits on at that time and all men were bored. So they sent a carpet seller to Sole, it having got about that the Captain had asked certain questions of his cook about the purchase of a good carpet. After bargaining, Sole agreed to pay six hundred shillings for one carpet, but the next day the merchant, on the advice of the chiefs, asked for seven hundred. This threw Sole into a rage, but after argument he flung down the seven hundred shillings and stared into the merchant's eyes. "Now get out of my office," was all he said.

Thus it was established for the chiefs that stupidity in money matters was a real part of Sole's character, and it was well known that a man who was stupid about money could be stupid about anything else. It was merely a question of finding Sole's weaknesses. One of them, it seemed, was not women. Countless times Yassin was asked by men, especially by chiefs, just what was the position regarding the Captain and women. Never had he been known to send out for a woman. He took a white medicine, though, ever so often, Yassin had reported. This medicine was to kill the desire which most normal men felt for women. Sole, mixing bicarbonate of soda for a stomach soured by bad food and water, liquor and cigarettes, did not know that each use of the mixture was faithfully reported to the chiefs and elders of whichever village or camp they were staying in. And the chiefs considered it wrong that Sole should spurn women, for it would be a good thing, each chief knew, if the Captain took a woman from his particular tribe. But during his stay at that last station Sole had never showed the slightest wish for a woman's company. The chiefs had been upset and had chattered to each other like a group of old hens over a piece of grain. All the officers had had women. Some slyly, and with the greatest precautions and secrecy. Others had hired them openly, permanently. These latter officers had been easier to handle from the chiefs' point of view, and the servants would vouch that life in the house was quieter, much more pleasant. There was less bickering over dusty tables, much less bad temper, and if you made friends with the Captain's woman, she defended you, warded off trouble. There were sometimes other pleasant rewards too.

Yassin sighed when he thought about it. Of course, if the Captain hired a shrew, a vulture woman, then life would be a torment. The Captain as a bachelor was easier to live with than if he found a wrong woman. The Captain had not a great deal of time to watch the house. He worked hard in the office and his goal was always to get out into the bush among the people, to show his face to them, which, because of great efforts in the office, he was able to do every two or three weeks. He could not watch the servants and the kitchen too closely, but he was cunning, though, sometimes walking straight across from his office and into the kitchen. He might find strangers there and then he would rage, and he would wear a hard face for Yassin for many days. You never knew the moment he might discharge you, so you were always on the watch and life was miserable. A good woman would soften all this. But not a white woman. White women were devils, they never rested, they were on the move through the day and half the night. That time he had worked for six days for a married British officer in Korma. The white

woman had nothing to do, like all white women. White
women were like white men. They were free and full of talk,
drank and smoked, were in no way subservient to their white
men. They did not have to make baskets, gather firewood or
drive goats. They had nothing to do. Their only duty was
to sleep with the officer when he came home tired and angry.
So they were in the kitchen from morning till night. They
weighed the flour, the sugar, the coffee. They knew all the
market prices. They locked cupboards. When you wanted
cooking fat you had to ask for the key, so that she always
knew when you were using the cooking fat. This meant that
you could only use it when you were cooking for the officer
and his wife. These women examined the corners of rooms,
inspected your nails, and they screamed like hyenas if they
found dirt there. That six days. No sleep because of the
eternal worry that the other servant might have got hold of
the key and helped himself to sugar or flour, precious things
in a desert country cut off from supplies by the war among
the white people. On the sixth day he had left and the white
woman had fixed her pale-blue eyes on him, eyes like those of
a wild cat, and had hissed and boiled like a pan of milk on a
fire. Never again would he go through such torture. Out
here, in the desert, he had food to put in his belly, while the
majority of the tribes had not enough. He had cigarettes
and clothes and peace, provided he watched the Captain. And
good money, and a certain amount of power due to his
position as a government officer's servant. There were many
who coveted such a job. You had to watch them, for they
would throw you from your position to the ground. They
could carry tales about you to the Captain and get your job
if the tales were convincing enough.

Now the Captain was angry, in that quiet way, like a low
fire in a sharp wind. He had drunk too much of the Christian
drink and he was sick and angry as usual. Yassin, on such
mornings, would warn the chiefs or the merchants who might
request interviews with the Captain. Such warnings were

worth money which the chiefs and merchants grudgingly paid. But here, in this stinking place, full of the smell of camels and their filth, one need not warn anybody, for this was not the Captain's station. It belonged to the Colonel. It was the headquarters of the area. But soon he and the Captain would be in their new station for twelve long months, and the money would add up month by month, for there was nothing to buy, not even cloth, unless the Government sent special consignment to the Captain for sale to the stupid and ignorant savages whom he ruled. Yassin was not a nomad. He was a town-boy from the coast a thousand miles away. He could spit in the faces of such people as these. They thought a tin of pineapple was from God, and it drove him mad trying to explain that it was not so, but these savages knew everything. They would never admit that anything was new to them, or a surprise. It angered the British officers, this arrogance. It was the same when you watched an officer teaching recruits how to take a machine-gun to pieces. They would not listen. They just wanted to get hold of the gun and tear it into pieces, and when it would not come apart they grew angry and sullen. So you could stand and watch until they were forced to admit their ignorance and were ready to listen. By God, how a man despised these savages with their stupid ideas about everything.

Yassin sat down near the truck which many shouting men were loading. They could do nothing without shouting, these people. They were packing the Captain's kit into the truck. Yassin considered whether it was worth going over to the truck and using his authority. But they all knew he could come and give them orders whenever he wished. No, there was more to be valued in just being seen sitting down nearby, watching quietly. He thought he might shout something to them in any case. Some order about being careful. No. His eyes closed. With one long, thin, black hand he scratched himself carefully under his left armpit, his face sullen with approaching sleep. He had had a late night. Dressed in

Sole's best civilian shirt and white trousers, with new squeaking sandals, he had been admired by all who saw him. He began to snore softly in the shade of the broken Italian eagle of white stone. The shouting continued as the men quarrelled with each other about the method of packing.

There was a sudden silence as Sole appeared. Tall and thin, grim now, and pale from the night's drinking, he nevertheless looked smart and commanding. He wore a well-pressed khaki shirt with brass badges of rank, starched, well-creased shorts and long khaki puttees over brown, nailed boots. His Sam Browne had the dark liquid glisten of age. On his cap the badge of a British regiment flashed. He still liked to wear the badge of this regiment of which he had trained and lost one platoon.

The packing continued in silence as Sole stood with his hands on his hips and watched. God, he was so tired of it all. The long hours in the truck, bouncing and jolting over rocks, the glare, and the ache in the small of the back, and the sweat-blinding, enraging business of changing a burst tyre in the company of boasting, shouting savages, who argued as to which of them knew the most. It would be a hellish journey to El Ashang, the least coveted of all the outposts of the Empire which now seemed senile, and ready for the self-inflicted death which it had sought for so long. Even though this place, this ocean of sand and scrub had belonged to the Italians only a year before, it could now be counted as part of the vast British Empire which Sole wished to give away. To whom? To anybody, but preferably to the people who lived in it, the natives. Let them kill each other.

When he looked at the savage, wherever he found him, in Africa, or in his shaving mirror, or holding a tube of the latest shaving cream in an American magazine, Sole felt the worry of death. What to do about it all? The doubt had come early to him. It came when he condemned an African to death two years before. He was a Bantu from a primitive tribe. And he had been asked " Guilty or not guilty ? " and had stared into

Sole's eyes. God, one remembered the sad, puzzled look, like the look of the monkey sitting in a silent zoo in a silent city on a rainy afternoon. Like a monkey far from home, in an artificial jungle built in the midst of the stone and concrete city. " Guilty or not guilty ? " The African did not understand. He had killed the two men. What did the white man mean ? And that warning about cross-examination. If he admitted himself guilty then he would not be questioned, cross-examined. The mystified dark eyes, full of the sadness which Sole had come to loathe, sad and human and accusing. Only a god could kill a man, coldly, legally, satisfied in the thought of duty done, backed up by the printed official version of other men's thoughts. Men dead a hundred years, or several hundred, or five. Men who had never been caught in the dark, frightening nets of somebody else's soul, or in the hands of some god who needed blood or corn, or an extinguished life to make him happy. One must not occupy a position of authority and grave responsibility, while pursued by the thought that one might be wrong, despite the written law which lay on the desk before one ; despite the weight of hundreds of years of other grave men's thoughts.

" But I did it," said the African. " I told the other officers who caught me. I did it. How can I now say I didn't ? "

Well, when he looked at this shouting mass of savages now loading the trucks, he knew that they were the same as the Bantu. The same as all those other people on the earth who drew knives to avenge the insult, who could not curse another without being ready to die for it. It tended to make a man glad he was English, of the race which had learned tolerance because of the twenty miles of water which had separated it from the continent of borders, conspirators, embittered idealists, giants who wished to die for their countries because life was not enough, was dull, was meant to be sacrificed for those who would come after. It only tended to make a man glad he was English. But now, you had to be prepared to accept hatred all over the earth because you were English, because of what grandfather had done, because there were many Englishmen in power who still believed grandfather was right and did old-fashioned things all over the earth in the name of the English people. Those people who stood in village shops and talked scandal, who were orderly and with a tendency to fairness in quarrels, who were almost absurdly willing to abide by the rules. Who knew hardly anything of the good and evil which had been done in their name all over the earth. Who only saw foreign lands when they went in uniform to die in them.

There was too much information in the world which was not ready for the daily shock of it. The shock to the conscience which was not equipped to deal with it. One half of the world had at last found out how the other half lived, and could do nothing about it, save read dumbly of how it was starved, wrecked by flood and fire, driven by whip or bomber, or killed by the orders of men who were certain that God was not about his business.

The truck was ready. Sole called the sergeant-major, a lean, brown man of below medium height, but who seemed bigger than all those about him. His name was Abduruman, and he belonged to Captain Turnbull, who had sent him to escort the new political officer.

" Sergeant-Major, go over and kick that sleeping man. His name is Yassin and he's my servant. He's idle, and it's time to go."

The sergeant-major saluted, eyeing Sole thoughtfully. The Captain might really mean him to kick Yassin. He would like very much to do it, for he did not like most of the officers' servants he met these days. Dirty, lazy, undisciplined and thieving dogs, most of them. Like most of the war-time soldiers. He stood beside Yassin and flexed his right foot inside his sandal. Then he kicked the snoring Yassin in the left buttock. Yassin screeched and leapt to his feet, saw the hard expressionless face of the sergeant-major and looked frantically about him. What had happened? His eyes were full of fear and wonder.

"It is all right, dog," said Abduruman softly. "You are not yet found out. It is only time to go."

CHAPTER THREE

A HOT wind sprang up every evening at El Ashang. Dusk there was the desert dusk of greys dying into blues and fierce, bronze scarves of fire. And there was a curious silence at that time as though all men, women and children were quiet and listening to the wind, which softened and then quickened into sand-laden blasts; or as though to the dusk which seemed to hold mystery and loneliness. The hot wind came in from the desert, blowing the dried dust of camel dung and sand into the air, tearing some more of the hard shale skin from the earth, until long ridges of limestone appeared through the shale like the bones of the earth. When the moon came up these bones showed themselves white and grey against the reddish sand. The wind died quickly and the darkness rushed in, hiding the huddles of several hundred skin and splinter huts, and the low stone buildings of the merchants, the wooden coffee houses and the crumbling mosque.

By day it seemed too small to matter, a handful of small mud boxes on the face of the enormous plains. At midday it began to swim from the ground into the burning, moving heat, and the traveller saw it resting slightly above the edge of a beautiful lake, a mirage of water and trees which dissolved as he neared the town.

El Ashang existed only because of its well, which had supplied water to raiding bands from ancient times. The raiders had always brought their plunder back to El Ashang, where they quarrelled and fought over it for months. Here they had circumcised their pagan prisoners and branded their looted camels. The little men of outcast tribes had settled here to make spears, swords and daggers, or bracelets of soft, heavy silver, or leather armlets for the raiders in which they secreted sayings from the holy Quran to save them from wounds and death. Slave-traders in their voluminous white garments had used the town as a base for raids on the pagan peoples whom they took to the coast for export into the Yemen and the Hadramaut.

El Ashang had never been prosperous. It had lived always on excitement and loot, but the main reason for its existence, a permanent supply of clear, though bitter, water, had never failed.

The first white men had settled far south of it in the early part of the present century: the *Italiani*, who had conquered the flat-nosed, black peoples with little trouble. They had sent two expeditions into the country near El Ashang and these had been instantly wiped out. Then the Mad Mullah descended upon the country from the North with his thousands of fast-moving dervishes mounted on camels and ponies. The tribes joined him in his holy war against all infidels, black and white. They raided far south into the fat colonies of the Italians, where for the first time they came up against the white man's machine-guns. They were not the kind of people to retreat before these new guns. The Mullah himself said that he must have one, and his dervishes returned to him with several. He caused great slaughter with them among the tribes.

Tribal legend agreed that it was these raids into the Italian territory which had caused the conquest of the whole country by the Italians.

And then one day the Italians came to El Ashang in hundreds of trucks. They appeared to come from all directions, so that the two main tribes, the Omar Bilash and the Yonis Barra, had no chance against them. For the first time the tribes of the Ashang desert experienced artillery fire. They saw the two forts of the Mad Mullah, now dead some fifteen years, crumble under a hail of shells, and the Italians came into the town at the head of hundreds of flat-nosed, black soldiers. An Italian chief, a fat man with a white beard, called the townspeople to assembly in the centre of the town and told them about the White King across the waters. He told them they had been wicked to make war in Italian territory. But the White King understood well that it was because they had been misled by the Mad Mullah that they had done this. The White King had sent his soldiers to protect the peoples of Ashang from people like the Mullah, and to teach them new ways. It was after this that the Italian chief had spoken of the bravery of the Ashang tribes. " We want you as soldiers of Italy," he had told them, and from that day the Italian flag had flown over El Ashang until the arrival of the English only a year or so ago.

The Italians had rebuilt the town. Although they were Christian they seemed to admire Islam, for they built a mosque for the people, and they consulted the *Kadi* in all cases involving tribal or religious disputes. They built a great fort on the edge of the town so that it dominated the scattered huts of the people and the precious wells.

In the town lived tribesmen of the Omar Bilash and the Yonis Barra, who had become traders and merchants. The elders and chiefs of the tribes were helped to build houses there by the Italians, who could instruct or consult them as they wished. The new Government built a market and installed a Government Market Master, who kept order and inspected the meat before it was sold. They built a small hospital, laid aside land for a cemetery, and even gave money to build sepulchres there for holy men and chiefs. Because they quartered hundreds of troops in and about the town, there was much trade in mutton and milk, grain, hides, incense and cloth. And when the Italians were ready and had won the friendship of the tribes, they recruited the best men into the *Gruppo Banda*, the roving bands under one white officer which were then used for the final conquest of the lands in the North-east. By then the White Government owned the whole of the country until the English came and drove them from power.

Now El Ashang had changed. The English had only two officers there and fewer than a hundred soldiers, all flat-nosed save for the non-commissioned officers, who were from noble tribes. The first English officer who came to El Ashang had landed in an aeroplane, and he had hoisted the English flag and made a short speech.

"We have come here because the Italians declared war upon the English," he told the people. He then read them a proclamation which was full of rules and warnings. It said that the land was a war area and was now under the rule of the English Army. Anyone carrying guns, assisting the Italians, damaging roads, vehicles, guns, telegraph wires, carrying explosives, holding meetings without permission, or in any way offending the English Army, would be severely punished, even by death.

The officer said that the people were to live in peace and were free to live their normal lives, for they were now living under the flag of England.

Soon two English officers came with flat-nosed troops and they began to govern the country.

El Ashang never rested, was never truly at peace. Two warring tribes mingled there, the Omar Bilash and the Yonis Barra. Each tribe was rich in camels and fighting men, each tribe treacherous and mistrustful, both pledged to a hatred now only held in check by the memory of British disarming operations a year before, two months after the retreat of the Italians. Held in check also by the uncertain grip of Captain Milton, and by the threat of Captain Turnbull, "the stone one," the hard-mouthed one.

Turnbull waited for them, they knew that. He watched them, quietly training his troops, and a chief could not tell how much he thought or knew. The chiefs had once seen him tear a door from its hinges with his hands, during a search for arms. He was not tall, but he was broad and as well-packed as a sack of flour. How long Turnbull would stay there was a question that was argued in every coffee house of El Ashang. Sometimes an officer came and went quickly, or he grew sick and was transferred. But it seemed that Turnbull would stay for a long time. Men asked him many questions about this matter, in many ways, but he never answered these questions but just stared until his eyes were cold and a man changed the subject. He was a cunning one, telling a man what was on that man's mind, and answering a question before it was asked. He behaved as though he did not like men, and once he had told three chiefs who were boasting of their tribal fighting prowess : " I know six men of another race, Moslems, too, a long way from here who would wipe out your whole tribe with their swords. The mouths of the fighting men here are as big as their shields." He said that in the strange Arabic he used. Not the Arabic of the Yemen or the Hadramaut which the chiefs used, but an Arabic which some Arab traders had said was of the far North.

They knew his personal habits. They knew that he was neat in his room, in his dress, in his office. His servant was an Abyssinian, and they knew he had chosen an Abyssinian because they, the Moslems, did not like Abyssinians, had been continually at war with them, hated them. There could be no friendship between this Abyssinian servant, Belai by name, and the tribesmen of the area. He was silent, black and secretive, and careful of where he went, of what he said and what he did. He was completely in the power of his master, who trusted him a great deal, though not absolutely. Captain Turnbull trusted no one absolutely, not even his sergeant-major, the hard-faced Abduruman, who wore as many medal ribbons as Captain Turnbull himself, and who made no secret of how much he looked down on the tribes-men and their chiefs. There was only one man in the village who had been a soldier of the Italians for as long as Sergeant-

Major Abduruman had been a soldier of the British. This was Yussuf Mohamed, who had been a sergeant-major also, in a much more magnificent uniform than the plain British khaki worn by Abduruman. And he had hated Abduruman since the incident in the market. In the market-place while marching at the head of the company, Sergeant-Major Abduruman had pushed Yussuf out of his way by prodding him with his silver-knobbed cane. As it was the policy at that time to complain to the British about everything and anything, Yussuf, who had power in the village, who had been wounded in battle for the Italians seven times, went to complain. This was to show the village a man's feelings, for the insult was deadly—to be pushed with the end of a cane as though a man were a dog or a flat-nosed one.

Most white men liked to be considered great and wished all men to think that the white race, but particularly their own race, was the race which could conquer all. But the first Italian sergeant-major Yussuf had seen drunk, vomiting, reeling near the fort and then collapsing into the sand, had disgusted him. It had also made him proud to be a Moslem. He was twenty then, an " *ascaro*," a private soldier. He had never felt the same about white men since. When their senses were gone in drink they lost their power, were like children. It was thirty years since he had heard the drunken Italian choking and roaring like a camel, had heard him curse the country and the heathen savages in it. That had meant Yussuf too. But after one year of the British, he, like the others, wished for the return of the Italians. He had thought that the Italians were too proud, had despised black people, but the British were worse. They were cold and detached and hard. They never enthused, never became truly excited, and they did things secretly. The Italians laughed more and sang more, were honest about their need of women, were friendly and did not mind sitting down in a man's house for a cup of tea. If a British officer did that, he was doing it for the sake of policy, and he was not enjoying himself. That stiffness and coolness never melted. Yussuf remembered the tea party which Captain Milton, the political officer, had given for the chiefs under the casuarina tree outside the guard-room of the fort. He had given it because the headquarters of the Government at Korma had written instructions to all the officers all over the country telling them to meet and entertain the chiefs and notables more often, to cultivate their goodwill. Abdul, the clever one, the thin, short-sighted clerk in the Captain's office, had passed the word round that it was the wish of the Government that British political officers should make friends with the chiefs.

Yussuf wondered if the English knew all the small troubles, jealousies and old hatreds which made up the daily life of dreary, crumbling El Ashang. For Yussuf often found life dreary in this village of ignorant people, but they were his people, and he consciously and deliberately enjoyed the plotting, the never-ending intrigue between his tribe—the Omar Bilash—and the Yonis Barra. Things had been quiet for too long. Men felt that matters should come to a head, that there should be a killing. Men had begun to understand the British ways. They saw that the British wanted men to live in peace. Now they were trying to make friends with the chiefs, whom they had treated badly, and the British excuse, when the chiefs complained, was that all troubles were caused by the war. But the British were clever. They knew how to hurt men. They ignored them, forced them to wait outside an office and forced them to take their place beside lesser men as though all were equal.

He thought of Captain Milton's tea party. After a speech in which the most influential chief, Kalil Abukir, the chief of the chiefs of the Omar Bilash, had praised the British and particularly Captain Milton, as being wise, generous, brave and all-knowing, Captain Milton had replied through an interpreter that all the things the chief had said were true, but further, that the British were the most powerful people in the world, but the defeat of the Italians was nothing, for the

Italians were like women on the battlefield. Their troops were no good. By God, it had been hard to stay silent, Yussuf remembered, and yet there was no doubt that the British had defeated the Italians in this land in a few weeks; but he could not believe that the British were really better than the Italians. No, he could never like them, and he would never forgive them for anything. Since the defeat he had grown to like the Italians more than he could have imagined possible, because the British were contemptuous of all peoples with darker skin than their own.

In his cold speech, with the hate for the Italians in his eyes, Captain Milton had tried to anger the chiefs, two of whom were *Cavaglieri* of the Star of Italy, honoured for service performed during some of Italy's Colonial wars. When the Italians had wanted troops they came for the best to the Omar Bilash, and to their enemies, the Yonis Barra, though they never were expected to serve together in the same regiments. But the British, who were recruiting troops from these tribes also, made no distinction between them. They made men of all tribes serve together, even putting inferior slave peoples with flat noses and thick lips among men of ancient and noble blood. But there would be trouble.

Now Yussuf stood before Captain Turnbull to tell his story against the Sergeant-Major Abduruman. Behind Yussuf were two chiefs he had brought as witnesses, so that they could tell the village of how Yussuf had addressed the Government. They stood gravely behind Yussuf in their long, white cloaks, their white turbans speckled with colour, grave as becomes the chiefs of powerful tribes now under the heel of a power more foreign, more powerful than the Italians.

Captain Turnbull sat behind his desk, playing with his thick, yellow hair, and never taking his eyes off Yussuf's face. The hate surged in Yussuf's heart when he thought of the misery and failure of his life. His pension gone, his right to wear medals gone, his life of long service counting for nothing. He told Turnbull his life story, and then he began to make his complaint against Sergeant-Major Abduruman, who had pushed him with a cane as though he were a dog. Did Abduruman think that because he was a British senior non-commissioned officer that he had the right to push men about? Yussuf knew that this was the first time a man of the El Ashang peoples had spoken thus to a British officer, but the excuse was perfect. He, Yussuf, was a notable of the town, and it was important that Captain Turnbull realise this. Turnbull said nothing for a whole minute. He just stared at Yussuf, who could not resist shifting his feet uncomfortably.

"You have a big mouth, Yussuf," said Turnbull. "And now you have used it. I now know your feelings about many things, but you do not know mine. You will find them out if ever you make trouble here. If you stand in the way of my troops again, then again you will be prodded, not like a dog, but like a man who stands in the way of marching British troops. It is simple. It has nothing to do with the Mullah who fought the British, nothing to do with how many years you served the Italians, and nothing to do with the long and interesting story of your life. I do not care how many years you served the Italians. But you must control your tongue. Perhaps you have said too much. Do you think so?"

Yussuf plucked his greying, pointed, Italian beard, and smiled angrily.

"I have told you my thoughts. I have concealed nothing," he said softly.

"That is your mistake," said Turnbull. "There is much you should conceal which you have not concealed." He stood up, straightened his Sam Browne belt, and jerked his head to the waiting soldier, an Arab, who stamped to attention and opened the door for Yussuf, who raised his hand in salute and walked out, tall and dignified, grinding his teeth in anger.

God was just and all merciful. One day he would end all this and bring Yussuf back into a powerful position again. He would send the English away from here. He would make the Omar Bilash the most powerful tribe again.

One could not tell what lay in the heart of the Captain Turnbull. He too was a soldier of long service. He was cunning. He was careful and he planned everything he did. He was ruthless and cruel, as a soldier should be, but would the British Government ever allow him to be so? Yussuf smiled and cracked his fingers together. There would be trouble one day. He knew his people. They would fight if they were led. If only there were some Italian officers still fighting in the country. Then the tribes would rise and fight the British. They were bored with keeping the peace, and the hatred between the Omar Bilash and the Yonis Barra was growing every day, and this was the fault of Captain Milton, who favoured the stinking, crawling and treacherous Yonis Barra. The woman who kept him awake in his bed was a Yonis Barra and there lay the trouble. To take a woman of the Yonis Barra, knowing them to be enemies of the Omar Bilash, was thought by some of the chiefs to be a studied insult to the Omar Bilash. Aurella, the woman, pretended to be detribalised, pretending not to care any more for her tribal pride, but no man believed this. The Captain Milton was influenced against the Omar Bilash, though he claimed to be fair and just. The chiefs of the Omar Bilash had expressed their annoyance with the Captain's choice of a woman, but only in the form of parables. They could not tell if Milton had understood or not. He said nothing, only thanked them for their words and then dismissed them. But they were not afraid of him. They knew he was weak about women and drink, and they had even seen him frightened by the strong words of angry chiefs who had disagreed with some of his decisions over the use of water-holes. He had tried to calm them when he should have been angry. They saw this at once and seized upon it, discussing it for nights. They knew also that the Captain Milton and the Captain Turnbull seldom saw each other at night. They stayed in their houses, Captain Milton keeping his woman near him, in the room in which he drank, as though she were his wife, a white woman. It seemed that the two captains did not like each other. Anyway it was unusual for a political officer and a soldier to like each other; it was the same among the Italians. The soldier was proud of being a warrior. The political officer was vain about his subtlety, his intelligence and his power of administration. The soldier he treated as an arm to be used in a time of trouble, and the soldier resented it, feeling that ultimately everything would depend on him when the political officer had made the mistakes that would lead to trouble among the people.

Yussuf hurried to the house of Issa Samantar, an Omar Bilash chief. He wished to pass on his story before Sergeant-Major Abduruman started telling his own version in the village. He felt weakness, a kind of faintness sometimes, when the hate came upon him, so fierce was it when he thought of Turnbull and the British. He was tired of ignominy. He had had enough of the inability to tell men what they must do. He had been used all his life to giving commands, to instant obedience. He was sure that he was meant to influence his people. The idea had formed in his mind since Captain Milton's decision over the water-holes. He had allowed two sub-tribes of the Yonis Barra to water their camels at water-holes formerly the sole property, agreed with the Italians, of the Omar Bilash. There was anger. There was enough water for all, but that was not the point. It was pride. The Omar Bilash would never agree to the sharing of their water-holes with the Yonis Barra. Trouble would come, and Yussuf could smell power and leadership in the distance. It was like the approach to a well after long thirst.

CHAPTER FOUR

IF one could hate something or somebody wholeheartedly,
openly, it would save so much trouble in the end. If one
could say to a fellow that one could not bear his presence,
then how simple it would be. There were so many reasons
why Captain Milton could not like Turnbull. Turnbull
always looked at him in a curious way, not contemptuously,
not quite that, but in a cool, steady way, so that while Milton
talked he was continually groping about for a means of
dominating Turnbull. A means of making Turnbull realise
that he, Milton, was superior in many ways, belonged to clubs
the inside of which Turnbull would never see, had had and
spurned opportunities for which Turnbull would give his
soul. But how could one convey this to a chap who spoke
casually of how he had delivered sacks of coal from door to
door of a small town until the army gave him his chance?
That was the thing which annoyed Milton, the way in which
Turnbull talked about it, as though he assumed that you
knew such ways of life, realised there were such situations in
everyday life. It was an assumption which infuriated Milton
sometimes, if only because of the manner in which Turnbull
described having been hungry during the slump of 1931, or
the unresentful way in which he described how a " gentleman " had lent him a pound to see him on his way to the
army recruiting centre. If Turnbull had spoken angrily or
bitterly, then one could have defended one's class, one's
knowledge of the fact that not all men were equal. But when
a fellow laughed about it, treated it as though it were something that could happen to anybody, there was not much
you could say. Turnbull hid nothing. They had met in
evening discussions over a drink, possibly on three occasions

in the last three months. Turnbull had now been four months in El Ashang, and had another eight months to go before leave and reposting. Turnbull did not even hide the fact that his wife had been a factory worker when he married her. It had made her hands very rough and coarse, and she had worried herself unnecessarily about it until Turnbull, as he explained to Milton, told her to stop worrying about it. He, Turnbull, did not mind if her hands were ugly. Would Milton have minded? Milton said that he really did not know. It was an unusual question. One could not tell what one would feel. As far as women's hands went, he liked them soft and long and slim.

"You're married, aren't you, Milton?" Turnbull had said directly, almost curtly, it seemed. For Milton was not sure if Turnbull knew about Aurella or not. They had not discussed women. Being addressed as "Milton" by Turnbull made Milton uncomfortable. From Turnbull, an ex-sergeant-major who had delivered coal until the army gave him his chance, it hurt. Turnbull had that directness and simplicity which seemed a part of the long-service non-commissioned officers of a certain type. The type who had educated himself, learned about the good things he could afford to buy. He was almost a new kind of being, not fitting in anywhere. He was scrupulously clean and neat, almost stupidly honest, hard-working, and childishly faithful to his wife, the King, his regiment, his old commanding officer, and the army in general. That was what happened when a chap had no school to be proud of, no club, no father, no land. They were a special kind of human being, these N.C.O.s. Machines who executed orders, who would put their own mothers into the guard-room if necessary, and who could not hide their affection for the gentleman type of officer : but as officers themselves they showed their limitations. They could not use life as the vehicle it really was to a gentleman, any true gentleman. They could never grow used to being in power, being looked up to as a gentleman. They only knew, perhaps, how to make men of their own class into imitations of themselves. Killing machines to be led by officers.

There was something in Turnbull which had begun to get on Milton's nerves, a sort of coolness, an impudence it seemed sometimes, which forbade anything in the nature of explaining who was who, and what was what. It was not that Turnbull need have been subservient to Milton, or even called him sir. But, somehow one would have thought that an ex-regular N.C.O. would have taken a certain attitude, would have felt slightly inferior to one who was a gentleman by all the standards which had been safely understood for years. But Turnbull would listen to one of Milton's opinions about politics, about a certain lost battle in Libya or somewhere else, and even if he disagreed, never took that careful line which regular N.C.O.s took out of habit : not disagreeing, but, perhaps, just saying, " Well, er—yes," and so on. But not Turnbull. He once said, " That's moonshine, Milton. Where did you get that idea ? From a staff college ? " His laugh was open, with regular white teeth. There was something about him which almost forced one to like him but for the resentment one felt for his familiarity. Milton hid his anger and invited him to drinks no more. He noticed that Turnbull had never invited him in return for drinks. He had waited, having already written his chit of refusal in his mind, but no invitation came, and it made him angry.

If only one had been able to dislike him with an open tongue, to have told him really where he stood in this administration. He thought he knew too much. Also there were many things going on lately which Milton would have liked to discuss with Turnbull. He had an idea that Turnbull was beginning to interfere in matters, political matters, which were not his business at all. The chiefs brought Turnbull's name into their talks with him, sometimes saying, " We know that the army Captain Turnbull is our enemy and our friend as well. A man does not quite know the Captain sometimes, but he has warned us that in the event of trouble among the people we will be taught our lesson." Here the chiefs, with that two-faced innocence which the years of intrigue had developed in them all, spread their hands and said, " We thought that such words should come from you, the political officer, and not from Captain Turnbull. But we said nothing. We listened and then after thinking between us, we came to you, to ask for guidance. To request interpretation of the threats, for such they are. What is it we have done to receive these words ? "

Then they looked grave and were silent. These were the chiefs of the Omar Bilash. The speaker was Kalil Abukir, tall and emaciated, with one leg crippled, the result of a sword slash in one of the many tribal battles in which he had fought. He was the first chief of the Omar Bilash, more cunning, more patient, more thoughtful than those other chiefs now grouped about him. His lined and ravaged black face seemed to hold within it some hollow hunger, some fierce anxiety which the two large black eyes used as a fuel. These eyes fascinated Milton. He could not resist staring at them. They were like the eyes of some demon of his childhood nights, smoky and hot, flickering against the brownish eyeballs. When he looked into them he saw killing and torture and felt a vague presence near him of unrest, the eternal unrest of the savages who did instantly what came into their minds when excited. Kalil Abukir wore a short beard, grey now, and carefully trimmed. His turban was snowy white and carefully wound, beautiful above his black, frightening face. He carried a curved Arab sword, a gift from an Italian general with whom he had served as a political adviser. Now gone were those days ; and the colour, the money and the power had gone with them. In these days a man did not know where he stood, for the British made it clear that they did not wish to be here, but were here because they had captured the land from the Italians who had declared war against them. And the British did not trust anyone, not even him, Kalil Abukir, old and tired with experience. Sometimes Kalil suffered bouts of self-pity when he thought of the other days of power, when the Italians had backed and respected the noble fighting tribes, of whom the most noble and powerful was the Omar Bilash.

He awaited Milton's reply. His clan chiefs were silent behind him. They stared at the white man who used a woman of their greatest enemies, the Yonis Barra. How could he be fair to the Omar Bilash?

Milton stopped playing with the ebony ruler and placed it carefully on the desk, lining it up with the edge of the blotter. He appeared to come to a decision, to have made a choice of some importance.

"I shall look into this," he said with conviction. Kalil's eyes held his, piercing into them, waiting for more words, but none came. Deliberately, the chief shrugged his shoulders and twisted his mouth. It was the only way in which he could express his great anger. Having planned secretly with his chiefs to make war on the Yonis Barra at the first opportunity and on the first excuse, Turnbull's words had frightened him. Did Turnbull know something. Was there a spy somewhere in the village? And now Milton said he would look into it, had not even shown anger, the righteous anger of a political officer who had discovered that an army officer is interfering.

The shrug and the twisted mouth were something new. It gave Milton a queer scared feeling in the stomach. He had been here twelve months and things were going wrong. He knew he had not done all he should have done, had not gone out among the tribes enough, had grown slack. He knew, too, that something was being planned, that there would be trouble between the Yonis Barra and the Omar Bilash. And Aurella in his bed at night, her big, black, doggy eyes glittering, would argue for more concessions to her tribe, the unfairly treated Yonis Barra. Not until she had finished her tirade against the Omar Bilash and had heard him promise to do something, would she open her arms and allow him near the black, exciting body which had become part of his life's

furniture. She knew his tastes, of which she had taught him
not to be ashamed. She had eaten through him. He loved
her and was afraid. She wore two hundred pounds' worth of
gold about her neck. He had paid for it willingly for only
then would she really submit to him. She knew how to hurt
him and how to ease his pain when she was ready. She was
wonderful. He had to admit that she was the most wonderful
bint he had ever known in his life.

Kalil left the office with his chiefs. There was a bad atmosphere. There was going to be trouble, Milton was certain.
Panic came to him, climbing on to his back frantically and
urging him to go, to leave this place before the trouble started.
When would relief come? That bastard, Sole, was no doubt
sitting comfortably in the Officers' Club a thousand miles
away drinking brandy, waiting until he was thrown out by
final command before he would leave for El Ashang. Milton
shivered. He knew what these people could do if they started.
He had seen one or two bodies of their victims.

It was evening and the desert was pink and alive as though
exuding a soft warmth, and the sky was fantastically coloured.
It made him lonely and afraid again. He was a long way
from help if anything really big started. There was only
Turnbull and one company of troops and that insufferable
fool, Lieutenant Cuddy, on patrol with a camel platoon about
one hundred miles to the north, near the big water-holes.
Turnbull would probably bring him in if Milton hinted at
trouble, but one had to be sure before requesting such a
move. If there was no trouble, then in the eyes of all he would
have shown panic, would have been a scared fool and discredited in the eyes of seniors and juniors.

Now the wind came, dashing sand against the office door,
sighing, saying alone, alone, alone. An *askari* came in and
shuffled his sandals on the sandy floor. He wished to close
the office, but Milton hardly heard him, his eyes were vacant,
staring into nothing, thoughts rushing up from the dark pit
of experience, memory, the driftwood of years flinging on to

the beach of his half-consciousness. Fear ? It was probably only the result of too many months in El Ashang listening for three hundred days to the lies, the maddening, worrying, half-convincing lies of the paid chiefs, the unpaid chiefs, the deposed chiefs, the cheated tribesmen, the venal contractors, the people who had been year after year to sell their stores to Italians and Englishmen. Those who were full of smiles and anxious to please yet never losing sight of their main objective, gain, injury to an enemy. Those others who were fierce and uncontrolled, tortured with jealousy of another who had been shown favour by the Government. And those who were sent by chiefs to feel out the ground, to assess the present mood of the officer, for it was necessary to know if the next move in the months-long intrigue was safe. And day by day it mounted up, this river of words, false words larded with mutually known truth, so that one halted and thought and the thin, black liar watched you falter and rushed to smother your hesitating mind with the greater lie, the lie he had saved for this moment. Then rage might engulf you and he had won if you drove him from the office, for he knew that at heart your duty was justice, and after anger would come doubt, and you might send for him and in remorse grant him the undeserved favour. Lies, millions of them, eating like acid at the foundations of simple official morality.

But he had fallen several times and it was known. He had played one chief against the other and been found out. He had accepted the present of a carpet, for Aurella had urged him to take it. He must not think it a bribe, she told him, it was only a gesture of friendship from chiefs who wished him well. They were the chiefs of her own tribe who were looking into the future, who knew that the Omar Bilash were arming, were enraged with the neutral attitude of the British to people great and small. Milton knew that the carpet was a bribe, that the request for favours would come later, probably from somebody else, somebody who had not been present at the carpet giving, so that one would not be sure that the carpet was expected to help in the decision. But he had been weak, had not resisted her breasts, her sharp white teeth, the shiver of the limbs under the silk he had bought for her. And he could not fight her any more, for his desire for her was mingled with his fear of the dark, wolfish people outside who sat of nights in their huts, talking, remembering old history, pride, rights, deeds of blood. Gradually, as fear came, born mainly through the complete inability to pierce through the skeins of lies to the truth, the wish to please became strongest. Smiling falsely to the chiefs when they came into the office to pursue the question of their tribal rights. Laughing at the slightest excuse, being jolly with old men and watching anxiously with darting eye for an answering smile from one of the others who sat listening. And knowing all the time that none of this must be too transparent, for those pairs of brooding black eyes were watching, and the fast minds behind them, born and reared in intrigue, would see the weakness. Then the growing anxiety for flight from the gathering trouble which he still could not assess clearly, but could only see in incidents like that contemptuous shrug of Kalil Abukir's, the sneer of one who has found another out and despises him for weakness.

It was nearly dark now and the *askari* was coughing, watching Milton, who unknowingly was clutching his head with his hands.

Was it too late, Milton wondered, to go out now among the tribes and *do* something, show the flag, some strength, hold a meeting over the question which he suspected was at the bottom of the growing troubled atmosphere. The question of the water-holes at Nalang, granted to the Omar Bilash by the Italians. The Yonis Barra had been using them too since shortly before the British arrived and when the Italians were breaking in defeat. Then the Yonis Barra had been as well armed with discarded Italian weapons as the Omar Bilash. But in the first disarming operation by the British, the Yonis Barra had surrendered most of their arms, weakly and wrongly they now thought, for the Omar Bilash had stayed obdurate and had denied possession of more than the few they surrendered.

There had been incidents at the Nalang water-holes. A few stabbings between thirsting tribesmen of the two tribes, one or two unexplained killings, and now the interminable claims for blood money, one hundred camels for the life of each man. But neither the Omar Bilash or the Yonis Barra would agree upon how the men had died, as to who had started the quarrel, and Milton dreamed of them at night, sometimes frantically, their gleaming teeth, their wild passionate eyes and their crowns of thick bushy hair moving through the dream mists.

The *askari* placed his hand on Milton's arm and shook it gently. "*Effendi*," he said, " *Effendi*, it is dark and time to go."

Milton licked his lips and sat up quickly, sensing the chilled sweat on his head, the soaking neck and back of his shirt, usual at this time, but now colder, making him shiver. Stiffly he got up and walked out of the office, Kalil's face in his mind, contempt on it, and danger in its eyes, the eyes of a savage animal with a man's intelligence. He half ran across the thick sand from the office, into the light of his room, the hot white light of the petrol lamp, into the presence of Aurella. She would pour him a whisky to drink before he bathed. She would wind the gramophone and put on that worn Italian record he liked so much, " *Un giorno ti dirò*." He did not know what it meant, but it moved something in him, brought a happy feeling with the whisky, into his heart.

She would be good to him. She would give him the illusion of a home in the midst of these savages, and she would woo him from his restless fears.

CHAPTER FIVE

TURNBULL was shaving when the clerk came to the bathroom window and gave his usual discreet tap. Turnbull made the clerks, the orderlies, the company cook, and the sweepers report to him at the bathroom window while he shaved in the cool of the first dawn light. They had not liked it when he had first given the orders for this routine. Now they were used to it, and had given up the attempts to wear him down, to make him regard such an effort on his part as hopeless, and to change his mind. When they came to the window he knew that the machinery of order and stability at El Ashang was awake and functioning. The clerks to their papers and stores, the sweepers to the lines, the orderlies to the office and the armoury, and the cook to the cut-down petrol drums in which the food for the troops was cooked. About the sergeant-major he never worried. He was a soldier after Turnbull's heart, clean, hard, trained to his job and utterly faithful to his superiors.

When Sergeant-Major Abduruman handled a rifle during instructional periods for the troops, he had that appearance, that unmistakable appearance of the highly trained non-commissioned officer, which gave Turnbull immense pleasure. He handled the rifle as though it were part of him, his long tightly putteed legs apart and his gleaming nailed boots planted firmly in the sand, showing the troops the standing load, each slap of his hands on the rifle driving home his lessons. No soldiers whispered or failed to pay attention when Abduruman spoke. They had served long enough in the army to feel that curious fearful adoration for a good sergeant-major who would never let them go short of rations or clothing, who would show them everything they would need to know as soldiers, but who would inflict the heaviest punishment on a wrongdoer who may have considered himself a favourite of the sergeant-major.

While Turnbull shaved, cutting the lather from his red-brown face and noting the clearness of his eyes with pleasure, Haji, his chief clerk, talked of the new officer who was to relieve Milton. His name was Sole and he was a captain.

" Colonial or British ? " Turnbull asked while he bent with open mouth to the faded mirror and razored the corner of his jaw where it joined his thick strong neck. He was trying to place Sole, almost certain that he did not know him. It was always a strange time on an out-station waiting for a new officer to arrive. How would he look ? One would have to live in the same station with him for months, work with him, or against him, as against the useless Milton who was rapidly losing his nerve, if he had ever had any. Sole. No, it did not remind him of anyone he knew.

" I know Captain Sole, *Effendi*," said Haji eagerly. " He's a kind man. He was District Commissioner at Lamjang in the South six months ago when I was clerk to the lieutenant who died of wounds after the Italian battle. I don't know his name. The Captain Sole speaks Italian and he is a permanent officer of the British Government in Africa."

" Colonial or British ? " Turnbull said again as he wiped his face with a towel. He did not like Colonial officers when there were " natives " or " blacks " to be dealt with. He had known them before. One he knew had been a sergeant and had forced new African troops to salute him until he, Turnbull, had taught them the King's Regulations. The salute was for an officer holding the King's Commission, and not for ranks below that status. He remembered the bared teeth of the Colonial sergeant when he came to remonstrate, having found out that the failure of the African troops to salute was due to the order of Turnbull, then a lieutenant, an officer of the Imperial Forces, British, from Home.

" Who the hell do you think you are ? " the sergeant had

snarled. His accent was better than his own, Turnbull noted swiftly. Probably well educated, but ruined by life in the Colonies among primitive blacks. He remembered getting to his feet and in a voice of freezing anger saying, " Stand to attention when you speak to me." The sergeant had hesitated, looked at Turnbull's medals, the two pips on his shoulder, the hardened eyes, and Turnbull saw his mind working as he clicked his heels together and then Turnbull deliberately stared at the sergeant's hands until they clenched unwillingly and slowly came into line with the seams of his shorts.

The sergeant's eyes were cold and full of hate. At any time the Colonials disliked the British, but now he saw that the sergeant could hardly contain himself. With the official kindness of the long service N.C.O. who would not allow a drunken or angry man to commit himself, to injure his career as a soldier while he could be saved, Turnbull began to talk rapidly, his face hard and stern.

" I would put you on a charge, Sergeant, and you would lose your stripes, but there is one thing that stops me. You are a sergeant of little experience and you have been used to getting respect because of your stripes and not your ability. If you were a real sergeant you would never have approached me in the way you have. You would not last five minutes in a first line battalion, but only with raw Africans, this rabble out here, which you do know how to train or treat." Seeing the sergeant's lips move, Turnbull read his mind. " I know what you all think of *Imperial* officers and N.C.O.s," he said, stressing the forced scorn in his voice when he used the word " Imperial." " You think we do not understand African troops, because we treat them as soldiers and not slaves. But get one thing clear in your mind, Sergeant. What you think or feel has nothing to do with regulations. Once a man has signed on as a soldier, he gets the same treatment as any other soldier as far as we are concerned, whether black, brown, yellow or white. There's a war on, and all the troops are in it, no matter what their colour. Remember your rank and be respectful to all officers whether you dislike their nationality or not. When you do that, your troop may do it for you too." He paused and the sergeant, now more subdued, nodded, and Turnbull continued in the same hard voice. "If I find that you make one more African soldier salute you, I'll break you. I'll have your stripes off before you know what has happened."

He knew that the sergeant, now watching him with eyes full of wonder, was waiting for the final words, the friendly words which would show that there was no real ill feeling. But while Turnbull knew how to do that as did few officers, he decided to surprise the sergeant.

"Now fall out!" he snapped, and he hid his satisfaction as the sergeant stiffened and saluted, turned about and strode out, angry and puzzled. He did not care whether the sergeant was now his enemy or not. Turnbull went by regulations, and by humanity only when it was really required. The King's Regulations were given for soldiers first and humans after. Any N.C.O. or officer who tried to get along in the army over a long period while ignoring regulations and rules was a fool. King's Regulations had all the knowledge and all the rules. When you knew them, no one could shake your position. If these Colonial sergeants resented the " British " officers and N.C.O.s, they would learn better later. True, the Colonials understood African people, but they obeyed also the unwritten Colonial rules on how to keep them from progress. An African was a menial, a child, a nice chap while you watched him and checked him, the Colonials thought. But Turnbull was certain that if you asked an African to lie under shell-fire in a country far from his village, to use the bayonet on strange people of whom he had never even heard, then you were breaking the rules and you must break them thoroughly or not at all. You must give him good pay and rations, treat him with the justice as written in the rules, and never lie to him, even if it was unfortunate that after a life of ordering Africans about as a civilian white man, you were only made a sergeant when war came. You must not lie to him and expect him to treat you as an officer when King's Regulations laid down the rules of a private soldier's behaviour to a sergeant.

Therefore, any white man was wrong who did not behave towards a soldier, no matter what his colour, according to the rank he held and the justice which the army ordained he must administer. It was simple. No soldier could go wrong if he lived within the King's Regulations.

He folded the soap-scented towel carefully and smiled at the clerk. Had he revealed what lay in his heart, he would have said, " We will be glad of this new officer, won't we ? The present officer is a failure, and useless, has sold himself. He is a disgrace to the British Army and I am ashamed of him."

He was ashamed of him. But he said nothing. He knew from twenty years' service in the army that a man who did not play straight, who surrendered to the enemy (and the enemy was everywhere, bribing, lying, whining), would fail and would be found out. Such a man could not sleep nights, and the greatest joy, Turnbull knew, for a man in a responsible position, was to be able to sleep nights.

Haji was talking about Captain Sole. Turnbull listened while he thought his own thoughts. It became a habit when one was dealing with gossiping menials. You listened for the facts, not the legend. It seemed that Captain Sole was a good fellow. Haji said he was kind, and he had been a soldier before he came to the Military Administration. He knew there were bits of information which Haji was not giving him. He could get them as if he asked for them, but he would not ask for them. The bits about Sole's private life, which he knew the " natives " loved to know and to relish. He could wait until Haji thought that it was safe to talk openly, and if Haji became too intimate, he could check him. Thus, face was saved on both sides. But Haji would not come into the open. Turnbull resisted the slight twinge of annoyed disappointment, and he smiled at Haji. Anyway, Sole sounded a good fellow. God, it would make such a difference to El Ashang, where the atmosphere was thickening, where he, Turnbull, could not interfere, because he was not the political officer. But he knew nearly everything that was going on. He could feel the growing danger like a smouldering heap of ash, and nothing was being done. But he had everything ready. Reserve rations, reserve ammunition, stocks of water even— private, perhaps foolish, preparations, but if things went wrong, there would be real danger, and he was ready. He knew the fanatics, whether they lived in Palestine, India, or here, in the loneliest place in which he had ever served. He had only a few private fears, and they were not concerned with this rotten, corrupt and hateful place. They were to do with his two children and his wife, now living under bombardment in Britain, while he served here in potential danger, but doing nothing against the actual enemy, the Germans, of whom he had killed six to his certain knowledge. But it was duty and that was that.

One day he would get the transfer for which he applied every month. Transfer to an active theatre. But this place would become an active theatre very soon if something was not done. If only Milton had been found out. If only Colonel Casey knew how the atmosphere of El Ashang was deteriorating, and about Aurella, the whore, that cow who had wound Milton up into the web of the Yonis Barra tribe's secret ambitions—victory over the Omar Bilash. If trouble started, it would be fast and bloody and full of danger. He knew these people. They were all the same. Pitiful and dangerous, overcome at times by the love of a God whom they did not know. He wanted to like Moslems, but when they were poor and ignorant they were the poorest and most ignorant in the world, as merciless and cruel as they could be generous and gracious. He had seen them tearing a man to pieces with their hands in Palestine. He was sick and tired of fanatics. He had had to shoot and beat too many in order to save a hundred others from death and wounds. It was the price of being a British soldier, a soldier of a power which was now loaded with hundreds of millions of human beings who had come to realise their rights, their needs, their due rewards of freedom, that curious state which nobody could really describe, or value.

Haji did not know when Sole was coming, but he would need an escort from the Colonel's headquarters at Malak. Probably the signal asking for the escort would arrive from the Colonel for Milton to-day or to-morrow. Haji said he knew that there were three civil prisoners to go to Malak on the next truck and that Sergeant-Major Abduruman had mentioned that he would like to see the one section of Captain Turnbull's troops now stationed with the Colonel at Malak, if he could get permission to go. Quick as a flash Turnbull said, " Did Abduruman ask you to ask me, Haji ? " and just as quickly Haji denied this and Turnbull believed him. Nothing surprised Turnbull. If Abduruman had done such a thing, it would be a disappointment, but only in line with all human failings, including his own ; and he knew all his own failings. He tried continually to weed them out from his character. From the time he was given his first stripe years ago he had tried to make himself into a man, what he thought was a man.

He had known the strange humiliation of being a British private soldier in India, cut off from the kind of English who were now his comrades and brother-officers. He had driven past their clubs in India in rickshaws, a young thick-set " Tommy " in clean, pressed khaki and topee. Those English had looked through him on the streets, did not know he was there. He never forgot India for those things nor his own companions of the barrack-room, good and simple, but like himself uneducated and unequipped for any life but that of taking orders.

The man who had really helped to change things for him was Captain Sallow, the adjutant of the battalion. He told

3

Turnbull that with his intelligence he should advance himself, take the educational chances which the army could offer him. He asked Turnbull what books he read and was agreeably surprised when he was told, but surprised in a way that pleased the sensitive Turnbull.

In so far as it was possible for an officer and a corporal to be so, especially in peace-time, Captain Sallow and Turnbull became friends. They lent each other books, and any army manual which Sallow could obtain he lent to Turnbull, who studied them, weapons, tactics, drill, regulations, rules of pay, even Field Service Regulations. He read of the Peloponnesian War, of Stonewall Jackson, Napoleon, Alexander, Cæsar, Suvorov. He grew to love Suvorov, the mad, capering soldier of genius.

The army became his life, but did not claim him completely. The other side of him, the side that regular soldiers were supposed to take to cinemas, pubs and brothels, he saved for himself. He saw the inside of India, Hong Kong, and Malaya, places which were known to few British. He ate and talked with the people. In Malaya he fell in love with an Anglo-Malay girl. She was well educated and unusual. He was a sergeant then, and they pursued each other for several months.

For twelve years he soldiered abroad, maturing, forming the habits for a lifetime. Up early in the morning, scrupulously shaved, fresh and fierce for the day's work. Because he was inclined to fanaticism, which he recognised early, he had to watch himself with troops, especially young troops. Not to expect too much, not to drive too hard, not to wither them with the trained scorn expected of sergeants, and of which he knew he could be a master. He was told quietly by Sallow, " Sergeant Turnbull, my friend, watch that tongue of yours. Don't be too sharp. Remember your mind is twice as fast as all those young minds out there on the square. That man who dropped his rifle. You cut him to the heart. Shout at him, yes, but not in that quiet merciless way you are inclined to use."

"I know, sir," he said, "it's true. I know that about myself. I was thinking of something else."

"It's boring for you, sometimes, I know," said Sallow. "The eternal instructing, teaching the same stuff. But you *do* produce trained soldiers."

Turnbull knew that was true. He did produce trained soldiers, he was sure of that. He would not let them go until he had taken the fat off them, weeded the dolts out, and with the rest he had always worked until he was satisfied that he had earned his pay and his right to retain his three stripes.

Palestine changed him more than any service he had known, even more than the Indian North-west Frontier. He became pro-Arab quickly. There was something, *something*, he did not know quite what it was, about the Jews which he did not like. For him they were alien, and the Arabs were not. He began to understand the Arabs from the start, and even when he saw them butchering and burning, he still retained his sentiment for them. Something about nomads and their desert, the simple way of living, hospitality or enmity, they were thorough in both.

He knew that the Jews made factories, made the desert fruitful, worked hard and long, but they were alien to him. He knew that a great many officers and men were pro-Arab and he tried to understand why it could be, but nobody could say. Yet Jews were kind to him. He took Jewish girls out for coffee sometimes, but he was at home with the Arabs. The Jews could change the Middle East if allowed, but Turnbull did not want it changed. He was sick of the huge cement cinemas, swimming pools, brassières and pants, breasts and sandals and dark glasses. He thought the Jews would force that sick culture on the Middle East which he had grown to love. If only he could have rid himself of that feeling that the Jews were alien to him and cut off from him. If only he could have felt certain that the Jews did not think of him as an outsider, a non-Jew. So he made Arab friends over coffee and interminable talk. He learned to speak Arabic fairly well. It was his greatest adventure—actual lingual communication with a people of whom he had grown fond. As the pleasure in the Arab language heightened in him, so also did the small joys of discovery—customs, sayings, subtleties— all the intellectual excitement of a foreign language opening a new culture to him after what seemed barren khaki years.

One night during the troubles he fought two Arab gunmen in a cellar and killed both with a pick-handle he was carrying. It was the first time he had fought hand-to-hand, and it was easy when you knew you were right. He locked the cellar door and left them, rejoining his patrol. He remembered the frightening crack of the pick-handle on the heads of the two snarling, weaving Arabs, and then, leaning against the wall of the dark cellar, soaked with sweat, nervous and happy and triumphant. He had suddenly felt at his best, young, fit, well trained. A feeling that was to come again for him when he lay in a Belgian ditch, his rifle, the rifle he knew so well, pressed into his shoulder, and watched his first two German soldiers stagger and fall as he shot them at two hundred yards' range. Not too much foresight, the blade of the foresight level with the shoulders of the backsight. He knew he had hit them for he did not hear the noise of his shots, which was the sign for him of good shooting. There was nothing more in killing men than that. They plunged and fell and were still. And the flat explosions of mortar shells, the savage thumping of the artillery, and the excitement of the machine-guns moving their chatter as the wind moved went from his mind as the German infantry tried to move in rushes.

He had told Lance-Corporal Bailey to collect every Bren-gun magazine and to cover the wood on their right with fire, and while Bailey did this, Sergeant-Major Turnbull, full of a cold hatred for the young Germans who he had been told were so confident, so tough and resourceful, waited. He wanted to kill a German officer and then suddenly he got one. There was plenty of room, plenty of time to try himself and his rifle. The German officer, young and tall, steel-helmeted, and even wearing black gloves, was trying to exhort men who were lying in cover. While Bailey was raking the wood, Turnbull drew a bead on the officer's head. Range, about one hundred and fifty yards. He waited until the officer turned the flat pale disc of his face, then he moved his rifle sights to the enemy's throat and gave the exact two-trigger pressures which he had taught others for years. The officer staggered and fell, the German troops hugged their cover, and as Bailey changed barrels on his machine-gun and continued firing, the remains of the company retired, fire and movement, drifting clouds of smoke and the earth-trembling of increasing shell-fire. He had known that he was doing his job well. He was not frightened. He knew that nothing could touch or scratch him. It was not his time ; and he would die in a bed. He knew that.

He sometimes thought he had had enough of soldiering, but could never be sure. Perhaps when the war was ended. He could never make up his mind. The thought of civilian life frightened him. Now, as an officer, he had the rank of captain, perhaps would become a major, perhaps would be court-martialled and broken if Milton's mistakes and fears recoiled and he, Turnbull, was left to do the dirty work. Assisting the civil power. Anything you did would be wrong. If you killed, that was wrong. If you did not kill and the mob ran amok, that was wrong too.

Those dark, milling, yelling mobs of thousands he had seen in India, massing at the end of the long wide street, screaming words of hatred, screaming for the freedom which the Government would not give them. He had always been glad to get out of those streets, as was every other soldier. There was something horrible there. People tired of white skins and pale supercilious eyes despising them.

He sent Haji to the office and went to dress. Belai awaited him with a freshly ironed tunic, the medal ribbon bright after a scrubbing with a petrol-soaked toothbrush, the buttons flashing.

When the rusting alarm clock showed ten minutes to six, Turnbull went out to take the first parade.

CHAPTER SIX

SOLE told the driver to stop. They had covered one hundred and eighty miles across the worst country he had ever seen in his life. White, glaring rock and sand with patches of thorn, and they had seen only one human being during the day, a bushy-haired savage with big, black eyes and a face like a god. He had waved his spear and pointed to his mouth. Sole told the driver to slow down, and turning, he shouted through to the sergeant-major on the back of the truck. "Sergeant-Major Abduruman, tell the escort to answer no questions this stranger may ask, and to ask none. They are not to talk. Understand?"

Abduruman nodded approvingly. He liked that. It showed that the captain had some experience, did not trust until he knew, kept his mind active and knew these treacherous and cunning dogs. He spoke sharply to the four *askaris* who sat opposite him gripping their rifles.

The savage approached. He was tall and thin and perfectly proportioned. Though anxious with thirst as Abduruman could see, he did not hurry.

"Water," he said, "water."

"*Ha!*" said Abduruman. "There's water. Drink, but do not touch the bottle with thy mouth." He handed a water-bottle to the savage, who rammed the butt of his long spear into the sand, smiling thoughtfully at Abduruman's words. Before drinking, the savage said:

"From where have you come?"

"From nowhere and we are going nowhere."

He shouted to Sole what he had said. "Shall I carry on like that, *Effendi*?" he asked.

"Yes," said Sole. "And then get any news you can."

The man drank, pouring the cool stream of water into his mouth. Then he paused.

"It is a short way to nowhere now," he said. "You are awaited." He laughed and drank again. Abduruman's lips tightened and he said nothing. The man was cunning, he could be hunting news for interested chiefs.

"I know you," the man said simply. "You are the Sergeant-Major of El Ashang. You are Abduruman, and you are of the Isaak, not of this land." He rinsed his snow-white teeth and squirted the water with a slap into the sand. He smacked his lips and flashed a look at Abduruman, who would still not be drawn, but who stared into the man's eyes and said, "You are of the Omar Bilash, are you not?"

"It is so," said the savage. He was wearing a long bone-handled dagger. Abduruman knew it would be as sharp as a razor and that almost certainly the other had used it to kill, and that long keen spear. He knew all about these people. He could imagine the other with his foot on a wounded man while he drew back the spear for the plunging thrust that would end the life of another enemy.

"From where have you come?" said Abduruman, "and what is the news of the land and the Omar Bilash?"

"The news is the same." The savage flashed his teeth and eyes, unable to withhold the anger of the one thing which no Omar Bilash tribesman could bear. "The Yonis Barra are still drinking our water," he said angrily. "The chiefs have told the Government of this insult, but the Government has done nothing."

"And what will the Omar Bilash do?" asked Abduruman meaningly.

"It will await the word of the Government," he said and then paused—"and of the chiefs."

That could mean anything. But what it really meant to Abduruman was that when the chiefs gave the word, the

Omar Bilash would begin killing. Abduruman laughed falsely, to anger the other, and he was successful.

"Do you not think the Government knows what is in the minds of all of you?" Abduruman asked. "Do you not know that the Government never sleeps, and that it watches all?"

"The Government of the British," said the savage, "is like a loaded donkey in these days. It is loaded with worry and war and trouble. It cannot think of everything. It must climb the hill."

"Who taught you to say that?" said Abduruman sharply.

"It is what all men say," said the stranger. "It is the truth."

Sole was in a dream, his sandalled foot dangling over the side of the truck. He could hear the buzz of the voices behind him. He had stopped listening. If only he could get his wife out of his mind, out of the pain behind his ribs that her memory gave him. Oh, Elizabeth, tender, cruel bitch.

The ache in his back had eased after the jolting, hot, miserable hours across the rocks towards El Ashang. It was cooling and the sun was going down in a red swoon of dusty cloud, that lonely silent sunset of the desert when you could hear the first sough of the evening wind. When it whistled in the thorns it gave him a strange exalted and lonely feeling, as though he had lived a thousand years, as though he were eternal. The desert could not purify him, nor burn out in its silences all the dirt and the rubbish of the thirty-odd years which had culminated in his failure with the one woman he had ever wanted but could not have. She had someone else, he was certain. If only he could know. He had handled it all wrongly, being moved by the hatred which is still love, burning, embittered and disappointed love. The kind of love that made him want to kneel before her and cry in desperation, or to kill her because he could not have her, could not kneel and ask for pardon for something which he could not name. He was full of a resentment, and so was she. A gulf of rage and yearning, of the depths of unknown and incommunicable personalities, which were not simple, which were complex and mazed with unspoken experiences, jealousies, fears and longings. Other men, other women, who had they been? How much had they meant? How did they look? How long had they remained in the " other's " life? Would it be a wise thing to ask the other if he or she had ever *really* been in love with those strangers of which one only knew something vague, something vague but frightening? Sometimes he looked at her and wondered and imagined, and it was like a knife driven into some nameless place, the base of feeling which became something real, almost fleshly, when one thought of the other, the beloved, the lover, the bringer of the agony.

He had never asked, but he had read hints from her voice. He had wanted to cut her mind in half. It would begin, her mind, at the point where he had come into her life, but he knew that her life before his arrival had been her own, and it was a gulf he could never cross. There had been others before him. She could not hide the knowledge of other experience, and this was a torment in him which nothing could heal.

Then anger came, blinding his mind, and he swore he would kill her if he found that she was unfaithful to him. He would like to walk in on her, surprise her, find her out, then kill them both. He would kill them both with his hands. It filled him with exaltation to think of it. He knew his heart would be destroyed, but he would rid himself of the enfeebling doubt and the misery, and the dry, burning lump of pain within him.

Can a man really give himself to somebody? Other quiet men did it, or seemed to do it. They sat all over the world in small houses, thickening, balding, contented, listening to the radio, poking the sleepy cat with a stockinged foot, while the woman sat nearby, intent on some sewing, happy because she was useful to a man. Perhaps these men were happy because they did not demand undying love and allegiance, and therefore got it quietly.

" Make tea," he called, " make tea quickly. We move in half an hour." The *askaris* jumped from the truck and set about the happy work of brewing strong tea for all. They thought they might like this quiet officer who seemed reasonable and without excitement or anger. They would give him what he wanted.

A woman was a physical necessity, Sole thought. Was there any doubt of that ? She was as necessary to a man as a religion. But a man could have a woman even if he could not have a religion. Yet God did not torture you in the same way, once you had accepted him, he felt. He did not worry much about God any more. God could come when he was ready. But the life which he had built privately, those few rooms in the mind reserved for books, birds, history, some music, some other stray interests, and the problem which grew mote urgent in him as time passed, the problem of the shrinking world with its increasing call to his conscience, had been eclipsed by the frightening pursuit of Elizabeth. Life had been so promising. A matter of certain kit, certain clubs, certain habits, all within the framework of a safe, official life which had gradually come to demand an answer from him. Was it right to rule when you were in doubt ? There was no one to whom he could talk about his doubts. He could never again go back to the life of a colonial official when this war was finished. The war might go on for the rest of his life. It was like living in another world which was slowly becoming familiar.

Abduruman was still talking with the savage, but when he saw the *askaris* fanning out in search of brushwood for a fire he lifted his right foot and kicked out with it behind him, so that his sandalled foot caught the sleeping Yassin in the stomach. Yassin yelped and sat up, staring into the sky. Without turning his head, Abduruman said : " Listen, dog, if you do not have tea ready in twenty minutes by my watch,

I will kick the skin from your useless, filthy body." Yassin jumped from the truck and began moving in slow aimless circles while his mind climbed over his fear of the sergeant-major and over sleep. Gradually it came to him. The box containing the cooking utensils, matches, a fire, these were necessary.

"What is it now, dog?" said Abduruman as Yassin crouched below him.

"I need to get things from the truck," whispered Yassin.

"Then get them," barked Abduruman. "And quickly, or I'll drag you up here by your hair."

Yassin moved like a snake on to the truck, anxious to do the right thing, wishing he were back by the sea in the South where no man expected too much work, or too much speed.

The savage had defeated Abduruman in cunning conversation and he raised his hand in farewell and departed. Watching him go, Abduruman straightened his tunic and belt, pressed his turban more firmly on to his shaven head and then jumped from the truck. He walked to the cab, stamped to attention, rammed his cane under his left armpit and gave his measured, unhurried salute to Sole. Abduruman's figure moved slowly through Sole's curtain of thoughts, becoming real, part of now, and Sole said, "Yes, Sergeant-Major, what is the news?"

Abduruman decided to take this chance of outlining what he thought was the situation in the country of El Ashang. This was a chance not to be lost, but he must talk in a way which would not offend the officer at the start. He must talk without giving the impression that Captain Milton was no good. A difficult thing to do, for to an officer in conversation with an N.C.O. an officer was still an officer, and was not to be judged by an N.C.O. But this was important, for the new officer, this reasonable and obviously experienced man, Sole, must start in El Ashang as an informed person, if it could be done, and he, Abduruman, was better informed than all others here, save for Captain Turnbull, who he knew had no influence over Captain Milton.

" The news is not good, *Effendi*," he said, still standing to attention. " It is not bad either, but it may be."

" Stand easy," said Sole, looking at him thoughtfully. " What did that man say ? " Sole examined Abduruman's face. He approved what he saw, for there was that firm mouth and those straight eyes. It was wonderful what happened when the will to serve was infused into one of the fierce, hawk faces of these fine-looking people. Intelligence, truth, straightness, the things which long association within a discipline could put into a savage face. Partly softened himself by such contact with the Western life, the changed savage would be kind to his wife, thoughtful about his children, less liable to steal other people's goods. That was when he was properly trained and unruined by contact with Western dirt. Abduruman had the look of an utterly faithful man. It was strange with these people. You could tell when they had surrendered themselves completely, when they were honest, almost safe from corruption. It was the idea of service, believing in a leader, fighting slovenliness and laziness. Abduruman had reached the point when he could not abide untidiness, when he could read a lying man, the fast and human intuition of a man long experienced in the handling of other men's lives over many years.

Sole was glad to think that Abduruman would be at El Ashang, the disturbed place which the bar-talk in the Officers' Club at Korma said would blow up if " something " were not done.

Abduruman patiently went over what the man had said. It was very interesting, said Sole, very interesting indeed. If only he could have been honest with Abduruman and asked him for the facts about Milton. No one would know more than this sergeant-major, and native sergeant-majors had spies and informers everywhere.

"Do you think there will be trouble here?" Sole asked casually, lighting another cigarette.

"Yes. I think there will be trouble, *Effendi*," said Abduruman without hesitation.

"Unless what happens?"

But Abduruman was wise and said, "It is not for me to say, *Effendi*. I am only a sergeant-major," and he smiled, but Sole was not to be put off in this way.

"Come, Abduruman," he said. "Why this mystery? You know a lot. You are experienced. I am new here. I have no false pride to worry me and prevent me learning. What do you know?"

Now Abduruman did not hesitate. His eyes narrowed slightly and he said, "*Effendi*, these people are savage and excitable people. Do you know them up here?"

Sole shook his head. "I have served only in the South."

"Those people down there are different, *Effendi*. They are slave people. But these people up here are fighting people who trust no man and whom no man can trust. When they kill, they kill many. Now they are preparing trouble. They bring lies to the Captain Milton daily. They, the Omar Bilash, wish to raid and destroy the Yonis Barra, who have stolen the water of the Omar Bilash. It is said that the British Government will not care if there is trouble. They are buying arms from tribes on the frontier and are digging out the many arms left by the Italians. I listen and I hear much."

"Tell me what you hear?" said Sole. He was interested and somewhere inside him he felt the breathtaking gust of some fear about the future. A sense of disaster and trouble, which he fought, but in which he believed. He sometimes said to himself that this kind of feeling was a part of the modern disease, the destruction of the personal responsibility, for himself and for other people. And with no god on whom to blame disaster, one was alone; sterile, preoccupied and alone, alone with the responsibility and the decision, and the fear of the decision. Was it right to do this? What right had one to make these decisions in this century, when all values were moving and shifting on the old foundations, as though one could see them dissolving like mud in flowing water? Memories of rivers, trees, rising suns and music, these were things that had little to do with the dilemma into which he felt his century had plunged him. The sense of responsibility, but knowing too much of the suffering in the world until capacity for horror, fright, concern, was destroyed. If five thousand were killed by air bombardment in an English, a French or a German city, there was always someone to remind you that many more had been killed by the same kind of bombardment in a Chinese city. It was a kind of new measurement of efficiency and scientific achievement, a new dimension of the qualities of appreciation for a job well done, for a fact of which there could be produced photographs, of the actual dead laid out in rows, until you believed it, though still in doubt about whether men could go on doing it. It was like the degradation and murder of Jews; it was true, must be true, that the Germans had so treated them for years before this war, but the mind, for some reason, did not wish to believe it, would not believe it, even in the photographs. Like those pictures of China, they might be fakes. Nearly everything was a fake to-day. People were driven desperately to new solutions, new gods, new pastimes. Colonic irrigation, new sexual techniques, new contraceptive methods, new murder, new misery and new violence. This must be why man had held on to God through centuries of sunlit and rain-cooled misery, through oppression and fear of life and death, the feeling that some power was there who would not show you a photograph of himself, the modern, yet doubtful proof of being, of fact. Yet if one *knew*, one would wish to die at once, for there would be no more doubt, no more reason to wonder and sin, and feel worry and wonder again.

Abduruman mentioned Milton's name, and Sole thought: " Well, we are here. There is trouble brewing. We will throw aside all the artifice and protection methods. Abduruman is a grown man and is sensible. He wishes to talk and help me. Not just gossip. He cannot talk while I hold this wall between fact and me."

"Captain Milton has a woman of the Yonis Barra, has he not?" he said, half regretting, but in his way glad because he had committed himself, for now he could unleash his fears and present them to Abduruman as intelligent searching questions about the country and the people, so that he could arm himself with some of the answers and be ready for El Ashang and its troubles. He did not want trouble. He had seen enough. He did not want any more struggles with the personalities of people, situations in which he was always afraid lest he was doing wrong to them, making unhappy decisions, wondering whether he had really understood their words, savages trying to explain to the Western brain, a brain choked with the sicknesses and agonies of a breaking world. A brain which was only half with them, which was worried about the minorities in Czechoslovakia, the peoples of India, the Indians in Africa, the Jews in Germany, the Eskimos and Indians falling under whisky and tuberculous germs, the women and children in terror over half the earth, and about the far body of Elizabeth, free in a world of hungry men. So that the mind was like a raging fire fed with continual disaster. These savages did not know what it was to be sick in the heart with your own civilisation. They expected help and what did they see in your eyes when they came to be advised, or helped, for they treated you like God? They came for help and assistance from calamity. What did they see there? Tranquillity? Kindness and knowledge or cruelty, the light of another jungle more frightening than theirs? He felt unfitted for this job. He would like a year on a green mountain somewhere, with just enough to eat and drink and time to ponder. But that was escape, cowardice, and yet the heart and mind were choked and unable to really help. These savages would go under the machines, under the cigarettes and the alarm clocks, under the germs and the cannon and the cinematic valuation of a woman's breasts. Uplift and the frightened twentieth-century look in the eye, the aloneness and the anonymity. No clan, no tribe, no family, no land. Only the vast world and the clock, the ache for a lasting peaceful house and the certainty of to-morrow's bread.

He and his companions were carriers of this disease, a disease which he could not name or describe. He only knew that he could go among unknown savages, reason with them, and they would be unhappy, would sicken earlier and begin to die. And in this land, from the Mufid river to beyond El Ashang, there was the effort to work for them and with them, when they were all against him. There was so much to learn about their grazing and water rights, but it was more difficult than it had been amongst simple Africans, for here the tribes lived in a continual state of war, and one could not get at the truth through the thick and cleverly woven curtain of lies. There was a temptation to give up and let them kill each other, especially when they had angered you for days with their lies and arrogance. And there was the fact that the country was really a part of the Italian empire and the British were temporary masters who did not intend spending money on an enemy desert, and the tribes felt this. They knew the familiar answer of the British officer who, uninformed himself as to the country's future, replied to many complaints, " You will have to wait for the end of the war for that. We are soldiers. One day there will be a permanent government." And very few officers wished to stay here. The country was hard and bitter and the climate harsh, and the people were a rabble of bloodthirsty, lying fanatics. Most officers wished to fight on other fronts, return to their regiments and the liveliness of an army preparing for battle. There were a few who would stay here, who would not jog the arm of the tedious machine which could transfer them if irritated long enough by repeated requests for more active service.

Sole was considered by Headquarters to be pro-Italian, because he had fought in a long correspondence for the freedom of an Italian who had been jailed as a Fascist. He had fought until a stiff letter from a colonel had silenced him. The letter said that there was a war between Italy and Britain, and that what junior officers felt about justice was sometimes less important than the decisions of those better informed. This colonel was sadly in love with an Italian girl, Sole knew. He, too, was learning how you could love your enemy. Many were learning this in the arms of women who were enemies and who were able to melt the frost of propaganda, and the memory of the stab in the back delivered by Italy in the summer of 1940. Some of the women wanted peroxide and lipstick, some wanted love, some wanted help of various kinds. The currency was loneliness exchanged in unlit bed-rooms, behind screens, for the military police had orders to stop fraternisation, but they could not stop it, for many of them were lonely and hungry themselves.

The Italians thought the Germans would win in the end and were afraid to mix openly with the British, even had they been allowed to do so. Few would co-operate and each watched his neighbour, and the Latin gift for intrigue and secrecy was given full rein. Lists of names of Italian girls who had prostituted themselves for British officers were found stuck on the entrance to the cathedral at Korma. Anonymous letters threatening death to traitors who worked with the British. Speeches made secretly in rooms to bored Italians by ex-Fascist officials.

"*Ritorneremo*," "*Credere, Obbedire, Combattere*," "*Vivere Pericolosamente*." All the old muscular, Fascist slogans were chalked on walls. And sometimes, looking sinister and exciting, there would be found red stencilled hammers and sickles on the wall of a church, on a memorial to some tired prince. The city was in a state of transition from conquest by the British to a decision as to which side to support. For the Italians, kind-hearted and hard-working by nature, life was difficult. They had not the cold, sullen metal in them which fights on, right or wrong. They had to laugh sometimes, for to continue with the scowl was like being a child.

Abduruman had let himself go. He told Sole the story of the water-hole agreements. He described the barren, hot land in which the two tribes lived, and he drew in the sand with a blunt, brown finger, the border line between the Yonis Barra and the Omar Bilash. The big water-holes were located here and here and here. He stabbed holes in the sand at three points. The distance between these three sets of water-holes was only a matter of a few miles, and in the days of the Italians over two companies of troops had been stationed there. Yet the Italians had thought of something else too, and had drawn levies of men from both tribes and had placed them under an Italian officer near the water-holes. This was after it had been agreed that the powerful Omar Bilash should have sole use of the water-holes, for it was estimated that the water-holes within the territory of the Yonis Barra were more than enough for that tribe's requirements. This had never been disputed again after the Italian decision, which was made at the water-holes following a meeting between chiefs of both tribes in the presence of Italian officers. The tribal levies, men of both tribes working together, patrolled into both tribal areas and they maintained the peace.

" But that meant that in any case there would be peace, for the Omar Bilash had the best of the bargain and were treated as powerful people by the Italians, does it not ? " said Sole.

" Yes, *Effendi*," Abduruman replied. " But the Yonis Barra do not fear the Omar Bilash. They would have fought if they could, but the presence of troops prevented that, as it also prevented the Omar Bilash from raiding into the Yonis Barra country. These people, *Effendi*, if they see there is no organised force ready to prevent them, will raid and kill as much as possible. They do not stand by agreements. They do not consider the cost of their actions. If an Omar Bilash man kills one of the Yonis Barra, then the Yonis Barra take up the matter as though the murder was an act planned against them by the whole of the Omar Bilash tribe. And the Omar Bilash would feel the same in the same circumstances."

"You mean that the only way of keeping peace among these people is to have troops at all important points?" said Sole, and Abduruman said that this was so. It meant, thought Sole, that these people would never be able to learn how to control themselves, would be able to live only in the presence of an authority, which, while benevolent in a time of peace, could be ruthless if trouble started.

Abduruman had told him about Aurella, about how she sent news to her tribe, of her insults to chiefs and men of the Omar Bilash, and of her power over Captain Milton. It had been hard going for Abduruman as Sole asked question after question. The sweat came out in beads under his turban, for he had never before discussed an officer with another officer. Sole saw his distress and said: "Sergeant-Major, you must not be upset by these questions. The situation sounds bad and therefore I must know as much about it as possible. I must know about this woman as well, for she seems to have a good deal to do with the situation. Better that I hear these things from you, and I trust you, than from the mouth of some informer or police spy."

He then asked for details of the present position at the water-holes, and Abduruman told him that when the British advance took place, men of all tribes ran wild, killing and stealing, frightening those who were peaceful and helping those who wished for violence. Some tribes fought their way through the territories of others, returning with great stocks of looted camels and arms. Small tribes who had never before been able to disturb the peace, joined other more powerful tribes of their own tribal groups and sought power.

These movements took place at a time when the warriors of the Omar Bilash were out in force and looting in the territory of tribes in the North-east. Therefore, when the Yonis Barra camel herds came to drink at the water-holes, guarded by laughing Yonis Barra men who waved Italian rifles, there was none to oppose them. The anger of the Omar Bilash was great, but they could do nothing, for in the area were thousands of British troops who were moving to attack the mountain strongholds to which the Italians had retreated. There were fast armoured cars with machine-gunners in the turrets, and a temporary supply base was formed near the water-holes, so that there were many British troops in the area for months, and the Omar Bilash hid their arms and waited. During this time, the Yonis Barra had surrendered many arms to the Government. They thought that the great numbers of troops in the country would always be maintained, and they had got what they wanted, use of the water-holes. They thought also that if they did not surrender their arms, then British columns would loot their camels, a threat made to their chiefs by a British officer who seemed to know they were well armed. They gave up large quantities of rifles, grenades, ammunition and several machine-guns, and looked to the British to be their permanent champions in a time of war and poverty.

The Omar Bilash denied the possession of arms when their turn came to surrender. They called the bluff of the British officer detailed to cajole and threaten them, and they said stubbornly that if the officer did not believe them, then he could come and search for himself. It would mean transport, rations, ammunition, water supplies, troops, and months of marching through a hostile desert, looking for arms among a people who had been ordered by their chiefs to surrender nothing. The army in front had come up against a hard patch of Italian resistance and every man and truck would be needed. The British officer appealed to his commanding officer by radio for permission to take camels from the Omar Bilash and hold them until the chiefs were willing to exchange rifles for the return of the camels. The British officer, alone, thought as all officers do in such circumstances, of prestige, of the necessity for an example of firmness, and was angered by the faint smiles of the chiefs who watched his helplessness. And it came about that soon afterwards the officer and his troops were recalled to take part in the growing battle in the North. A special political officer would be stationed at El Ashang with two army officers and a company of troops. These would be responsible for the peace of the country.

The angry British lieutenant, packing to move out with his troops, wrote in a private letter to his Colonel that the Military Government was mad if it considered that two officers and one company of troops could control thousands of square miles of desert inhabited by these people, who were enemies of the British and treacherous in every way. But his Colonel ignored the letter. He was worried about the coming action for his battalion, about the rawness of the new recruits from the depot, about poor rations and about promotion.

So the liveliness of hundreds of men and trucks disappeared from the Ashang desert in clouds of dust and glittering metal. The Omar Bilash watched them go with satisfaction, and the chiefs, the patient, aged chiefs moved the focus of their plans to El Ashang, about sixty miles south of the water-holes. They must feel out the ground, test the new officers, divine the plans of the British Government, which sat at far Korma on the sea.

An *askari* brought tea in a mess-tin and Abduruman took it from him and poured some into the green tin mug, which he handed to Sole, who thanked him and told him to drink what remained. They drank gratefully, Abduruman still standing easy, but in that ready respectful attitude of one who cannot really relax, who is not nervous and yet stands ready to do the instant bidding of his senior. It was a kind of muscular tenseness, so that he still seemed to be at attention and not truly at ease. He was thinking about Sole's eyes. They were very dark and piercing, they flashed keenly. They were not like the cold blue eyes of Captain Turnbull which he had seen staring through a liar, full of an expression which was like cold disgust for something bad, and yet saying nothing. Sole's eyes were warm and hot and full of movements. Turnbull's eyes were still and cold and altogether those of a man who always knew he was doing the right thing. Yet while Abduruman almost worshipped Captain Turnbull as a soldier, he already felt more warmth towards Sole than he had ever felt for his own officer, and he could not understand this. It might be that he knew where he was personally with Sole, and with Turnbull only when he was a soldier. Yes, that seemed right. He did not know Turnbull as he knew Sole, for although he talked much with Turnbull it was nearly always about soldiering and war. Turnbull would never ask for help as Sole had done and yet he felt no less for Sole because of that. It made him wish to help Sole, and to tell him more of what went on in El Ashang, but he got rid of this temptation and was quiet as he drank his tea. He noticed that he did not feel uncomfortable while quiet and unemployed in Sole's presence, which was a strange thing. Sole seemed to trust him ; probably he trusted all men like that until he learned all of them by experience. El Ashang would probably worry and puzzle him, but when they got there together all this relationship would end. He would be the Sergeant-Major of C Company under Captain Turnbull. He wondered what Turnbull would think if he knew that he had discussed the state of things at El Ashang with Captain Sole, the political officer : he might be glad. On the other hand, Turnbull might fix him with that cold, silent look and ask by what right and by whose order had he spoken thus to the new officer. As though reading his thoughts, Sole turned from staring at the darkening desert and said, " You need not tell your officer you have spoken of these things to me, unless you want to. He is a strict soldier, is he not, and he might be annoyed with you ? "

" Good, *Effendi*," said Abduruman. " Yes, he is a fine soldier and we have a good company. Captain Turnbull knows better than anyone how to train soldiers. He is stern and just, and if a man is dirty and a liar, or a thief, or no good, then he will not have him in the company. He transfers him at once."

" Good." Sole smiled when he saw the earnest, somewhat proud expression in Abduruman's eyes, as though he were talking of some hero of his tribe. " Are the troops of the same tribes as live up here ? "

Abduruman looked grave and said, " There are about a dozen men in the company who are related to the tribes up here. Captain Turnbull has tried to transfer them, but head-quarters don't seem to take any notice. They are good soldiers, but if there is trouble, it will be hard to trust them, for blood and tribal relationship is very strong amongst the tribes up here. The Captain wants only men from far South as soldiers here, for they have no bonds with these tribes. Most of the soldiers *are* from Southern tribes, though they do not seem to be able to go as long without food and water as these tribesmen here. That is because they come from a fat country which always filled their bellies."

" Yes. It is a hard country and the men from the South were not born in country like this. Here there is nothing. No grass, no water, no food."

" And the people who live here love their country, *Effendi*," Abduruman said and laughed softly. " They speak of it as a paradise, and they sicken in a fat country if they go there. It is a strange thing. Like when we take camels from one land into another. They may sicken and never work until they die. The most obedient and willing soldiers I have seen, *Effendi*, are Africans, but they cannot live without water, plenty of water, and women." They both laughed, Sole affectionately when he thought of the good, simple-hearted African peoples he had known and when he remembered their musical laughter and chatter. He noted that Abduruman did not seem to despise them because they could not go long without water. He knew the pride of these people in their powers of physical endurance. It was vain and boastful and cruel. And these people were cruel because their country was cruel and because in the early formative years of their lives they must live like wolf cubs, snapping at whatever morsel they saw. Brought up without discipline or the softening influence of happy people, they grew into violent and quick-tempered men and women, sharp and without pity, and were thus fitted to live in their barren, sun-beaten desert of rock and sand where all men coveted your camels and would kill you for their possession.

Sole threw the dregs from his cup into the sand and said, " We're off, Sergeant-Major." The driver jumped into the cab as Abduruman came to attention and saluted, and Sole smiled as he heard the different, metallic voice of Abduruman shouting orders to the *askaris*. An N.C.O. had two personalities and two voices ; his own, and the other, strict yet kind, hard yet human, for the troops.

Sole gripped the door of the truck as it began bouncing and heaving over the rocks on the last few miles into El Ashang. He was worried and still apprehensive, an officer going to take over a bad station, where things were " not right " and where trouble was awaited.

CHAPTER SEVEN

IT is one thing, Turnbull reflected, to write a report to headquarters in which such things dominate as the necessity of revising the ration scale, the supply of rifle oil, the morale and health of the troops, and the weather conditions obtaining in the area. But it is quite another thing to have to sit down and tell headquarters that something is wrong with their policy; and worse, that there is something wrong with an officer in the station, who belongs to a service generally considered senior to the service of the writer of the report. It is hard, thought Turnbull, for the soldier to write with subtlety

and care of the defects in the administrative methods of a
political officer, for the soldier is a tool of the political service
in an occupied enemy territory. This had worried Turnbull
for weeks, for there was no one with whom he could discuss
it. He moved the problem about in his mind each day, and
when he lay awake for those few valuable minutes before
sleep came, he sometimes felt immense courage. He would
not care. It was his duty to inform of a situation which was
spoiling the name of the British, which was sure to lead to
trouble.   And trouble would call for the use of troops,
vehicles, recruitment of levies, transfer of officers badly
needed elsewhere, and all those other small but important
necessities which devoured grants, which ate like an acid
through the money of taxpayers in a war which had already
passed the border of lunacy in matters financial. Turnbull
knew about it.   He knew, in his restricted but thoughtful
way, how the small things like the wear and tear of boots,
uniforms, and cleaning rags, incensed some little man who
had slaved for years in a Government office somewhere in
that other dimension beyond the fort, beyond the sands and
the rocks and the oceans, in a soot-blackened building towering above the friendly traffic of London. It was perhaps this
little man's decision which could cause a mutiny among the
troops because the issue of red pepper was cancelled in a time
of great need, or who caused joy because he saw no harm in
an extra shilling being spent on each soldier's footwear in a
land whose name brought only a mistaken romantic picture
to his mind, but not the hot, humid, scorched and lonely
reality.

To recommend operations, to advise that it was " time
something was done," would mean conferences in Korma,
the weighing of intelligence reports, conversations on the
experience, character and abilities of the man who had written
the recommendation in a fort a thousand miles away from
the atmosphere of normality in which these senior officers
discussed the alarming report. They would say, " Now, this

fellow, Turnbull, has said so-and-so, and so-and-so. Read this bit. What does that mean? Does he dislike Milton? Is Turnbull 'round the bend,' deranged, due for leave, inexperienced, frightened?" They would say that and then they would argue. There would be a friend of Milton's who might be a good talker, more politician than serving officer, who would sway the decision by his command of words. Or there might be too much talk until all were exhausted and it was time for a gin and bitters, and nothing would happen.

He would have to be careful and exact, prudent yet unafraid, restrained but conveying enough of the potential danger to alarm those who did not live in this atmosphere which now could be felt in the air of El Ashang like a kind of thickness or tenseness in which ordinary incidents seemed dangerous, full of menace, part of the intrigue and the coming violence.

It was time to write the report, whether there was a new political officer coming or not. It was necessary that his opinions should be filed, in writing, with his own military headquarters, so that even if they did not heed him and left him to the turmoil and the decision, they could later read that he had weighed the situation and had warned them, had done as much of his duty as they would allow. He had to control his anger when he thought of the hundred ways in which they could prove him wrong. He might ask for troops and full-scale disarming operations, and then trouble might not come after all, and there would be private laughter in offices at headquarters, scorn in the bars of officers' messes. It was the price of being a soldier in the service of the civil power, where curious mercurial diplomacies mingled in the same stream with swift brutalities, crass concessions at wrong moments, curious faddish innovations dreamed and forced into reality by some old official who had served too long among the Warumbo, or the Gonds or the Masai or the Jumping Jiwawas of lower Jiwawaland. These old men, relics of an age when a gunboat carried the angry voice of Britain's pride—these old men would not retire fast enough, and yet they were great men, men of character, puzzled in an age which had discovered the petrol engine, the radio, the aeroplane, and the fact that a human being was a being with certain rights, even when he was black.

It made him clench his fists to think of it. It was not that he would deny people their rights, even savages, but it was all moving too quickly. The headquarters people could not call him dangerous if he called for troops. No one could say he was anti-native or without understanding of uncivilised peoples. Rather had he been accused in the past of being too generous with rights and privileges for his native troops. They could not say he disliked coloured people, for he knew it had been said that he lowered the white man's prestige among them by some of his actions. Playing football with them and drinking the black, strong tea from the same bucket after the game, eating with them while on patrol, teaching them awkward facts instead of hiding them, even those which might show his white race in a bad light, and answering their more awkward questions.

No, if he wrote the report, there was his long and unstained record behind him. When they read his report, there would be those readers who would say : " All right. It's convincing. But don't forget he's only a sergeant-major really, an N.C.O., and it's his word against Milton's."

But what had Milton told them in his own reports ? What inkling had he given them of the trouble which was due to start ? How much of the truth had he told them, and how much did they know about his woman, that sly whore who had once scowled at him in the village so that his throat had dried with fury ? And if they knew about her, how much did they realise of her dangerous influence in a matter which in any case should have given them cause for worry and immediate and determined action ? If Milton had reported the tense atmosphere then things would not be so bad perhaps. But there was no sign that the authorities down in Korma had received such a report.

It all pointed to the need for a talk with Milton. It could be either a careful, half honest and therefore fruitless talk, or it could be open and direct, even with the possibility of quarrel and shouting. It was time to have it. For all the notice Milton took of the atmosphere between the tribes and between the Omar Bilash and the Government vested in Milton and Turnbull, they might be living comfortably in Brighton or in the officers' club at Korma.

When he saw the fingers of his watch pointing to five o'clock, Turnbull took out his pipe and began to fill it. He smoked only two pipes in the day; one after breakfast and one at five in the evening when it was cool again and the sunlight had softened and streamed through the window of his company office. Then the blue fragment smoke hung and swirled slowly on the evening light, heightening his enjoyment of one of his few and carefully controlled pleasures. Pleasure had to be watched carefully or it won and had a man at its mercy. There had been a time when he was a slave to the tobacco habit, and one day he suddenly decided to end this domination and he entered upon the agonised days without tobacco. He remembered how the day came when he could trust himself. When he had that craving on a leash, he had decided to give himself the harder test of only one pipe of tobacco a day instead of the shrilly triumphant ache of none. And this he had increased until two became his habit and he was safe and in charge of himself again. The five o'clock pipe helped him to think soothingly and he valued it as much for this as for the comfort given him by the slowly puffed smoke and by the calmness it brought to the ending of a hard day of physical effort and office routine. It was good then to think over the day and to see that it had been usefully filled, that he had earned his day's pay, his field allowance and his ration allowance.

Turnbull considered that the daily achievement of a man should be " to be able to sleep nights," as he put it. A man could sleep nights if he had done his day's work and had dodged nothing of his responsibilities. It was therefore time that he wrote his report, for the night, when it was silent and calm, was not now the simple experience it had been. He lay awake longer and framed the headings of reports he hesitated to write. Simplicity, facts, cold and weighed, these were the two secrets of a report. He tied phrases together in his mind until they rang satisfyingly true, but always he shirked the phrase which would describe why Milton was wrong. If only he could write the truth about Milton, his uselessness, his weakness, his having given up the attempt to " keep his end up." If only he could do this, yet sympathetically and carefully, so that none could accuse him of malice. He had probed and examined himself, had admitted that he personally disliked and despised Milton and had then cast that aside, leaving only the useless military character of Milton who was allowing the British Government to be mocked among, not just an enemy people, but an ignorant and backward group of savage tribes.

Watching the smoke curl in the golden bars of light which slanted to his desk, Turnbull decided to go and see Milton and talk it over ; find out what Milton thought of the situation, and then he would give his own views, and if there was trouble and a quarrel, each would at least know what the other thought. Milton would never make up his mind alone, and he, Turnbull, had reached a stage where he was willing to commit himself over what he considered to be a matter of conscience and duty ; if there was to be a quarrel, he was willing to be the cause of it.

Belai, his Abyssinian servant, put his head through the open window and said that tea was ready. He looked hard at his master, who was doing more thinking and staring these evenings than the usual things like playing the gramophone, or reading those piles of books which were in the black tin trunk, which he coveted so much and one day hoped to own.

He thought he knew what might be worrying the Captain ;

he wanted to go away from here to the war as he had often said when he, Belai, had asked where their next station might be. The Captain was one of those men who would always be sent to lonely forts where a man could not even buy a lemon and where the eggs were small and pale-yolked, and a chicken came like leather from the pot even after hours of cooking. There were other officers, too, who always were sent to these bad stations and the servants had to go with them or seek other masters. Belai was saving money, but the tribesmen here would never accept him because he was a Coptic Christian, one of the enemies of their Moslem god, and a drinker of liquor when he could get it. Captain Turnbull let him have one bottle of gin in the month from his own supply, and for that he was grateful, for he knew that most officers would refuse to keep servants who drank liquor. Belai and Turnbull were satisfied with each other. It was as far as they could go in association, but it made life easier for both. Turnbull did not lose his temper, or shout and curse if something went wrong.

Drinking the tea, Turnbull decided to go now to Milton's house and not after his bath. It would be more to the point to arrive there in shorts and puttees, working uniform, as though he were still on duty and that this was a duty visit. He wondered if Milton would notice a thing like that, what N.C.O.s called " on parade " and " off parade."

He stood up and buckled on his Sam Browne belt and told Belai to delay his bath. He was going to see Captain Milton, and Belai hid his surprise; the Captain looked determined about something, but worried too. With that intuition of servants who both like and fear their masters, he almost knew how worried Turnbull felt. He wished to delay him, but could not; he wished to consult him about many things, but dare not. Only when the master wished to talk could one really meet him and like him. He might ask advice, suggest a possibility for one's own future, talk with kindliness about one's wife who was thousands of miles away, or go over old stories of past places, past officers, the strange things they did, or of their virtues, generally their virtues.

Belai sighed as he placed charcoal in the open belly of his flat-iron. He was weary of the atmosphere in this place. In that last station, Captain Turnbull had been so happy, so pleasant, so easy to understand, but here in El Ashang these last two or three weeks, he had been different.

Belai had to watch what he said and did, for the Captain often sat unusually quiet and unemployed, and watched, with a queer expression, everything that Belai did. The dusting of chairs, the moving of books, the sweeping of the floor; he commented on it all, took more than his usual interest in things which really did not concern him and which, usually, he left to Belai. There was something wrong with the atmosphere. The Captain seemed to occupy his mind with things about which he had never previously worried, and he found fault where usually he had found none.

Turnbull walked across the moonlit sand towards the lights of Milton's house. He could hear the noise of Italian jazz, tinny, sad and irritating. Milton would be having a brandy now, and that bitch would be there, slim, attractive, depending on his hunger, and with the strange, unassailable confidence of the black woman who had power over a white man in the face of hostility from another white man. He knew all about it; could imagine what she would say to Milton when he had gone, asking for reassurance of something of which she was already assured. It was only a step, reflected Turnbull, from the bedroom to the office, the files, the scraps of knowledge for which chiefs would pay. If only the British could solve the undiscussed problem of out-stations without women, could even consider it, instead of taking the chance, relying on the character of men who must spend long, nerve-fraying months alone in places of sand and rock in strange parts of the globe. Suicides, disease, intrigue, no one ever discussed the problem openly. Perhaps the British were right to leave their marooned administrators to their own choice, to the many staggered hours of temptation and the sometimes comic yearning for a woman's company, even that of a black, gleaming smoke-scented girl with whom they could not communicate in any language, but who would look at them with huge, animal eyes and smile.

Oh, he knew all about it, had seen it so often, had learned what it could mean and what good it might do, and what harm and dangers it could bring. He did not mind, did not even care whether a man kept a native woman or not. He understood the desire, more spiritual perhaps than animal, for this sad and undignified relationship with a woman; a woman—meaning just that—the opposite to a man. So he did not despise Milton for his failure to live intact and alone, he was sorry for him where " that " was concerned. The bed was one thing, but the government was quite another, and it was Aurella's power which enraged him and caused him to despise Milton as an officer. And if it became necessary, he would say so, and he would be interested in Milton's reply. Milton could not, obviously, see what was happening before him any more. He seemed merely to hope that everything would go along peacefully, and that balancing the two tribes on the rope of his soothing words would keep things going until his time for transfer to another station came, until Sole arrived. Milton thought he could leave Sole holding the baby, Turnbull felt, and that was the most despicable thing of all.

He knocked on the latticed door, and listened to the jazz and the fat Italian voice singing. It was like treacle and honey, and it was about *amore*. Aurella opened the door and smiled, but her eyes were hostile as she revealed her white teeth.

To have to ask if the Captain was in, to have to ask this primitive, Italian-varnished whore if he could see Captain Milton. Christ, no, he could not do it. He walked past her into the room, taking off his cap, standing a moment, then he called, " Milton, are you in ? " then more loudly, a trifle less apologetically, " Hello, there ! Are you there, Milton ? " He heard splashing water, then silence. Milton called, " Who's that ? " Turnbull told him and there was a long silence until Milton spoke.

" I'll be right out." Then, " Is anything the matter ? " There was worry in the voice and Turnbull's lips curled. He knew what worried Milton. Had the Omar Bilash attacked the Yonis Barra yet ? " Not yet," Turnbull called in his coldest voice. Best to get off to a good start. He could imagine Milton sitting in the soapy water thinking about that silently. " Not yet." It gave the whole picture.

Aurella stood with one hand on her hip, angry and dramatic, waiting for Turnbull to turn and look at her when she could show him her feelings, but he knew this, and ignored her. Instead he sat down in a basket-work armchair and folded his arms. Aurella walked over and stood before him, having tightened the native skirt about her beautiful hips, and the white, smooth cloth wrapped about her waist and over her breasts was fastened at one shoulder. She knew that most Europeans would have stared hard at her, for many whimpering Italians had been unable to resist these parts of her so dressed. She wore a black, silk headcloth, bound tightly around her short hair, and the lamplight threw gold lights on to the exquisitely moulded face, the large, black, liquid eyes, and the short, straight nose. Her black skin had a velvety bloom, and a glow as though there was a soft, dark heat within, so that he who touched this skin would expect to feel the texture of a peach's skin, but he would have felt a cool firmness, almost cold, and would be reminded of an eel, or like Milton, only of his desire.

" You do not like me, do you, Captain ? " she said in broken Arabic.

" I do not understand," said Turnbull. He lay back in the chair, his arms still folded, looking at her with the faintest expression of distaste on his mouth. She repeated what she had said, and again Turnbull told her that he did not understand. He saw her small nostrils widen and her purplish mouth quiver for a moment.

4

"I speak in Arabic," she said angrily. "You speak that language, why do you not understand me?"

"I do not understand," Turnbull said again, frowning slightly.

Aurella's eyes became glassy and they narrowed. She turned as Milton came into the room, buttoning his shirt. His thinning brown hair was brushed flat on his head, and he had the bright look of one freshly bathed, though his fat, pale face was gloomy, even slightly hostile.

"The Captain does not understand Arabic to-night," Aurella said sharply, in the voice of a shrewish wife who has grown used to a weaker man.

"What's the trouble?" said Milton. He was surly, but he smiled quickly when he saw Turnbull's cold, almost transparent blue eyes turned on him.

"Which trouble do you mean?" said Turnbull. "About Arabic or about out there," he jerked his head. He was angry, and he expected Milton to send his woman away, and with that intuition which weak, clever men often possess, Milton saw this at once.

"Go into the kitchen," he said to Aurella. She stared at him for a second and then walked slowly and awkwardly from the room.

Milton rubbed his hands and as he bent to sit down said jocularly, "You've come for a row, I suppose, Turnbull. Is that it?" He laughed engagingly. He was too fat for a man in his thirties. There was a small, hard paunch bulging from under his belt. It would be pale, thick fat, bred at a desk in the shade, Turnbull thought. And the cleanly-shaved double chin, the well-padded chest and ribs over which the shirt was tightly stretched. He had put on even more weight since the last time Turnbull had drunk here.

"What makes you think I have come for a row?" asked Turnbull as pleasantly as he could, pressing down the anger he felt rising in him.

Milton laughed awkwardly. "Oh, I don't *know*," he said.

" You looked cross when I came into the room, that's all. Sorry about the woman. Did she annoy you ? "

"Yes. She did," said Turnbull. " But I really came to have a talk with you about the situation in these parts. I'd like your opinions on certain matters that affect us both, and may affect us even more in the future."

Milton raised his eyebrows, and his eyes watched Turnbull's face carefully, reading it, worriedly but shrewdly. He could tell that Turnbull wanted a serious discussion and once more he felt resentment of Turnbull, the ex-coalman, the ex-barrack-room ranker, who wanted a talk as though he were determined to have it. He was about to speak but Turnbull cut in and said quietly, " Before you get angry, Milton, I just wanted to tell you that I won't stand for any slick talk, or any attempt to show me my place. I knew my place long before you knew yours. We have avoided each other and probably by mutual consent. Now, we must discuss this place as simply two officers on the same station. That's all. And—if you're not worried about the situation here, I want you to know now that *I* am. Do you see what I mean ? "

He had leaned forward and Milton sat back, smiling, but nervous, anxious to retain his position over Turnbull, but anxious to please too, for he was frightened of El Ashang and he knew that Turnbull was worried too, if not frightened. He would have liked to make friends at once with Turnbull, unburden himself of all his fears and worries, ask for help, but some stubborn resentment deep in him forbade it.

"I see what you mean," said Milton, his voice shaking and then recovering its usual tone. " You seem to be *very* worried."

"And you can cut that stuff out too," said Turnbull in the same quiet voice. " Never mind if you wish to think I'm *very* worried and you're cool. Have it your way. First thing I'd like to know is, have you told Korma that there may be trouble here ? "

" No, I haven't," said Milton sharply, sitting up. " Why ? Do you think I should ? " His mouth trembled.

" Yes, I do. Because I'm going to ask for troops if you don't."

" You can't, unless *I* ask for them." Milton's voice rose and his brown eyes were hot. " *You* can't ask for troops until I say so ! "

" Then say so," said Turnbull. He could not withdraw the contempt from his voice. " Say so. Or is it your opinion that we won't need them ? Do you expect that when the trouble starts that I will be Joe Soap, with one company holding the baby ? That you refer the matter to me, when it goes wrong for some mysterious reason ? " Milton tried to speak, but Turnbull said, " Wait, I haven't finished. There's a lot I'd like to say, but it may not be necessary. The main thing is that I want to know what you are going to do. I know you are expecting your relief any time, but you've been here for a year nearly and things are now going wrong. Or don't you think so ? I want to know what you think, so that I can do whatever I *must* do. It is up to you to say. Do you believe the situation is dangerous or not ? That's all I want from you, your opinion on that."

Suddenly he felt a kind of pity for Milton, who sat with his lips moving, unable to speak. It was like seeing into the private, secret life of another human being, making him ashamed of himself and of his victim. But this feeling was removed when he thought of the violent nomads who, once they had ceased to care about the Government power, would slake the appetite of their tribal pride until they were exhausted, or stopped by a greater violence than their own.

" Do you really think it is so serious ? " Milton then said. " Don't you think you are overdoing it perhaps ? "

Turnbull saw into Milton's eyes and into the fervent wish for escape from this place. Milton's time was up here and he was losing his nerve. If anything did start, he would probably be a nuisance, like an old lady in a night club, like a padre in the sergeants' mess.

He had seen them before, this type, put into a position of authority for which they were too weak, and they were seldom found out. Many did well for themselves and for their country, providing the crisis did not come which would demand more of them than they had to give. Like this one in the cane chair here, sweating and wanting to be relieved, wanting to climb into the truck and get away from it all. The glaring heat and the endless sands and shale upon which the sun raged from dawn until dusk, the danger and the undone work, the sense of surrender to fear, failure and weakness. It was only a matter of being willing to kill, to stamp ruthlessly on ruthless people, for their own good and for the good of countless weaker and helpless people. That was the way Turnbull saw it. It was when you had been weak and had let it go too far, that you had to stamp on people and thus punish them for your own weakness. He, Turnbull, would have to do it for Milton, for Milton's weakness, and it made him furious.

"Fancy having to ask for troops *now*," said Milton. He appeared as if he might break down. Turnbull would know what he was thinking about. He was thinking about what they would say in Korma, in headquarters, in the officers' clubs and messes, at parties.

"You mean you are worried about what they will say down in Korma?" said Turnbull. His voice was innocent.

"Yes," said Milton in a quiet voice. "They'll gas about it for weeks."

"How terrible for you," said Turnbull acidly. "How terrible if they say things about you. Is that all that worries you? Isn't there something else perhaps?"

"What do you mean?" Milton shouted. He jumped to to his feet, glaring, one hand plucking at his shirt pocket. His face had reddened and the sweat suddenly darkened the tight sheen of his khaki shirt.

"Oh, sit down, for Christ's sake," said Turnbull wearily.

" To hell with Korma and to hell with your feelings too. You *did* this. You created this situation, let's face it, but I want you to know this, that you send for troops before you leave this station, or I'm going to write in a full report. I don't give a damn what you do with yourself, but in my opinion you're dodging your duty, and you're trying to plant it on me, and on the new chap who's due to relieve you." Now his voice was angry and full of contempt. Milton sat down, his teeth showing in a kind of still smile of fear, or terror, and the colour had gone from his face.

He listened to Turnbull fascinated.

" But," said Turnbull in a calmer voice, " you're not going to get away with it, nor that black tart, either."

" Don't speak like that to me," shouted Milton, but Turnbull took no notice.

" You mean mentioning a woman's name in the mess ? " sneered Turnbull.   " You and that tart have ruined this station. When the tribes do blow up I'd like you to be here, in command. How would you like that ? "

Milton did not reply. He was staring before him, thinking about how easy and good life could be sometimes.

Suddenly he burst into tears and as he cried his sharp, bar-trained mind awaited the hand on his shoulder, the softened voice and the words of compassion. But Turnbull said in the same steely way, " You useless bastard. Shut up and listen to me and don't behave like a bloody woman in pod."

It stabbed him, deeper and more wounding than anything ever said to him. The humiliation lifted him to a frenzy and he got to his feet, screaming and cursing, yet conscious all the time of each fresh shame, each terrible revelation of himself and his failure beside this hard, cold, neutral machine from the ranks.

He did not know what he said. He was holding his left wrist, his face wet with tears, ugly in the yellow lamplight, and his mouth was wet and broken, as though the will and the spiritual muscle had been taken from it. Turnbull sat, cold, but fascinated, wondering why he was not more kind, remembering Captain Sallow of years gone by. What would Sallow have advised? Kindness? It did not matter. He would now do and say as he felt.

Milton cried out about unfairness and lack of understanding, and about lies and treachery and mistakes made at El Ashang in the past by other officers. The hand on the shoulder would have helped him, would have allowed him to sit down, cry a little, get over it, be brave. Then Turnbull could ask him softly to be reasonable, to consider, to remember that he, Turnbull, understood. It was the strain and so on. But standing, having made a fool of himself, and Turnbull silent, watching him, and waiting to go on with his cruel merciless talk, left him alone, stripped, beaten. He cried now from his heart, partly from remorse for his failure here, and for the past, the untidy, unplanned past, and it filled him with pity and a frightening loneliness. He could not cry any more. He wiped his face with his wrists and sat down, dazed, the pupils of his eyes enlarged to great blackness, his face wet with tears in the bright sobering light. He was like a child who has been beaten and who recognises the power of the father and now he looked at Turnbull, and felt defeated and alone. They were silent for nearly a minute, Turnbull leaning forward with his elbows on his brown knees.

" You're a useless, snivelling little bastard, Milton, aren't you ? " he said in a calm voice, as though what he had said was a fact, irrefutable. " Well, your time's up here "—he paused—" on paper, that is. But you will carry the can back with me. Expiate yourself and your sins, just like in one of those bloody novels about Captain Carruthers of the Ninth Lancers on the Frontier. The honour of the regiment and all that. Too much bed with a woman weakens you, doesn't it ? You must not mind me rubbing it in, but I know you bastards so well. Nice face, nice manners, nice talk. You say in the mess that the British N.C.O. is the backbone of the army. How bloody true." He scratched his shin, digging through the short puttee with his broad nails, wincing with pleasure. Then he said, " Write a signal asking for troops. Write it *now*."

" All right," said Milton, " I'll do it now." His relief had changed his voice. He sprang from the chair and hurried away to his office.

Turnbull smiled, watching him go. Then he did something which surprised him, but with which he agreed, for it was a special occasion. He took out his pipe and began filling it. Just this once. He was trembling and he felt a tiredness as though someone had frightened him badly. There was nausea in it. He thought again of how frequently in his life he discovered that he was not the hard creature he had grown to imagine himself. This tiredness and this curious fluttering feeling inside him was like the almost thankful exhaustion after battle or after a safe escape from prolonged bombardment. And there was the same selfish thankfulness, for having survived, or as now, of having done his distasteful duty. A touch of uncertain regret also for having failed to hide his contempt for Milton, but could it not be that his contempt had been the very weapon which had shown Milton his error and weakness ? How could a man ever really know these things ? It was seldom that he allowed himself to wind these cocoons of doubt and conjecture around the simple machinery of an ordered mind. But he did not like the inside workings of other human beings. It was shameful and somehow sickening. A human being was an unknown thing which should stay unknown. Much as he disliked and despised Milton, he did not know whether to blame himself or Milton for the shameful breakdown which had turned Milton into a weeping, pitiful child. He knew too that Milton would try to avoid him now, following the outburst, the humiliation with all its social implications, all its threats of scandalous talk in the future.

" But perhaps he knows me better," thought Turnbull. " He must know that I would never discuss this thing with anybody. But I'll report it if necessary." If a senior officer, in the line of duty, asked him what he thought of Milton, then he would say what was in his mind. Milton had that right too, but probably he wouldn't care if it was an official right or not. " If he had anything bad to say about me, he would say it anyway, anywhere." Turnbull sucked his pipe, his eyes unseeing. He felt weary, and anxious for peace, a fireside, the kids playing, the radio on, and the snug, shut-off fireside away from the world which had shown him little but harshness and trouble. But what was peace, and where was it to be found ? He missed his wife so much sometimes, it was like being very sick. The wish for peace and a need for ordinary, normal situations, requiring ordinary and normal decisions, about bread and clothes, and the electric light bill, if you had electric light. Sometimes in her letters he had seen this thing, this almost desperate preoccupation with the holding of the fort, *her* fort, against all comers, against loneliness, against occasionally voiced physical longing for him, against bombs and years and the hand of time which slowly changed her face, her body, her mind, which was always lost and anxious without him, though courageous and full of hope. Yes, he saw all that, but what could he do about it ? The most important thing in life at present was Milton and duty. He knew what it was to wonder if there was *any* sense in life at all. To want one thing so much, with all his heart, but to be doing another—with all his heart. When you realised that you fell back on facts—like " I am here. It is like this, I want and wish so much to do that—but I must do this. It is my duty ! " He supposed that anyway a man never got what he wanted, but what prevented him from being with his wife ? The war, yes. But before the war, he had been separated from her, and would be again after it. Day after day, writing letters, getting older. But there was no sense in it. Better to be delivering coal again with a home to go back to, and the kids, and probably less money, but at least he would be growing old with his family, he, changing slowly before them, they, his wife and children before him, not changing while separated for years and then meeting as strangers almost, dumb, and full of unspeakable longings and hopes.

Then he heard Aurella's shrill voice, rising in anger from one of the rooms at the end of the house. He could not distinguish the words, but they were angry, scornful, and probably they fell like a whip on Milton. He must have told her of his decision to call for troops. She would not want that, not seeing, shrewd as she was, that the Omar Bilash would kill many Yonis Barra if the trouble started. She only knew that the Yonis Barra had the use of the water-holes and felt perhaps that if troops came they would move the Yonis Barra back into their old water-holes to the south. She preferred the present balance and probably imagined that, under her influence, Milton could keep the peace.

Sitting in the cane chair, Turnbull could hear Aurella's angry voice and Milton's reasoning with her. He felt a great longing for the power to punish Milton. If only he was a Colonel. He would have had Milton broken.

In his bedroom, Milton tried to quieten Aurella, but her fury frightened him. "But I *must* send for troops," he said to her. "I *must*. Things have become dangerous. The Omar Bilash will attack your tribe otherwise, and drive them from the water-holes. You don't want that, do you?"

She spat on him, quivering with rage.

"You said you would not bring the troops. You promised me. My chiefs and my people have believed me when I said you would not bring troops. If the troops come they will drive my people from the water-holes. Always it has happened in the past that way. When troops come they stand up for the Omar Bilash and drive my people from the water."

"But, Aurella, I *must* bring troops now," said Milton. "Please understand!"

He tried to get hold of her, but she struck his arms from her. "I promised the chiefs," she snarled. "I swore that troops would not come." She considered telling him of the large amounts of money her tribal chiefs had paid her for her work, but she changed her mind. If he sent for troops her work was finished. The thought of what the chiefs would say when she told them made her wish she could stab Milton on the spot. She had sworn before her chiefs that she could influence Milton in any way she wished, and she had done so nearly a year. And now, in the last stage of Milton's service here, while the chiefs were discussing what they might do about the officer who would replace Milton, this fat dog was calling for troops. She screamed abuse at him and Milton turned pale when he saw the hate in her eyes. She was trembling, her hands clenched, while she shouted above his protesting words.

"You will regret," she screamed, thrusting her face against his. "You have let the army officer frighten you, and you will regret."

"But Aurella," he pleaded, "it is for the best, I swear. The troops will protect your people from the Omar Bilash, who are getting ready to fight."

She bared her teeth and cursed him in her own dialect which he did not understand. She and the chiefs had many plans which now would come to nothing. She spat in his face and Milton stood before her, frozen with shame and anger. His face turned a greyish-white and she backed away from him, calling him a hermaphrodite dog, a *kants*, the greatest insult among her people.

There were tears in Milton's eyes. He was torn with grief and misery, with a familiar tender lust for her, and with shame for the spittle on his face.

"Aurella," he pleaded hoarsely. "I love you, I love you." He came towards her and she saw the tears on his face. They fascinated her. She had never seen men of her own race in tears, only one or two of the white men she had lived with. These tears in the eyes of men disturbed her, moving something in her which she did not understand, but Milton's face revolted her. She wanted to strike it, claw it, in some way hurt it. She struck his hands down as he struggled to clutch her. She could see that dumb, tortured look in his face, like that of a sick animal, the look she knew so well, prelude to what the white men called love.

"You are going to call the troops?" she shouted. It was the last attempt and she saw the battle in his face.

"I must, Aurella, I must," he pleaded. He tried to embrace her, but again she avoided him.

"You will regret," she said, and ran from the room.

Turnbull heard an angry hand on the door-knob, fumbling, and when the door opened, he saw Aurella, taller, slimmer, her face distorted with rage, near hysteria. She screamed at him in English and Arabic, accusing him of interfering in the affairs of Captain Milton and in the political affairs of Milton's office. She advanced until she stood over him, her small hands clawed, spittle foaming at the corners of her mouth. Turnbull stood up and struck her hard with the palm of his right hand, knocking her across a cane chair. She fell to the floor, and he saw her eyes distended with shock. Then he took two paces and looked down at her while she crept to her feet, her large eyes fixed on his, ready to obey, changed into the tribal woman who knew only the power of men. She held her left hand to her cheek and some tears flooded her eyes, probably of pain, Turnbull imagined.

"Get out of this room," he told her, "and don't come back while I am in it." She almost ran from him, leaving the door open. He could not know whether he had made an enemy or a willing follower. You could never tell with these bitches. She would go and think somewhere, reckon up the odds and perhaps act. Then he felt a need of her, a shudder of desire for her, perhaps because of her eyes after he had struck her. It was a queer thing and it did not anger him, for he still felt weak and in a way frightened of something. The row with Milton, his nervous state which had demanded a pipe of tobacco, and then the release of his violence and despair in the blow he had struck Aurella. But he could not deny that he would now be kind to her were she to appear before him, that there was a tender but animal feeling in him for her—until he remembered that she belonged to Milton. If only they could all go home—home, and be left alone, in peace, with bread and light, and wives.

He did not know whether to go or not. He stood and stared distractedly at the cooling pipe in his hand. Then he walked out into the sand, and he was still worried, for even though Milton had decided to send the signal, there would be many days before troops could arrive. Korma was a thousand miles away, and Korma did not always do things at once. Down there conferences dragged along, people yawned more easily and time seemed to fly so that it was time for a gin by the time a chap had opened his file of the case under discussion. No, it would be all of fourteen days before troops could arrive. He hoped there would be good officers with them, and that they would have petrol, rations and ammunition. It was sometimes frightening what stupid things the base *wallahs* could do when equipping troops for a fast move. When he reached his office, he sat at the desk and drew up another plan, for it was best to have an alternative.

Already Turnbull had accustomed himself to the idea of reinforcements arriving at El Ashang. He considered the possibility of accommodating them in the old Italian Air Force workshops. Then there was the question of water supply. It would mean the employment of camels to carry the water from the already overtaxed wells to the reinforcement camp. The problem of fresh meat rations with mangy sheep costing seven and eight shillings each, but, and a cold smile moved his lips, whichever tribe started the trouble would feed his troops on sheep and goats, either seized or requisitioned at an operational zone price of one shilling. Nomads who lived on camels and goats were hurt in their tenderest and most vulnerable spot when you took their animals. They liked you to chase them and hunt for their rifles, but suppose he did not chase them as they moved at speed in the trackless bush, but drew up in the rear with their slow-moving flocks of sheep and goats, and then his troops devoured these flocks and moved off for a fresh flock ? Suppose he did that ? Well, it would do two jobs, it would feed the troops and save the taxpayers' money, and it would hurt the tribe so much that they would either voluntarily surrender their rifles, or at least listen to the order for their surrender in a reasonable state of mind. But these tribesmen were even tougher than Arabs or Pathans, for they lived a harder life. Even their scarce water was bitter and aperient. In a thousand miles of country beyond El Ashang there was one fresh water spring, and when Turnbull had once drunk at this spring after long weeks of patrol, the taste of the water was so good that it made him think of the wonders of the universe and even of the goodness of God. At times like that, or when you wished to halt during a hot midday march and fall flat on your face in shade that was never really shade because the thorn trees had no leaves, you saw the hardness and cruelty of the nomads' existence. But Turnbull never let it soften him too much towards them. For over two hours he studied the maps, guessing future tribal movements. Then he closed the file containing his operational plans and walked across to his house. He felt lonely and in need of action.

Reaching his door, Turnbull did not resist the feeling of pleasure which had been growing in him since Milton had agreed to write the signal to Korma. Now everything would change. The signallers, all natives, would pass the word round that the Government was sending troops, and the chiefs would hold secret meetings and would be in doubt and in fear.

Whistling softly, he turned up the wick of the hurricane lamp by his bed, and in the armchair near him he saw Aurella.

She stared at him and smiled, and a terrific trembling began inside him. His throat dried up while he looked at her and he wanted to shout at her. But suddenly it was too late and his stare became different. He could see her bronze softness, alone with her in this silent room, and the sound of her breathing drew him, for she was more beautiful than he could have guessed.

CHAPTER EIGHT

IT was as father had said, " There'll come a time when you won't be so smart, and when all your smart friends have deserted you, and you will be alone and you'll wish you had listened to me. I'm an old man," and so on ; but had the old man been right ? Milton lay face down in the darkness of his room, his hands pressed over his ears so as not to hear the howling of the jackals who swarmed on the edge of the village.

" Am I really a failure ? " he asked himself, but he could get no answer. But things were moving closer to him, half frightening things, closing in, making him want to run away. Again Turnbull's words echoed in his mind, shaming him : " But you'll carry the can back with *me*," and the bitter, cruel words about expiating his sins like a novel about the Frontier. For he knew that Turnbull would make him do his will now, and he wished to obey, he wished Korma would immediately appoint Turnbull to command, freeing him of responsibility, and of the galling humiliation of being in command and being called a snivelling little bastard at the same time by Turnbull. The memory of Turnbull's words, driven by a hard will, humiliated him afresh each time they crossed his mind, making him bury his face in the pillow. He thought of shooting himself. Several chaps had done it and he had been present when the living, who discussed it, had called those suicides " fools and cowards." It would only take a minute, but when he thought of the hard, cold muzzle against the bone of his forehead, and the jolt and shatter of the explosion, his heart turned in him; and what about the other side when he had done it? Death. What about hell and heaven and falling into the hands of that fearful God of his childhood? He sat up in panic, breathing quickly, and his dried throat seemed to close. The terrific weight of the night and its darkness seemed to lean down on him, as though he had been cast out by men and was utterly without hope, without friends, without to-morrow. It seemed to have eyes full of longing and compassion for him. Had he been evil in his life? Was it really evil to avoid responsibility? Had he not always paid his share when he could? Had he not been willing to pay for the things he had done and which in his childhood he had been taught to regard as wrong? Was it wrong to love Aurella? No, people would not understand it, but he loved her. And love was being unable to do without somebody. It must be, for what else could it be when the thought of not seeing Aurella again, of losing her, gripped his heart like a powerful hand and squeezed the will from him so that nothing seemed worth while.

The feeling of failure was new to him; often he had had doubts, but not this feeling of complete aloneness, for now he would have to lose Aurella if he sent the signal asking for troops. And he could not bear it, he could not do it. It was the one thing she had asked him not to do, the thing she had fought against. Somewhere in his mind he knew there was the voice which disputed this, the voice which could tell him that the time had come for a decision, and that Aurella had nothing to do with the decision he should make. But he could not make it. He would lose her, and he could not face it. He moaned. He rubbed his forehead in the pillow to wipe the sweat from it.

Aurella had gone, probably to her room. He heard his heart beating, throbbing through the bed, and he breathed deeply until he trembled. If he sent the signal, he would lose her, and he could not, could not, could not bear it. He was beating his clenched fist on the pillow, and as soon as he saw once again that she was his master, not his mistress, he as quickly denied it. It was only that he could not bear living without her.

He decided not to send the signal, but to wait, for what he did not know, but only to wait, and to see what would happen. There was Lieutenant Cuddy, the huge ape-like man whom he had seen only twice, who had been patrolling the water-holes for four months with his platoon. Surely with Cuddy and his platoon in the area the Omar Bilash were unlikely to attack the Yonis Barra. He began to reason again as to why the Omar Bilash should make trouble now when the Yonis Barra had been using those disputed water-holes for over a year, but he knew too that these people would fight at any time. Yet he ignored this doubt. He could not send the signal because he would lose Aurella.

He felt somewhat relieved to know that he was not going to send the signal, but Turnbull appeared like a shadow across the faint light of his optimism. He would have to lie to Turnbull, invent some story about lack of troops at Korma, but the thought of Turnbull's hard, cold eyes watching his while he lied made him shiver, and aloud he sighed, " Oh, God, oh, God."

He fell asleep muttering, and the jackals crying did not reach his ears. His dream moved in his mind, making him writhe as though disturbed by pain. Outside, the moon was full now, and poured a flood of light on to the sands, and the fort became a block of silver which shimmered against blue shadows and softly glowing shale. Nearby, the village huts huddled around the mosque, and against its white purity they appeared shabby and squalid. Milton's house showed the only glow of light.

From the shadows of the last village huts one figure moved across the bright moonlit sand until it entered the shadow of Milton's house. Here, the man rested for a moment, looking about him. Then he took off the grey, cotton skirt which was his only garment and stood up. His body gleamed with goat-fat so that he could slip from the firmest hands. He was young and lean; in his right hand he held a long, sharp dagger, and tied on his arm was a *tariq* wrapped in a pad of leather. Aurella had given it to him and it would protect him from all harm.

Some time after dusk a man of his own clan had called him from his hut. "Our chiefs have sent me for you," the man had told him.

He went to the house of the Government contractor, Elmi Farajalla, and there he had found four of the chiefs of his tribe, the Yonis Barra, squatting round the Government woman, Aurella.

"Come here," she said to him. "You are the son of Haji Ahmed?"

"Yes," he said, "I am Fara, his son."

Aurella took an egg from a wooden bowl near her and broke it on the stone floor.

"That is the Government Captain," she said, "Captain Milton. Like this egg, he is broken. You are to kill him, Fara, like this egg." The chiefs nodded and he looked into their old eyes as they sat huddled in their cotton robes.

"Like that you will kill him," they said one by one.

"We have called you to do it because your father killed two Italians in the time of the Mullah," said Aurella, smiling at him. Fara smiled back with pride. "You are strong, and young and brave," she added.

"Yes, I am," said Fara excitedly. "I am. What will you give me for this?" The chiefs and Aurella exchanged a look and Aurella said, "Many camels we will give you if you kill him."

"I will kill him," said Fara fiercely, and Aurella began to give him instructions, making him repeat them after her in the same way that the Mullahs had taught him the Quran. "He will be asleep," said Aurella. "It is the right time to kill him," and the chiefs nodded. Fara was excited and he drew his dagger. "I will kill him with this to-night," he said, and it was agreed.

Aurella sat rocking herself, clasping her feet. She felt pleasure in the thought of Milton's death. He had made her wealthy, but now his time was over. She had never felt remorse in parting from the white men whose beds she had shared. This one had to die. The Government would blame the Omar Bilash and arrest their chiefs. No greater blow could be struck against that tribe. They would not then carry out their long threatened attack on the Yonis Barra. And what would the strong Captain Turnbull do? He hated Milton. Captain Turnbull was a man. She felt her cheek burn where he had struck her. She wanted him now, those strong, cruel hands on her. She had seen a look in his eyes after he had struck her, the white man's look, not like that sharp look of the men of her own race; the white man's look was soft and sharp at the same time. But Turnbull's look was not like the other white men's looks, he was like a warrior. If she could have him she would make him a friend of the Yonis Barra.

She had bathed in hot water and then had stood naked over a brazier in which she had cast fragments of the precious scented wood from Persia, the *Ud*, which would impregnate her skin with its perfume for days. It was for Captain Turnbull. She would give him pleasure while Fara killed Milton, the frightened *kants*.

Fara loped along beside the Captain's house until he found the open door, and he went in, crouching and slow with caution. The light from the lounge helped him and he saw the low open window which Aurella had described. This window led to his quarry, the first white man who would fall to his right arm. He asked God to assist him, and then he peered through the open window. Silence and darkness. After a time he could see the end of a white man's bed, its wood gleaming softly in the almost complete darkness. He measured his next movement with his eyes and then in two long, silent leaps he was in the room. He stood absolutely still until he could hear a soft ticking and he thought about this for a time until he realised with pleasure that it was the sound of the white man's watch. He traced the position of the sound, and it was from the bed which he could not yet distinguish beyond the faint shape of the wooden bed-rail. Then he wanted the watch. It was a deep wanting, for he had seen several on the wrists of Italian officers, and now he could have one for himself. He could wear it and he could listen to its sound. His heart was suddenly full of happiness with this knowledge, and he knew that the white man was wearing the watch and was lying in the bed only a few paces from him.

He knew too that the white man had a revolver. Aurella had said that he kept the revolver under his pillow now, for the white man had become afraid of death. But Aurella had not told him why. "Kill him," she said, "and I will give you much. You will have camels to spare and I will be the cause of your wealth."

He stood, gripping the dagger, listening, and suddenly he heard the slow, steady breathing from the bed. He listened to it for a few moments and then, sharply, it stopped, and then it began again, but it was different now. It was faster for a moment, it stopped, was slow, and then the breathing moved and quickened. The white man was awake.

Milton turned slowly on to his back and listened. His heart stumbled and raced. The last few hours rushed into pictures through his mind. There was someone in the room, he was sure. It could not be Aurella. He was sure there was someone in the room. It was a feeling of not being alone, of being watched, yet it could be the worry and torment in him which made him so afraid, but he could not console himself. Slowly and carefully he sat upright, making not a sound, his right hand moving quietly until it found the cold shock of his revolver butt, and he gripped it, but resisted the temptation to thumb back the hammer. There would be a click and the unseen " somebody " would hear it. The trigger was cold against his forefinger. The fear made his mouth open and

he said in English, " Who is there ? " but no one answered,
and the silence rolled back over him, black and deep and
terrifying. He pressed his fist holding the pistol against his
hip and stared into the blackness, and he could feel somebody
there watching him, waiting to move to him.

The other waited, straining his eyes. He knew that the
white man was now sitting upright and that almost certainly
he had a revolver in his hand. He took one long, slow pace
forward into the deeper darkness, and again he asked God to
help him, so that he could kill safely and gain the things he
coveted and which he had been denied for so long. He
crouched now, holding the dagger far out from his right side,
his arm drawn back, ready to stab with all his force, and he
felt the growing urge to kill the white man behind whom
stood the camels which he had never possessed. He had
nothing now save his dagger and he had no wife, no camels,
no goats and soon he would have all.

He could see the white man at last, the soft, momentary
glow of moving eyes and the faint flicker of a brass button,
and he crouched lower. Milton's breathing was deep and fast
and his hunter could smell the fear in the room, and when he
was sure of the distance, the poise of his dagger, and the
gathered spring of speed in his muscles, he moved in a long
swift glide, and drove the dagger into the white neck. He
locked his left arm around the white man's head and stabbed
him deeply in the back, feeling the power of the blows
shuddering in his clenched dagger hand and in the struggling
body of the white man. Milton uttered long moans until he
fell back dead from the grip of his killer, who knelt beside
him while feeling for the watch. He wiped the blade of the
dagger back and forth across the bed-sheet, while his groping
left hand found the watch, and the gold links of the strap
puzzled and then angered him. He gripped it with both
hands and pulled, shattering the links which went tinkling on
to the stone floor ; he held the watch to his ear, hearing its
strong tick, and he laughed aloud with pleasure.

CHAPTER NINE

CHIEF KALIL ABUKIR of the Omar Bilash sat waiting for arrest. He was wearing his best turban of soft yellow silk and he sat cross-legged in the cool half-darkness of his sitting-room, watching the bright sunrays moving across the floor towards his sandals. A lump of incense smouldered in a white clay charcoal-pan in the centre of the room and the blue fumes filled the air with pleasure for him, helping to calm the turbulence which seethed and milled behind the mask of his black, emaciated face. His eyes seemed struck still and dead, but occasionally a light burned and quickened in their depths and went out again.

He had done everything he could immediately after hearing of Milton's death, though he did not know who had caused it. Soon many dead Yonis Barra tribesmen would lie around the water-holes of Nalang. When he thought of the dead body of Milton, he could hardly bear the pleasure it gave him. But his hate was still unsatisfied. He would have given much for possession of the body and to see it savaged, cut up and flung to the jackals. He screwed his face up and shut his eyes tightly as the joy of Milton's death warmed him again and again. He rocked to and fro, his arms locked round his knees, and he thought of his life, of when he had been young and had led the marauding bands of the Mad Mullah. Oceans of yellow sand and the horsemen galloping, shouting that there was but one god before they attacked the *zariba* of the white men. In that time a man had all the possessions he ever needed ; good weapons, good saddles, women and camels, and the excitement of owning the land and of having power, the power to move and roam at will, to kill and punish those who did not belong to the way of the Mullah. And for years there was that power, and the deserts of many-coloured sands to the north and the east and the south were the raiding grounds of the Mullah's men. Then the English and the Italians joined their forces against the Mullah's men and brought English and Italian, Indian and African troops against them, for so great was the Mullah's power, and his barren lands so hard for the white men. But they could not defeat the Mullah's men, nor could they establish themselves in a land hostile to them, for nearly always they were tied to the water-holes, and when they ventured far from their bases they were at the mercy of the fast-riding Mullah's bands whose scouts were everywhere. It was not until after the first great war fought by all the white men in the world that the power of the Mullah declined until finally he was beaten, mainly through treachery. But the white man could never find the Mullah himself, nor did they ever find his grave, and even now no white man knew where the Mullah's body lay.

The chief's eyes flickered and he told a few beads, his mind far from the prayers. He knew that to-night he would be in gaol, but he would not be there for long. He had ordered the chiefs to tell the people that it was time to drive the Yonis Barra away from the water-holes, to oppose and worry the Government and to show their will to all the British, for the land was tired of white men, of rules and orders and restrictions. Men could not pay off old scores and they had to endure insults from inferior people because the British officers said that it was justice. A man's tribe counted for nothing now, and it was white men like Captain Turnbull who were the enemies of the powerful tribes, for his cold eyes measured all men as the same ; but he was powerless to work his will because he was a soldier and not an administrator. Now, with Captain Milton dead, he would be in control, but only for a short time. The clerk in control of the signal station had said when questioned that there was a new officer called Sole on his way to El Ashang, and he would arrive at any moment. And with him was that soldier-pig, Abduruman, returning to El Ashang. But when Sole arrived he would find much to worry and distract him, for in a few hours the Omar Bilash would be moving.

All men over the age of fifteen years would be moving with rifles, spears and bows, and if necessary the two machine-guns would be brought from the cave near the Moon Spring in the rocks at Gaban. He had told the obedient Hashi Eleyu to rouse the people and to tell them that now was the time to drive back the Yonis Barra, even though their chiefs might be in gaol, and to await the return of the Italians, who, when they had defeated the British, would be driven out in their turn by all the tribes. Eventually the land would belong to the powerful tribes, and the most powerful would be the Omar Bilash.

Kalil crooned to himself, rocking to and fro. He was old and wished to see the Yonis Barra defeated and driven back into their land, so that the British would learn that the land did not belong to the British, or to any white man. The land would be full of death and fire, and the Omar Bilash would have the camels of the Yonis Barra.

While the chief sat awaiting the arrival of the soldiers who would arrest him, Turnbull paced his office, torn between exultation and worry. He had what he wanted now, but some of it frightened him, it had come so quickly, an avalanche of trouble driving him to files, to the armoury, to the barrack-rooms, to Milton's office and house and back again, giving orders, sending signals, driving the sergeant and the corporals, and finally the maddening, enraging, almost unbelievable discovery that Milton had not after all sent the signal requesting troops. Turnbull had gripped the chief signaller by the arm and shouted at him: " But you must have sent it last evening. It was urgent. The Captain Milton must have given it to you, you fool." He had shaken him as he would shake a rag, but the signaller swore before God that he had received no signal from Milton. He showed Turnbull the neat, numbered signal copies and it was not there. Then the search through Milton's house and through his office, but there was no signal, and he cursed the dead Milton into hell as a treacherous, lying and useless eater of the King's rations who not only could not do his job, but who shirked even the keeping of his word given in snivelling tears. Turnbull went to the room where Milton still lay, stuck to the bed by his dead, congealed blood. The dead man's skin was snow-white for his wounds had drained him, and his eyes, dusty with death, looked up and saw nothing.

Turnbull stared at him, his lips moving, rehearsing the military funeral drill which he had not performed since Palestine. It was different in battle. The dead piled up and were trampled upon, forgotten, and they could not have the proper thing; the bugles and the reversed rifles and the saluting. But this useless bastard would have it all, and it would be done slowly and deliberately, and gravely, so that the savages could see the burial of a British officer, for which they would pay.

He sent an urgent signal to headquarters, copy to Colonel Casey, requesting the despatch of a company of troops, saying that Milton had been murdered and that there would probably be heavy raiding.

Turnbull rammed his hands deeper into his pockets and frowned. Then he twisted his face up and spoke aloud. " But good Christ, surely you could have at least sent the signal off. I admit I was a bit bloody to you *sometimes*," he said, addressing the office, " but you are a *bastard*, and you know it, don't you ? " Then he frowned again and stared at the cement floor. Millions of thoughts rushed up again, but at the back of them all was the satisfying yet infuriating thought that he had been betrayed. For the first time in his life he was undecided about what action to take concerning his duty. This was something which did not explain itself to him as did the matter of rations, ammunition, family allotments for the troops and so on, " and so on and on and bloody well on," he shouted to the empty office. He banged his fist on the desk again and again, and aloud he said, " I wish to Christ I was back with the coal-cart." But it was no good to wish that. He was here, alone, and outside there were things going on about which he could only guess. He had declared a curfew in the village, and he had stationed two standing patrols on the two highest buildings in the fort, as well as a small patrol of half a section which had orders to move gatherings of more than five people in the town. He would not arrest the chiefs yet. He wished to give them time to make a mistake. He hoped that one of the chiefs would send messengers to the tribes and that he could catch one of these messengers. He had never approved of police methods, spying, suspecting, scheming, but now he must do it. He knew that the chiefs were expecting arrest because they had told one of the *askaris* so earlier that morning. They knew about Milton's death within half an hour of the terrified cries of the dead man's cook, who proclaimed it as he ran to call the guard. The rush of the *askaris* across the sand and the shouting as they fell in to the shrill whistle of the sergeant; and Turnbull had felt the flutter of panic in him as he tried to imagine what it all meant; this intrigue, this hostility, this perplexing mixture of lies, pride and greed ending in the killing of Milton. It could only be the Omar Bilash who had caused his death. The aggrieved and brooding chief, Kalil Abukir, would know all about it for it must be he who had planned it. Turnbull struggled with the wish for a personal revenge on this chief, the insolent one, the liar with the black mask of hate and bitterness.

It was nearly midday. A vulture hung like a speck of dust high up against the fierce yellow globe of the sun, and the machine-gunner in the tower sat over his gun, black and sharp against the sky. He moved his head from left to right, watching the village in which only a dog moved moodily, sniffing at rubbish, scratching itself unhappily.

It was silent and hot, and the giant sun approached his zenith until the desert surrounding the village was a sheet of glaring whiteness and the village looked shabby and grey and utterly miserable.

The machine-gunner wanted to kill somebody. He was not of these people. He had a flat nose and thick lips and he came from the big river in the South. He had not eaten fish for several months and he remembered the times when he had trailed the pot of poison-bark in the river until the fish came blinded to the bubbling soapy surface and to his clever hands. Up here in this wilderness there was no river, no fish, there was no family, there was no peace. These people hated him because once his flat-nosed people had been their slaves and now he was their master, behind a machine-gun, and they had killed the white man. He sighed for a woman and hens near a hut, for green trees and the smells of his home near the brown swirling river. He licked up the drops of sweat that crawled to his lips. "Do not fire until you hear my orders," the Captain had said. "If you see anything strange, shout and then cock your gun, and wait for orders." But nothing happened; he watched crows flying lazily over the mosque and then he saw the patrol marching slowly between the huts near the market. They carried their rifles at the trail and the lance-corporal was secretly smoking a cigarette as he walked behind his men. The machine-gunner envied him as he thought of the smoke and the taste of it. He thought of how he could inform the sergeant of the lance-corporal's indiscipline, but it was too much trouble, too dangerous. He would have to wait another hour for his smoke. The sound of the Captain's iron-shod boots walking up and down the office reached his ears. What was the Captain going to do? Nobody knew, save the sergeant, and all he did was curse the men for a gang of idling thieves.

Last night the Captain had had a woman in his room, it was said. The night picket announced the news in the barrack-room at dawn. "Our Captain is now a man," he had shouted. "He has slept with the cast-off whore of the political one. She came tired from his room and I saw her with my eyes."

It was some time before they believed him. They were still discussing it when the whistle blew, and they tried to realise that it was the alarm and they heard the hard voice of the Captain shouting orders. The machine-gunner saw that the Captain was wearing a pistol and as he buckled on his equipment, Jama Fugas, the company cook, said, " While the whore lay with our Captain, death came for the other one, the fat Captain. Someone has killed him by the knife." Now there would be trouble, said the cook. It was the Omar Bilash who had done it. They had sworn to have revenge for the loss of the water-holes, and now they had killed the Captain who had kept the whore of the Yonis Barra. Why did she sleep with our Captain on the night of her owner's death ? There was much that a man could not see in it. The cook laughed until his belly shook. He said there would be much killing and " I will cook your food," he said, " safe in my kitchen."

The gunner watched the dog move down the alley between the huts and then he turned his eyes to the crows which were wheeling and hopping into flight, pointlessly, as they had done for an hour. The village, which seemed emptied of all human life, made him feel afraid, for he knew that the huts were full of the handsome, contemptuous people who hated him, and he felt alone, even behind his machine-gun. He tried to remember what he had been taught about the various stoppages which might occur during firing, but he could only remember one of them. He ran his hand over the heavy belt of brass cartridges and they were hot to the touch. Then he asked God earnestly to send him home to the big river, but God did not answer.

Turnbull could bear it no longer and he called for the sergeant, who came clattering into the office and slapped the butt of his rifle.

" *Effendi*," he said.

" Go and arrest the chiefs of the Omar Bilash," said Turnbull. " If there is any trouble give three blasts on your whistle. If a crowd collects, do not fire into them. Retire to the fort, but not without the chiefs. Be quick and quiet. The men will charge the magazines of their rifles but they will not load unless it is really necessary, and only on your order. Do you understand?"

"I understand, *Effendi*," said the sergeant. He slapped his rifle butt, turned smartly about and went running to the waiting section, who were standing easy outside the office.

"Now it is done," thought Turnbull. "I have done it." He longed for the arrival of Captain Sole, who was due at any time now. He thought of sending a truck out to look for Sole, but decided against it. He might need it for other things. Had he done everything possible to ensure against a surprise attack? Ammunition, rations, water, the signal station, the wells? Yes, he had complete control of the village wells and the three thousand people of the village could get water only at four o'clock in the evening, and then under the eyes of the *askaris* who guarded the wells. But his troops were thinned out on the various duties which the situation demanded. There were never enough troops when there was trouble. Troops must sleep, must be relieved by others.

Now he must bury Milton, but first he must see the chiefs safely into the gaol. Milton would soon be stinking to high heaven if he did not plant him. It did not take long in a hot climate for your best friend to revolt you when dead and left above ground, never mind Milton. It was a funny thing, death. The first time he had seen friends killed, he had grieved, but as he became more experienced he knew that it was just a matter of not seeing a chap any more. He was dead and you were not, and you wrote him off. His kit was collected and flogged to those who would buy it in the mess.

He tried not to remember Aurella and his angry surrender to her. But he could not help it. All the years of effort had melted, and it was like a fire blazing in him when she came and put her arms around him, dissolving all anger, all pain, all days and months and years, so that the fort and the danger and the duty disappeared before this engulfing fury of the cheated and long-patient body. His mind which was not really there heard her murmurings, and her false words of love, but they were part of the machinery of purely physical love, and he remembered them from other times he had known when younger, before he had married, in Egypt and India and Malaya, when it had been important to sleep with a strange woman. And now in the middle of a forgotten desert he experienced it again, and with it the crushing loneliness and disgust he had not known before, as though, after all, he were not the master of himself, but only the slave of a body which had waited years to show him this fact. It was better to be like Milton about these things. The need of a woman was like the need of food or water, purely physical, and when you had to have it you bought it and ate it. But he thought of his wife and the kids, and he knew with regret that now he would fall again and again, whenever opportunity permitted, until he could return to them and the peace and normality which they had long promised him.

With that surrender something precious had gone from his will, that part of a man which gives loyalty to things that cannot be seen, and which Turnbull could not properly describe even to himself. Like shaving every morning, even when there was no one to know if he had evaded that duty, like being present at parades when they could easily be avoided, and like keeping promises to people who would not really mind if they were forgotten.

No, he had said in anguish, it would spoil everything, watching her rise from the cane chair, her large eyes no longer flat and black and cowlike, but lit with the desire she sensed in him. The enormous forces of life had seized him, from deep within his structure, from the abyss of ignorant torment, like forces which in anger took his will and destroyed it, leaving him helpless at last so that he went to her blindly, mumbling and cruel, whispering pathetically.

He was as she had guessed he would be, and she was silent while the released hungers within him grew, assuming his shape, becoming him, so that he forgot himself and was lost in that force which had caused him, but lacking its tenderness, so that the animal was altogether convulsed in fierceness and all was forgotten in the red mists which hid his mind.

When he thought of it now, he put his hands over his eyes.

"Why did you come here?" he had asked her when he woke up. It had been dark and cold then, and he had shuddered in her presence, yet humbled before her as she sat cross-legged on the hard Arab pillow at the foot of his bed. He could not ignore the beauty of her nor the innocence of her smile, but greater than this was the feeling of shame which made him shout at her:

"Why did you come? Answer me."

"Because you needed me," she said earnestly, her voice soft. Then he remembered that she belonged to Milton and she saw his face change. She thought it was anger she saw there, not knowing the civilised disgust of white people, and she shrank from it, for she was now afraid of Turnbull, having begun to want him for herself. For he was fierce to her, not pleading, unlike other white men. She mistook his angers for ardour, being content to be used roughly and thus appreciated, rather than be asked questions which she did not understand about his feelings.

"Go now, and do not come back," said Turnbull, then sharply he asked her, "Do you want money?"

"No," she said, shaking her head fiercely. "No, no, no. I do not want money. But if you want me to be your woman, you can call me and I will come to you. I have finished with this other Captain. I will come to you only."

Her words brought back the pattern of El Ashang and its troubles, and he shouted at her:

"Go. Go. And do not ever return here."

He tried not to look at her, but he was unable to resist it, and he saw her shame as she hurriedly dressed herself, casting him looks of secret disappointment and of what he frightenedly assumed to be affection. He had hid his face in the pillow as he heard her sandals scuffing across the room, then the click of the door. She had gone and he was left in the silence of the room, dispirited, knowing that he was not the same person who had entered it some hours before. Through the window he could see the first chill of light in the dark sky, no hint as yet of the fierce sun still lurking below the darkened rim of the desert.

He did not know which was worse, his broken vow to his wife, whom he loved in the only way he could love, a compound of great respect and almost unvoiced affection, or his unfaithfulness to himself, the self he had grown and trained since his marriage twelve years before. He could not make up his mind and it was necessary, for the damage was done, and all his efforts of the past years had been consumed in this room, and the woman who had assisted at this bonfire of his personality had gone, some savage gone back to a hut where she would eat, and curl up in sleep, not knowing what she had done with him.

For a moment he saw comedy in the fact that she had been unfaithful to Milton, but swiftly came nausea, making him jump from his bed so that he could wash under the primitive shower, as though to scrub the scum of other people's secrets from his body. He had almost moaned, not with the shock of the cold water, but with the horror of what he had done. There was no longer any point in trying, in the effort to stay what he had always considered as good. All his rules were now pointless. He could do what he liked and whenever he felt like it, he thought, for the effort had all been for nothing. He did not hate Aurella for this, only himself, for he knew that this night had long awaited him. No, he would not tell his wife, for she would forgive him, and he did not want that, and it would not help him anyway. It was something he would have to live with always ; the knowledge that after all he was weak and not safe from temptation, was like Milton and all other men, save that he had tried hard, but now suffered more because of that. He could not comfort himself.

He wrote out another signal to headquarters, telling them that he had arrested the chiefs of the Omar Bilash on the grounds that he feared an armed rising. Then he began to worry about Lieutenant Cuddy, who must be still patrolling in the vicinity of the wells, but there had been no word from him.

When Turnbull sent him on patrol to the wells of the Omar Bilash, Cuddy had still seen no active service. Turnbull regretted his going, for he liked his honesty and his serious efforts to understand the native troops who were new and strange to him. He could not learn the language, having no ear for sounds or music. He stared in bewilderment at them and at the language book in his big, red paw, but he could not learn to speak them and he fell into the hands of his interpreter. When he moved off behind the loaded camels and he saw the great, hot desert open to him, he felt fear and excitement. His orders were to keep the peace. Three weeks before he was due to move on patrol he had received an extra large delivery of liquor. It took two camels to carry it, but Turnbull did not know about it. The liquor saved Cuddy from going mad during the long, hot, silent nights in the desert, on the edges of enormous ravines, or perched on a cliff above some endless, dusty plain. At the end of two months he was eating with his hands, like his troops. They liked him. He never shouted, never complained, never got drunk, though they knew he sat on his haunches in the sand until midnight over the bottle. It was only then that he was happy. The scorching days of marching with a few thoughts knocking about like stones in his skull, almost drove him mad, for nothing happened. Nobody attacked him. They saw only small bands of nomads occasionally and the interpreter always told him the same thing. "They are going to look for water, *Effendi*. They say they are men of peace."

Sometimes a runner would come from Turnbull, carrying instructions and mail. The instructions were always the same: "Keep a close watch on the Omar Bilash near the wells."

Once a month came a camel convoy carrying rations and any liquor which had arrived for him at El Ashang.

And day died into night and night into day again, and there was no change, no drifting of one season into another, and they hid from the midday sun as from an enemy, curled up under the broken sparse shade of a clump of thorn trees. The lips became dry and cracked and the eyes ached, but the troops did not seem to suffer in this way. They could stare into the sun with their eyes unwrinkled as though that fierce glare was not there, as though they and not he were fit to live this life. And they never seemed to drink from their water-bottles when they trudged ahead of him through the red, hot sand, while he, by sundown, was suffering the early agonies of thirst. Sometimes they smiled sympathetically when they heard the gurgle of his water-bottle. He tried to harden himself, to be like his troops, but he could not bear his thirst. He looked forward to the great pleasure of evening when he could sit in the sand, clad only in a pair of shorts with the bottle before him. He frequently thanked God for the bottle, and sometimes he was frightened by the thought that he would run out of liquor, that the camel convoy would fail to appear. And often he wondered what would happen to him should he be attacked by, say, appendicitis. Then he would just die here in this waste for no help could reach him, and he consoled himself with the thought that it was his loneliness which brought these fears.

One night the interpreter came and squatted near him. His name was Elmi, and he had evil, smiling eyes. He had been a stoker in ships sailing from Aden to England, and he had lived in Cardiff, where he had learned to speak English with the accent of that city. Like all of his people who had travelled in the world, he returned to his desert and to the atmosphere of intrigue and blood pride, to the smell of camels and the warm, smoky taste of their milk.

" Sir," he said to Cuddy, " there is going to be trouble here."

Cuddy did not show surprise. He said, " But there is always trouble here, isn't there ? "

Elmi smiled patiently and stroked his short black beard. " Yes, sir," he said. " There is always trouble here, but this time the Omar Bilash are going to raid deep into the country of the Yonis Barra. You remember the men who stopped to talk to me to-day when we were resting ? They were of the outcast people, and one of them was carrying his bellows and tools wrapped in a skin. He was a blacksmith and he was on his way to the camps of the Omar Bilash." Elmi paused significantly, and then he continued, " He said that many blacksmiths have been called by the Omar Bilash chiefs. It's bad news, sir. Blacksmiths make spears and daggers and arrows, sir," said Elmi softly. " The Omar Bilash are going to make war on the Yonis Barra."

" Ah," said Cuddy thoughtfully. " Ah."

" Yes, sir," said Elmi. His mind was busy with the choice of two alternatives. Should he disappear now and head for his tribe before the fighting began, or should he stay and work for both sides ? He had amassed a great amount of money in bribes during the last year. He knew that with luck he might make even more in one month if he could reach the chiefs of the Yonis Barra, or he could sell information to the Omar Bilash.

Cuddy sat lost in his thoughts as though he had heard nothing. Elmi waited and then rose slowly to go, watching Cuddy for a sign or an order, but Cuddy had forgotten him and Elmi walked quietly away to his glowing fire.

The stars burned in a dark sky and there was no breeze. The *askaris* huddled near their cooking fires and talked in low voices. One of them was singing a mournful song about a well which had dried up in a time of evil. Cuddy sat on, trying to imagine what he would do if a raiding party tried to pass his post. But he could not believe that there would be trouble. The desert was so silent, so empty, so forgotten.

CHAPTER TEN

THE first man of the Yonis Barra to reach the water-hole at Nalang had dust on his mouth and in his eyes. He appeared to be mad, for he sang to himself in a cracked, high-pitched note, and he swayed slightly as he walked. He was young and his massive, woolly hair was red with dust. His last chewing stick protruded from it, forgotten, for he was exhausted and even the long spear in his right hand seemed to oppress him with its weight. He thought he was alone and he smiled when he saw the grey, dusty hole of the well yawning before him. The goat skin tied round his neck was empty now. He had drunk nothing for two days and he had travelled fast despite having been forced to make the long thirsty detour because of rumours of an Omar Bilash raiding party. The chiefs had warned the men to be careful and not to kill ; let the Omar Bilash make the first move, they said, and the Government would act.

The young man knew that a British officer with thirty men was patrolling only a few hours away from this well. He had expected to see men of the Omar Bilash at the well, but the place was deserted. He turned and shouted, " Come ! Come, and bring the camels." Dust began rising among a clump of thorns a few hundred yards away, and a small boy carrying a bow and arrows appeared. He was leading a long line of swaying, plodding camels. Like the man, the small boy was covered with dust, and his tongue was swollen with thirst. He had large soft eyes but in them was an expression of fear, or pain, or both. The man had beaten him twice on the journey because he had asked for water. " It is a time of war," the man had shouted as he struck him. " It is a time for boys to become men and not to whimper like women." So he had been silent and had sucked his swelling tongue, for they had marched in the heat of the day as well as by night, and now he wished to fall down and cry with exhaustion and shame, for he had discovered what it was to be a man in a time of war.

"Come," shouted the man, "and drink." He was smiling. "We must not stay long. We will move to that hill beyond the trees and we will watch the well to-morrow."

They threw the skin bag into the well and when it was full they hauled it up again and it came wet and glistening, bright water pouring from it. There was silence while they both drank, the boy remembering not to show his delight. He pushed the swollen tongue through his cracked lips and rested it in the water which he held in his cupped hands and he could hardly contain his joy. Then he drank and he felt the water run down inside his body until the feeling became like a tube of cold metal within him. He was numbed with pleasure. Then there was a soft thud and he heard the man gasp and saw him vomit a stream of water as he swayed about. A long arrow was sticking from his belly, and he fell squirming into the sand, gasping, tugging at the arrow with his left hand, but it was barbed and would not come out.

The boy dropped flat into the sand, and while he stared about him he saw a group of men carrying spears and bows rising from a clump of rocks nearby. The struggling man beside him shouted, "God saw this. God saw this," and then he began to thresh about like a wounded buck until he was hidden in a cloud of dust.

The warriors of the Omar Bilash came running, waving swords and spears, and the boy stood up to fight over the body of the dying man. Fitting an arrow into the bowstring, he drew it as far as his tired arm would go and released it. It drove itself half-way into the throat of the first spearman, who jumped into the air, hissing like a snake, and then crashed against a rock and lay still. There was no time for a second arrow. Two men seized him while another speared him. Then they began to hack the dying man and the boy into pieces and when they were covered with blood and satisfied, they screamed and shouted and ran laughing to the camels, the sun flashing on their brownish-black skins, and on the varnish of blood, the smell of which had driven them frantic with the desire to win, to destroy the Yonis Barra and to take every one of their camels.

A few miles to the west of the well, a cloud of dust was moving through the bush. On horseback and on foot, the warriors of the Omar Bilash were moving to the attack. Every man from the age of sixteen was a " shield carrier," a warrior. This raiding party consisted of about three hundred men, and they sang and shouted as they moved, dust on their sweating skins, and sometimes one of the young men in front would shake his mass of hair and leap into the air, spinning, his spear flashing, and the others would cheer and roar. A chief rode ahead, carrying a curved sword, wheeling his horse to receive the cheers and shouts of the warriors. He had a short red beard and small sharp eyes. He had waited over a year for this day, and for the last time, as he continually reminded his men, the Yonis Barra had drunk the water of the Omar Bilash. And at last the word to attack had come from the council of their chiefs at El Ashang.

" Kill," he screeched. " Kill. Kill."

The warriors loping behind answered him in a roar : " Kill. Kill. All. Kill all, all." They ran forward in bounds, stabbing the air, cutting it with swords, leaping and bounding, their eyes wide and fierce with the longing to kill and to show their women that they were men, getters of camels and slayers of lesser men.

Another party of raiders was moving from the South. Between the two parties was a large group of Yonis Barra, men, women and children. Scouts had warned them too late to scatter, and the old chief said they must stand and fight. Many of the Omar Bilash had rifles, the scouts reported.

" You should not have told us to give our rifles to the English, old man," shouted the young men. " Now we have no rifles and you will die with us because of your mistake."

The chief said nothing. He knew that he should not have surrendered the rifles of his group, but the other chiefs had said " Give them to the English. They will like it and they will protect us ever after," but the English had taken the rifles and had done nothing. The Omar Bilash had kept theirs and now they were ready for war and plunder.

The old chief sighed as he watched the young men cutting thorns for the barricade. They ran the camels and goats inside the circle of piled thornbush and then assembled. The chief said they must fight to the finish, that they had been faithful to the orders of the British Government, and now they must wait and trust the Government would help. The young men sneered and shouted. " You can trust a rifle, but not a government," shouted one. " We are here, with no rifles and no government."

" I have sent two men in different directions to find the officer from the patrol. They will be here in the morning. It is five hours' journey," cried the chief. " We will be avenged."

" It is five hours' journey for one of us, but not for soldiers," shouted one who was somewhat older than the others. " Soldiers are soft and cannot travel as can we. They eat and drink too much. We must not rely upon them. We are thirty-two men and twenty-three women. We will fight, but we will die and our camels will go to the Omar Bilash." A wail came from the women at these words and the men looked grim and thoughtful.

Again the man spoke out to the people and the chief.

" The Omar Bilash will have seized all the wells," he cried. " There is no water for us here, they will crush us and take our beasts. What will happen to the Yonis Barra ? "

" Yes," shouted another, " what will happen to the Yonis Barra ? They will destroy our tribe."

" All the tribes of our group will unite to avenge us," another called out. " From far South they will come, and it is only the foolish men of the Yonis Barra who have given up their rifles to the English and now we must die for it. The English are like all white men. They make promises but they do not keep them. They want peace, but they will not put soldiers to protect us. Of what use are the thirty soldiers and the English officer now? I tell you we must die because of our chief."

"By God, it is true," other men shouted, and a woman began wailing and screeching until her man struck her and said, "Enough."

"I tell you that the English Government wants peace," cried the old chief. "If the Omar Bilash are determined to keep their rifles and kill us, peaceful as we now are, is that the fault of the English?" There was no answer from the men and they held their spears and bows and looked at each other, not knowing what to say, until one Musa, who had worked much with the Italian Government in his time, shouted in anger:

"You speak as one who eats the Government salt. They give you thirty shillings a month to buy your ear, because you are a chief. In El Ashang it is said in the coffee houses that you are a friend of the English. Your father gave them a thousand of our people's camels in the time of the Mullah Ahmed bin Sala, so that the English and Italians could pursue him to his death. Always your family have listened to the voice of the Government, and now you have brought us death. A word is not enough for men. They must have a thing that they can see with their eyes or feel with their hands. You have brought us death, I say."

"Yes. By God. It is so," shouted others. There was a growing noise of voices as the men argued and called insults to the chief. He was old and afraid. All his life he had tried to keep peace and to work with the officers of Government, Italian and English. But it was different with the English. The Italian officers had all said the same things. They had papers from which they read the will of the Government, and though each Italian officer had been a different man from the one whose place he took in the governing of the area, their words and actions had been the same. But not so with the English. Each English officer was different and held different opinions, spoke different things, made different rules, and he seemed to be himself and not the Government. One English officer would make a promise to the tribes and the next one would break the agreement. It was hard for a chief to follow the English, for his people were violent and quick to anger, and the English officers did not seem to care for a chief's troubles.

"It is because of your lies," one English officer had screamed. This one was mad and later shot himself, for the English kept their officers for a year in the forts of the desert, and not for a short period like the Italians, and the Italians had always kept great numbers of troops and officers in the Ashang desert, while the English did not seem to fear the people so much. But they did not know what could happen in these deserts, and now, the chief reflected sadly, they would find out. "It is because of your lies," the officer had screamed at him, "that we do not care, as you say, what happens to you. For months I have listened to you all, in secret when you wished secrecy, in the open when you wished to proclaim your insolence. You have lied continually in order to get the Government to strike your enemies, and every man is your enemy. Here, among you, no man can trust another. How many of your people have come to sell me information, but I would not buy it. I despise you. I shall never know and understand you, for my heart is scorched with your lies and your trickery. You love money and camels, but you love no man or woman." The officer's brain was mad and on fire. That night, the chiefs and the people in the village had discussed his words, and some knew in their hearts that what he had said was true. Later, the officer killed himself in another village. Before he did this, he beat his servant for stealing cigarettes. He beat him until the servant's screams had been heard in the village. That officer was young, and when he first came among the people, the chief remembered, his words had been sweet and good. But soon he became mad and destroyed his life.

The sun was sinking. The camels sat patiently in groups within the stockade of thorns, and the men knelt and stood at their posts waiting for the attack which must soon come. It was time for prayer, and they prayed, while the women watched the surrounding bush and desert for movement of their enemies. After the prayer five men, led by Musa the big-mouthed one, came to the chief. The chief played with his *tusbah*, which the Sultan had given him. Its beads were made of the finest *mal-mal* and they gave off a sweet fragrance as his hand warmed them. Fifty-three *Ramazans* had passed since the chief had entered the world, and he knew now that he would not see another, for Musa drew a long sharp knife from his girdle and said :

" Old man, your time to die has come to you."

It was nearly dark now and the chief could see all the eyes of the five men staring into his. He said nothing. Musa said, " You know about camels and about men, but you are a friend of the Government which has now left us to the rifles of our enemies. Soon we must all die, but it is proper that you die at the hands of your own people whom you have sold to death. And I will give you this death, for we must all die, but it is not proper that you die as we die, at the hands of the Omar Bilash. We will kill many of them before they kill us, but first we must kill you to avenge ourselves upon you and upon the English whose money you take."

The men seized him, doing as Musa told them, for he had influence in his group, the chief had always known. Still the chief said nothing and Musa said to him, " Have you any word to give us, old one ? "

A silence had come upon the whole camp, not even the camels sighing or grunting, as if all men and beasts knew that death had come to their group.

" I have no word," said the chief. He felt weary and doubt

was in his mind. Perhaps his men were right. Perhaps it was a mistake to have worked with the Government, but it was the way of a man to do what he thought fit, and now his time and his influence were gone.

" He has no word," said Musa. His large eyes were shining. He drew his arm back as far as it would go, swinging on his toe and heel, the dagger black and sharp against the darkening green sky, and then he bared his teeth and stabbed the chief to the heart.

When the chief's writhings had ceased, Musa said, " Drop him. Now let us fight and die," and they went back to their posts behind the thorns.

After some time they saw red flashes in the distance and then heard the sounds of rifle fire. They waited and soon they heard the shouts of the Omar Bilash and they could not tell whether the raiders knew their position, or whether their scouts sought them. One man said, " Perhaps they are the soldiers who are driving off the Omar Bilash," but Musa sneered and said, " The soldiers would use their machine-gun if it were they. Hope not in the soldiers. They are eating their food and soon will sleep as they have been used to doing each night. It is the Omar Bilash who seek us."

But though they waited throughout the night, there was no further sound, and the camels were silent, as though they listened like the crouching men whom they kept alive, whom they caused, more than women and water, to fight, kill and cheat for their possession. Grey watery light went sweeping across the thick darkness, bringing chill with it, until the sky was like a sheet of wet steel, and soon a red smoky glimmer appeared over the distant rocks ; the first hot breath of the rising sun which would drink the dew and the chill in one fierce lick of his flame.

Again they prayed and waited. The women sat huddled in a group, some young and beautiful, but like their men, anxious to see the dead and dying of their enemy, some old and withered, tired of blood and feuds, but lost in a reverie of old times when the Yonis Barra had more power, more spears-men. An old man sat picking his foot, his mouth loose and toothless, grey bristles on his wrinkled blackish face. He would die here, he reflected, under the iron of the Omar Bilash, of whom he had killed many in his time. Until last night it appeared that he would die in the way usual with the old, falling down in the sand behind the line of moving men and camels, too tired and old to go on, and they would leave him there to die, no man looking back. They would have sent a Sheikh and a boy to find his dead body a day or so later and bury him. But now he was to die under a blade. He was not sorry about this, for it is written and it is so.

The Omar Bilash came out of the trees in a long straggling line, screaming, waving their spears. The riflemen knelt and fired and then moved forward. The men of the Yonis Barra did not move until the firing became heavier and more accurate, when they rose and crashed through the thorns to meet the Omar Bilash. Several fell dead and wounded, but the rest charged on, howling and yelping, their spears drawn back on their shoulders. The Omar Bilash raiders closed round them like a half moon, then became a circle in clouds of dust, and the killing began. With two strokes of his dagger, Musa defeated one man, but he forgot himself, and while about to throw himself on to his victim, he was run through by one of the Omar Bilash horsemen who had moved in with their swords. The dust rose in clouds as they slew each other, and the circle closed in upon the few remaining Yonis Barra. The last of them alive was held down while a young man tried to cut out his eyes, but the fallen one covered them with his hands, until another hacked off his arms with a sword, and the young one had his pleasure. He had been waiting for this hour most of his adult life. They savaged the dead and dying, being unable to leave them whole, so overpowering was their hate for these who had forgotten their place in the order of men. They stabbed and slashed, dancing among the bodies until one of them remembered the camels, and they charged in a great mass to the stockade where the women sat silently in a group behind the camels. While the young boys drove out the camels, the others stood round the women and mocked them. Nearby were heaps of water containers, made of wicker and glued mud. They took these and smashed them to fragments, the women watching, knowing that they would be left to wander and die of thirst. Then they killed the three apprehensive old men.

"The land is ours," the warriors screamed. They leaped and danced before the women, shining with the blood of the dead. Then they collected under the chief with the red beard and soon they were gone, moving south, deeper into the country of the Yonis Barra. The sun was well up and the women sat on until the first big vultures arrived, sailing down and landing in the thorns with wide slowly flapping wings, their eyes hard and unblinking. The women sat on stupefied, huddled, and as though afraid to move. They now belonged to no man and were cut off from their people. One of the old women lay down with her head under a patch of thorns which gave her broken shade. She decided to lie there until she died, and in a way she was glad, for her life had been long and hard and bitter.

When Lieutenant Cuddy had finished listening to the scout's report, he hardly knew what to do. Three reports had come in to his camp of the massacre of the Yonis Barra and of the southward movement of large raiding parties of the Omar Bilash. It was all happening so swiftly that he was not surprised when one of the Government levies came in, minus his rifle, and wounded, to tell him that his two companions had been killed and their rifles taken. All violence seemed in the order of things, after hearing of the barbarous mutilation of the slain Yonis Barra men, but when he heard that Omar Bilash had killed his levies and taken their rifles, he saw that the situation was one demanding immediate action. He thought this out in his careful way, smouldering and sullen, and angry too, because the even rhythm in which he had lived for the past months, though months of maddening boredom, was now to be broken by forced marches, and possibly danger, and danger for what? So that the war might be won more quickly? No. Danger because some savage tribesmen were discontented. It was all very well for the Government to say that such tribesmen were helping Hitler by tying down valuable officers and troops, causing the consumption of precious petrol and rubber tyres, but the tribesmen had never heard of Hitler. They were simply carrying on their life as they had lived it for centuries, since the soil and the trees and the grass had gone from their land, causing men to slay each other and the living to know continual hunger and thirst.

So Cuddy felt that death at the hands of these tribesmen would be as inglorious as falling under a bus in London. It came to him that here an officer must believe in himself in order to pursue his duty. The decisions would be his, and if he wished to expose himself to death or wounds because some barbarous savages wished to kill each other, it was for him to decide. On the other hand, he could march in the wrong direction and let them kill. The finding of information was also something which could be avoided. He need not hunt for this information. He could let the tribesmen find him and then he could dawdle along to the scene where the vultures would already be feeding on the dead.

He went over all this, but at the back of his furtive reasoning was an emotional sense of justice, the hope of administering a swift and painful lesson to the excitable and treacherous Omar Bilash. British justice, fair play, help for the underdog. It was all tied up with the history books at school and the bright sunlit adventures lived by the troops of Kitchener, Buller, and those others who had represented Britain in so many deserts, jungles and rocky wastes. Justice. For Cuddy it meant the British sense of order and proper arrangements about men's rights according to their abilities and efforts. He did not like the Yonis Barra any more than the Omar Bilash, but he was now sorry for the Yonis Barra, who, so far as he knew, had voluntarily disarmed themselves and now were being massacred by those who had waited to regain their former power.

He tried to feel a sense of history about these moments as he watched his soldiers loading the camels, shouting as they dragged down the bellowing camels' noses. He tried to feel that he was doing something British, something about the outposts, about justice, but he knew too that the politicians in London did not care about such stuff. They talked about "the native peoples," exploitation, trade unions for blacks who cut sugar-cane, grew coffee, hauled bananas on their backs. He remembered the old men in the club in London; how they had said that Labour meant the destruction of the Empire, the reduction of two hundred years of British effort to a few statistics about man-hours, hospital beds, calorific contents of cassava root, and the rights of all men to be free. It made Cuddy feel alone, for some moments gloriously alone and borne up as some lone knight of a decayed chivalry, as though the old men in the club would remember him and how he had shown the flag to savages despite the sneers of the docker K.C.s, and the Communists in their corduroys and long hair. But the exultation quickly went from him, for no one would know how he felt, nor would they care while millions were engaged in enormous battles across Russia and the deserts and jungles of the Middle and Far East. He was an ant on an endless plain, bored and in some small fear for his life, for perhaps he did not really believe as his fathers had believed. They had *known*; *he* was not sure if it was all worth it. Like most other soldiers, he was a civilian in uniform and he wished to return to his car, his radio, his wonderful bathroom. It was not good to feel like that, but he could not help feeling like that. There was so much to go back to. He was sure that in the excitement of a big attack under a barrage, with thousands of other chaps, he would not have felt this way. But here alone, forgotten, with the choice of a doubtful glory and a possibly messy and painful death among strangers whose language he did not know, it was so different. He did not wish to sacrifice himself for a horde of savages, who anyway were the property of the Italians and the temporary unwanted responsibility of the British. Didn't the British already have enough savages, without being loaded with the extra worry of these people, probably the most unruly and ungovernable of the bloody lot who stretched from Hong Kong to Nigeria? But it was no good. Turnbull would expect action and a clear and concise report, and he liked Turnbull, a bit of a rough diamond, but all right and likeable in his way.

As the sun reached to four o'clock and the burning heat of the sand diminished, the column moved out, winding slowly across the ridge, until Cuddy could see the plains stretching into the mists of blue and grey haze where the world's edges mingled with the sky, lost in the sun's approaching struggle with darkness.

He cursed the camels and their irritating amble, for as usual he found himself miles ahead of them where he had wandered lost in a thousand thoughts, those thoughts which so many millions of marching men have thought and of which they remember nothing when the march is done. He would sit down and wait for them. He missed the clack of their wooden bells. The sergeant had removed them all ; he, Cuddy, would never have remembered to do that, he knew. What a lot of simple things there were to learn in the world. The clack of the camel bells might bring an attack, but he would not have remembered such a thing. The sergeant belonged to this life. He, Cuddy, belonged to London and the world of good clothing, good food and drink. He could not live like a savage.

Three times he sat during the night until the plodding camels reached him, and each time he got up, walked along the line of troops until he reached the last pair of scuffing sandals, those of his small corporal, and then back to the head of the column, determined to walk slowly. But his thoughts quickened his feet and he forged ahead, one hand on his pistol butt for support, the other unknowingly shifting the weight of the rifle slung on his left shoulder. There were lions in this part of the country, he remembered, and this kept him on the watch, for a lion was more dangerous than an Omar Bilash warrior.

The moon was hidden in dark cloud and a few stars glimmered weakly. It must have been nearly two o'clock in the morning when he decided to sit down again and wait. He looked round for his orderly, who usually walked a hundred or so yards behind him, but he was not there. He waited a few minutes and then grew anxious. There was no sound in the darkness, and in his anxiety he pushed his sandalled feet deep into the sand, feeling it cold on his toes, but he sat on and waited until a half-hour had passed. Then he got to his feet, about to walk quickly back on his tracks, but he remembered from the adventure books he had read in his boyhood that it was fatal to rush about in the bush, for that was the way so many heroes had lost themselves. There was something about chaps going round and round in circles, often near their camp, until they fell exhausted and died.

The column had either gone in another direction, or something had happened. After a time, he felt frightened, for his water-bottle was only half full, he had ten rounds of ammunition in the magazine of his rifle and six rounds in his pistol. He had also a compass and binoculars, but no map, for the Italian maps were useless when it came to finding water-holes. He was lost, only knowing that he was somewhere in the desert south-east of the water-holes which were two days' march away, even if he knew the direction. He had taken no compass bearings, and the compass and map-reading had been his weakest points in the training unit at home. He did not understand the stars either. He felt exposed, found out, and he admitted that he belonged to London and the clubs, not to this dreary life, which one moment was safe and boring, and the next full of menace and fear.

If only they had put trained officers to do this work. Chaps who liked it, who knew about the stars and tracks and savages, and left the others to move in thousands to the attack.

Before he knew it, he was walking back on what he thought must be his tracks, his pace quickening with his fears, until he was swallowed in the scrub. He wondered if his troops had deserted him, perhaps because they did not like him, for it was strange that his orderly had left him. Yet, surely the sergeant, a model for a native sergeant in his way, would not have been a party to such a decision, but again you never knew with natives. He began running, holding his rifle in his left hand. He did not know for how long he ran, for he was strong and powerful and afraid. As the first wet gleam of dawn came into the sky, he fell exhausted between two high rocks, lying there panting, still strong, grateful for rest ; but more afraid than he had ever been in his life before.

When the sun came up, he saw the plains again before him. He recognised nothing ; it was all the same, reddish sand and grey scrub, with the waves of the sun's light travelling at terrific speed across it to the horizon until the heat began to rise from it in haze and quiverings of smoky yellow light. He got up and ran again, feeling certain he would find his column, and the sweat came out on him soaking his shirt, running into his eyes and mouth, the salts of his body, sharp and bitter, which he could not replace, and the loss of which would bear his powerful body down into the sand unless he found his men.

In the afternoon he sat in the shade of a rock, panting, partly from habit, partly from fear and the senseless efforts of his first day alone. He held the water-bottle in his hands : it was only a quarter full, and he knew he should save it. But hope, and the weakness of great thirst overcame his memory of what had happened to the chaps in the adventure books.

He drank it all in one gulp and then, looking defiantly at the empty water-bottle, he licked his wet mouth. He jumped to his feet again and went on at a lope, heading south, never to be heard of again.

CHAPTER ELEVEN

TURNBULL stood to attention at the foot of the new grave which the sweating *askaris* had hacked from the shale. Milton was planted, with full honours, flag, bugles and firing party. What more could he want? Turnbull saluted the grave, his face grim under the parade mask of years.

The cemetery had been started by the Italians during their last campaign. Iron pickets and rusting barbed wire protected the sun-baked graves of a dozen Italian soldiers from the jackals and hyenas. Near where Turnbull stood was a headstone on which was chiselled in Italian: " These of the column of Manini died in the shadow of the Roman eagle at Bund Gadu in combat with the barbarous foe." Their graves were untended, forgotten, as Milton's would be.

Turnbull felt sick under the fierce weight of the sun as he shouted orders to the troops, and while they marched quickly from the cemetery towards the silent, deserted town, he saw a truck appear from a swirl of dust. He almost shouted with relief. It was Sole. It could only be Sole.

He turned to the sergeant and said, " Back to the fort into your positions. Do nothing until I come. I think the new Captain has arrived." He ran towards the truck, which had stopped, and he saw an officer get out. They saluted and shook hands, smiling, and Sole began asking questions at once.

" The sentry says that Milton is dead. Is it true? " He seemed excited and incredulous.

" Yes, it's true," Turnbull told him sombrely. " They

murdered him last night. I've just buried him." He examined
Sole with his expert soldier's eye, still enjoying his relief at
seeing him, a new face, a new officer. He was glad that
Milton was dead. It was wrong to feel that, but he was glad,
glad. Sole looked alive and keen and he still did not seem
to be able to grasp the news which Turnbull gave him as
they walked towards the fort.

"Christ," said Sole over and over again. "What an end!
What a way to die! He was a bit difficult, wasn't he, Turnbull?" he said. "I mean, he was having trouble?"

Turnbull was silent for some moments. "Yes," he said at
length. "He was the most useless bastard I ever met. He
asked for it and he got it. It's made it very awkward for me,
you know," he said seriously.

Sole almost laughed as he looked at Turnbull's serious
face. "You mean Milton's death?" he said.

"I mean everything," Turnbull replied stolidly. "Milton
ruined this station and he's left us a mess, I can tell you."

"Yes," Sole said, half to himself, "of course." He was
the new political officer. He began asking questions again.

"Who did it?" he said. "Have you got any information?"

"The Omar Bilash, of course," said Turnbull. "Did they
give you the dope on things up here before you left? It
must be the Omar Bilash. They had every reason to kill
Milton. He was screwing his head off with a Yonis Barra
woman, and anyway the Omar Bilash have been threatening
to start trouble for a long time now. It could have been
stopped if Milton had done his duty, but he did everything
save kneel down and ask the Omar Bilash for mercy." They
passed through the great gate of the fort. "One good bash,"
said Turnbull, "and there'd have been no more trouble.
Now they've killed a British officer, the first they've ever
killed in the country since the occupation."

"Plenty have killed themselves, but you're quite right,"
said Sole, "this is the first they've ever killed. It's serious,
by Christ! What have you done?"

"I've put on a curfew, covered the wells, put standing patrols in the town, and I've arrested the chiefs of the Omar Bilash. That shook the bastards, I tell you."

Sole said "Oh," and then grew silent. Turnbull stole a side glance at him. He felt that Sole did not approve of something. His nerves tightened up again, a feeling of intense irritability entered his voice.

"Well," he said, "what's up? Anything you think I've forgotten?"

"Oh, no," said Sole quickly. "I don't know enough of the situation yet. I hope you're right in arresting the chiefs, that's all."

Turnbull's heart fluttered. It was the one thing he had found difficult to decide, the arresting of the chiefs. He knew it might be a match to the powder train, and yet it might be better that way. If it brought this long threatened trouble into the open, then it could only be for good. A bit of fire-power would be the answer, fast, powerful and ruthless. He had seen it work before; the shock of it on an excited mob was numbing, as though they had been hit with a hammer. They crept back into their holes after it, shaken and silent, each of them a person again, their powerful identity as a mob lost, destroyed.

"What do you mean?" said Turnbull. "Don't you think the chiefs should be arrested, or something?"

"Why did you arrest them?" said Sole in a soft voice. He could feel Turnbull's excitement, and the sudden doubt which had come into his voice.

"Well, Christ!" said Turnbull, "it's obvious, isn't it? They're the Omar Bilash. They've been gunning for Milton for a long time now. They hated him because he had a Yonis Barra woman who interfered and who had too much influence over him. He was pro-Yonis Barra all the way. It's obvious I'm right to arrest the Omar Bilash chiefs, if only to stave off the attack on the Yonis Barra," he went on anxiously, trying to convert Sole—too anxiously, he was afraid, but

Sole's attitude struck at the very roots of his own fears

"Well, what do you say?" he said.

"Have you got a drink?" said Sole. "I'm played out, and I'm thirsty as hell. We can discuss it all over a drink."

They entered Turnbull's living-room, and Turnbull began calling for Belai, telling him to bring a bottle of gin and some water.

Sole stretched himself out in his chair while Turnbull eyed him, quiet and expectant, his eyes suspicious.

"Well, I must say, it's a hell of a nice way to take over a new station," said Sole, raising one eyebrow. "I come in and find you burying the bloke I'm supposed to relieve." He laughed softly. "Christ, what a country!" he said.

Put like that, thought Turnbull, it was a terrible welcome for Sole. Then he felt relief as he looked at Sole. He could not be as bad as Milton, he was certain of that.

"Well, you'd better start at the beginning," said Sole. "Give me all the dope."

While they drank gin, Sole listened to Turnbull's story. It came in a rush of words, sometimes animatedly, and Sole began to notice his insistence on the need for a swift blow, a sharp lesson, a show of force. Turnbull might be right, of course, but Sole drew back from agreement. He dreaded violence now. The last thing he wanted was to take what Turnbull called "a strong line."

"Are you sure they need what you call a bashing?" Sole asked him. "Is it really too late to make them see reason?"

"Reason," said Turnbull coldly. "Reason? The bastards have just murdered a British officer and you talk about reason! Now listen——"

"Wait a minute, Turnbull," said Sole, waving his hands. "Keep calm. I know you've been under a strain, but I just can't arrive here and start getting tough until I know what it's all about. First of all, how do you know the Omar Bilash killed him? What about the woman? Couldn't she have killed him? Where was she? After all, she lived with him, didn't she? Or didn't she?"

Turnbull was pale. It was a shock to him. " I never thought of that. But she—I don't know, really. Surely it's obvious that it must be the Omar Bilash. They had every reason to do it."

" Well, you've arrested the chiefs, you had better arrest the woman as well."

Turnbull said nothing. He stared at the smoke rising from Sole's cigarette, his mind in turmoil. How could it be Aurella? She was with him for hours. He suddenly found he was not willing to believe her guilty of Milton's death. She had been in his room when he arrived last night. The memory disturbed him again, making him want to hide his eyes. He was afraid that his weakness showed in his face. He began to fret about this while Sole looked at him through his cigarette smoke.

" What's the matter, Turnbull?" he said, curiosity in his voice. " What are you thinking about? Have you thought of something you'd forgotten? What about this bint of Milton's? Where is she?"

" I don't know," said Turnbull.

" Has Korma reacted to the news yet?" Sole asked. " Any signals coming in?"

" Nothing," said Turnbull, relieved that the subject had changed. " I'm worried about Cuddy, who is patrolling the wells. We need more troops. Korma must send them soon. What with patrols, pickets and guards, I'll have no one left soon. They'll be worn out."

" What's Cuddy like?" said Sole.

" He's all right, but I think he's going off his chump. He's started to write some queer stuff in his reports. He hasn't a clue about this kind of life, but he's got plenty of guts. He can't speak a word of the lingo, either."

Turnbull poured himself another gin, and he watched Sole pour four fingers into his own glass. In his mind he said,

" Aha ! " Sole did not look like a boozer, but you could never really tell. Perhaps Sole was just played out and was badly in need of a hard drink. Sole drank the gin in three gulps, and then said, " D'you mind ? " and then he poured an even bigger one, but he was going to take this one more slowly.

They went over the story again, the miserable story of Milton. He had been useless, and now Turnbull said so. Sole watched him closely, and he could feel the misery of what he heard, though it was against his will to hear this flood of bitterness about the dead man. Turnbull had been under a strain, perhaps. Oh, God, this bloody, miserable life of forts and sand and killing ! Why had they ever captured the land from the Italians ? No wonder Mussolini wanted other lands. His empire was a desert full of thieves and murderers.

They drank on, going over and over the story of Milton's death. " When did you last see the woman ? " Sole asked. " That's important."

Turnbull was silent for a moment. " Last night, when I saw Milton," Turnbull replied. " She's known as a dangerous bitch, even among the Italians. She's well known. The Italians exiled her after she tried to rob some pathetic old general of theirs who got tied up with her while he was doing a tour of the country's defences."

Sole swilled the gin round his glass. " She's a bitch," he said. " They're all bitches, these women."

Now that he had something to hide, Turnbull felt the change in his life, in the new approach to it of the liar, something which he had not known before. It humiliated him.

Turnbull was silent, and Sole looked at him sharply and read something in his face. He was not sure of what he had read, but there was something. He gulped down the gin and poured some more. He smiled at Turnbull. " I'll give you back a bottle to-morrow," he said pleasantly. " I've got plenty." Sensing what he thought to be disapproval in

Turnbull's eyes, he said casually, " I drink rather a lot, you notice."

There was an edge in his voice which Turnbull did not ignore. He decided to show less of what he felt to Sole. This bloke was a mind reader, a smarty, though likeable. He would have given all he possessed to be able to talk freely and openly about Aurella, but last night had crippled his honesty and he fretted. She had sickened his mind. She had deliberately seduced him. He wanted to know where she was, but he was afraid to ask his *askaris*, for he knew that they knew about Aurella's visit to his house. She had probably told them.

" There's bound to be a hellish flap in Korma when they hear about this," said Sole. " The Area Commander has a wife who will smell dirty work at once : sex, I mean. How women alter an army. Korma is like a big parish hall nowadays, with sewing-bees and tea parties, and sex is bound to be the cause of Milton's death. Everyone down there knows about sex up here. Every bloody white woman wants to know which officers employ black women. It fascinates and upsets them. They'd like to ask a chap what is the difference in bed, but how can they ask ? " Sole's voice was hard and sharp, and it cut into Turnbull's heart, for he had so lately tasted the difference, and perhaps Sole knew in some way. Sole grew more pleasant as they drank.

" Yes," said Sole thoughtfully, " they'll gab their bloody heads off down there." He turned and looked Turnbull in the eyes. " The chiefs," he said. " You've putt them all in gaol ? "

Turnbull nodded. " Yes," he smiled. " I wish I could find out who did Milton in, but the chiefs all deny knowledge of it. Kalil Abukir, the king of the bloody Omar Bilash, gave a speech before I put him inside. He would not leave the office until he'd had his say. He told me there would be trouble : that because a jealous woman caused the death of an officer, was it right and just to imprison the chiefs ? Was it right that they should be imprisoned because of a used-up whore?" Turnbull could not tell Sole of how Chief Kalil Abukir had looked at him in silence for a few seconds and then said, "Other men will use her now, for she has finished with the dead Captain. Find her and you will find the murderer, but lock us up and you will have trouble." "There's been silence since I put them inside. Fourteen of them. I got them in before they could hold a meeting in the town." Turnbull wiped the sweat from his forehead. It was a relief to talk about it all to someone who was able to understand, someone who was not like Milton. "But I'm worried," said Turnbull. "I think there'll be a big raid by the Omar Bilash against the Yonis Barra, and I don't know what Cuddy can do about it."

"What's Cuddy like?" Sole asked, but he was thinking about his wife again. How terrible it is to need someone so much, he thought, like a lump of burning, jagged iron in the centre of his heart. It was devouring him and yet never destroying his craving for her. He knew that he was becoming drunk, and he could hear Turnbull's voice droning on. Poor Turnbull! He was a bloody good chap, but if only it would all end soon. If only one did not have to force oneself to perform duties which daily grew more odious, more useless, more and more against one's will.

Then the night and the musing were swept away by a long burst of machine-gun fire which came from the turret above their heads. The frantic string of explosions ceased, and they could hear the shouts of the *askaris*, whistles, the running of boots across the sand.

Turnbull's face was white. He turned at the door and shouted, "It's started! This is it! I think they're going to try and rescue the chiefs from the gaol."

As he ran from the room the machine-gunner fired two short bursts, one left and one right, Sole could tell by the diminishing volume of sound. The flashes lit the windows of the room. He ran into the courtyard, unbuttoning the flap of his pistol holster. He was half drunk, he knew. He could not remember whether Turnbull had the right or not to arrest the chiefs, and he hoped the machine-gunner had killed nobody. He wondered if someone would kill *him*. It was possible they might overwhelm the garrison if they were determined enough. He began climbing the stairs to the machine-gunner's turret, and saw Turnbull sitting crouched over the gun. The *askari* machine-gunner lay slumped in the corner, his black face glistening in the starlight, blood on his mouth.

" What's this ? " said Sole.

" I've just flattened him out," said Turnbull without moving his head. " I told him not to open fire without orders from me, but, of course, like all these bastards, he thought he knew better. In a show like this *I* like to run the time-table. It comes in handy later. I can't see anything moving yet, I think he covered the whole place with fire just to keep them back. Can you go and find Sergeant-Major Abduruman and ask him what he knows ? I'm frightened now to let one of these chaps handle the machine-gun. It's more than my commission is worth."

That gave Sole something to think about as he descended the steps. One's commission, of course. If anything went wrong it would mean a court martial, the old British sacrifice and no complaints. He would have to trust Turnbull for a time, for he did not know enough of the situation to give orders. He would now back Turnbull, and the chiefs would stay in the gaol. If they, the people, thought they would get them out of the gaol, then they were wrong there. Hate came up, becoming like a wall of muscle within him. He clenched his teeth and the violence that belonged to this tortured and tired desert moved him to a quiet and dangerous wish to punish, to beat down and to subdue. All the desire for his wife was sucked up into it, so that it reinforced his hate, and was charged from the battery of his loneliness and desire. Then he was sorry, wishing to be reasonable again, and the light-headedness caused by the gin left him, and he felt the fingers of panic touch his heart.

The *askaris* began shouting again and he heard one of them slam a round into the breech of his rifle.

"Don't shoot," he cried. "Don't shoot until I order you." He heard his voice drown all other sound, and the *askaris* were silent.

"There's a crowd moving," he heard Turnbull's excited shouts. "Come up and have a look."

Sole raced up the steps again and looked over Turnbull's shoulder. A great mass of people were moving to the gaol, and low, soft roars came from them. People moving, angry, savage, blind to reason. Turnbull waited for Sole to speak, but Sole said nothing. He just stared, fascinated and afraid, trying to think of something which would prevent the need for violence.

"I told Sergeant-Major Abduruman to hold the gaol. I hope to Christ he's all right," Turnbull panted.

"Fire a burst across the front of the crowd," said Sole quietly. "That'll shake them." He could hardly control his voice. It was like the night he gave orders before the attack on the German position, wanting to be cool, yet being unable to speak properly. His sudden fear of using force almost overwhelmed him, and he could feel the sweat running on his face.

Turnbull swung the gleaming barrel of the machine-gun to the right until it pointed ahead of the crowd. He could see the gleam of spears or swords; so they were armed. Aha! That was different. He pressed his thumbs on the trigger and the flickering whip of fire lit the turret. He tapped to the left, one more burst, and the crowd moved back like a wave, like a swirling, breaking cloud.

Turnbull sniffed up the scent of heated oil and burned cordite. Even now, he remembered that it was his favourite smell. Suddenly he could recall the pleasure of the smooth, well-cut rifle butt pressed into his shoulder, and the perfection of the grip, the small of the butt tight in his right hand, and the two slow, smooth pressures prior to the kick and thrust of the shot. It reminded him of the pleasures of being a young soldier, learning his job, knowing it, his first stripe, being clean, young, fit, fit for service in any part of the world. And now that long journey of twenty years through depots, barracks, transit camps, battles and boredoms, had brought him to this, where, as a captain, he sat over a machine-gun, because he was afraid to trust his troops. And that crowd moving back below him could tear up his achievements of twenty years. They might force him to kill them, and that could easily mean the end of his army career. It would mean freedom too. It would all be done in a court martial by strangers, and he could go back to his wife and kids, knowing he was a sacrifice, but that in truth he had done his duty. For if that crowd down there asked for it, he would turn the machine-gun on them, giving them death, as he had given it to many others. It was up to them, and it depended on how badly they wanted their chiefs. With the chiefs in gaol there was bound to be peace, so they would stay in gaol.

He began to sweat. There was no breeze. The crowd halted near a cluster of huts and he could hear the murmur of their voices, as though they argued among themselves. People all over the earth were like this, until you beat them and forced them to go home and get on with eating and sleeping and loving and hating. Home was the thing. God, if only they could *all* go home.

" They're having an argument," said Sole in a low voice. " They're scared, but they've got arms. They'll have another try. Did you say that the sergeant-major was in charge of the gaol ? "

" Yes," said Turnbull, suddenly happy that Abduruman was back and that Sole was here. " I don't know what he's doing, though. He's sent no message, and I'd like to know what's going on there."

Sole said he would go and see. He said it because it would

save Turnbull the trouble of asking him. Turnbull seemed
to feel that he was in command here. But there was something
Sole felt he should say. It was difficult, but it had to be said.

It was a matter of who was to take the responsibility for
killing if the crowd continued with its movement towards
the gaol. This business of killing civilians, even civilian
savages, was something about which there was no definite
policy. You were not supposed to kill; you killed only if
forced to do so. And when was one forced to do so? Only
a God, Sole felt, should be allowed this decision. When could
you know that it was time to fire into a crowd? When they
threw rocks? When they appeared ready to overwhelm the
soldiers? When you had tried everything and had lost your
temper, your sense of proportion: when your judgment
was overborne by fear and rage, and the worry that you were
about to lose your authority—which once lost could never
be regained in its old form? To lose face was dangerous. Face,
in the structure of the Empire, was all important. There were
still people in England who expected it. They still wished to
be proud of being Imperial, despite the sun which had been
setting for years on the Empire: proud of being British,
because if the millions of Asiatics no longer wished to stay
in their Empire, it must be the fault of the Asiatics who could
not appreciate a good thing when they had it. All these
crowds who had gathered at times all over the East in front
of young British officers, who stood ready with their trained
platoons to " restore order," induce a sense of civic virtue,
" get the situation under control "; all these crowds were
tests of power. " I am diseased," thought Sole. " I am not
fit to administer because I do not believe in the religion of
Empire. And now I must decide what to do." A mixture of
doubt and fear would decide for him.

" They're moving back," whispered Turnbull. He was
very excited. Sole saw his thick, yellow hair hanging loosely
across his forehead, dark patches of sweat on the back of his
khaki shirt. He noticed the tattooed heart and dagger on the

big hand which gripped the right traversing handle of the machine-gun. Poor Turnbull. There was something about him which touched Sole, something of service and absolute reliability, something about caring for his responsibilities as a soldier, but something hard and cruel, too, the cruelty of the white man who is challenged by dark men who have forgotten the rules.

They watched the crowd moving in the open space. Turnbull thought: " I could wipe out the lot." Five or six long bursts of fire and he could scatter them dead and wounded and broken, and wiser. That was the power of the machine-gun. It was what it was for.

Sole was thinking: " They can have what they want as far as I am concerned. They can have the chiefs, if they can get them." He was tempted to let things take their course. He was tempted not to look, to hope for a painless solution.

" Perhaps you shouldn't have arrested them, Turnbull," he said. He watched the muscles clenching and unclenching in the other's jaw, and he wished he had not said it. He felt resentment for being sent here, a sacrifice on a shoddy altar.

" It's a bit bloody late to wonder that now, isn't it ? " said Turnbull crossly.

" Wonder what ? " said Sole, and then remembered. " It might have been a good thing if you had not arrested them. If you had waited for me."

" What would *you* have done ? " said Turnbull. Sole thought about that and then laughed softly. " I don't know," he said. " I haven't a bloody clue. I suppose you knew what you were doing anyway."

Turnbull turned his head at that, and Sole saw his cold, pale eyes.

" I always know what I'm doing," he said. It was Turnbull's official voice, Sole knew. He was on parade. Turnbull swung the barrel of the machine-gun until it pointed ahead of the crowd. He had forgotten Aurella. They were shouting and screaming now, but they appeared aimless and without a leader. The shock of the firing still affected them, but they would not disperse. Turnbull knew that when a mob loses its fear after the first shot, it is time to start killing. It would be time quite soon. The hairs on his arms prickled and he shivered. It was up to Sole, he supposed. The army must ask the political officer what he thought. "When do we shoot?" he asked.

"I will go to the prison and talk to them," said Sole. "But no shooting. I forbid you to open fire without an order from me." He had said it at last.

"You forbid me, do you?" There was no sarcasm in Turnbull's voice, and Sole liked him again when he looked into the serious eyes. They listened to the roar of the crowd for a few moments.

"Yes, I forbid you," said Sole.

"That mob means business. You think you can do something by talk, but there's been too much talk up here. Me, I'm all for shooting them now. Remember there will be trouble in the bush if they get away with it here."

"Hang on here. I'll go to the prison and have a talk with the sergeant-major." Sole ran down the steps, leaving Turnbull sitting behind his gun, worried, and mouthing soft curses at the mob.

Turnbull pushed his wife's face out of his mind. No time for that now. The world was too full of people who did not wish to live in peace. But one day he would be free of it all, in his garden, a pint of bitter at the local and——

"Who is that talking to them?" Turnbull shouted into the darkness. There was a silence and then an *askari's* voice replied, "It is one of the wise men, *Effendi*. He's saying, 'Once we were like a dog, but we had a master and he fed us and we knew the master. Now we are a dog and we have no master. The master is gone. The new Government does not care what happens to us. We are a dog without a master.' The master, *Effendi*," shouted the unknown *askari* nervously, "the master was the Italian Government."

" Christ ! " said Turnbull aloud. " And who wants *this* dog ? This mangy, mongrel dog." He knew that a mob could quickly smell indecision and fear. Soon they would smell it. Was Sole frightened, he wondered ? Was there something wrong with El Ashang so that everyone lost his nerve ?

The machine-gunner behind him lay still, conscious and afraid, conscious of his split and swelling lips, but feigning coma. He thought of home again and the river, the big brown river where people were happy ; tears oozed from his tightly closed eyes. He was half afraid of the things he felt around him, but this fear did not override his misery about his home near the big river, for he was not of a martial race.

CHAPTER TWELVE

IN the warm darkness the roar of the crowd swelled as the old and the very young began to swarm from their ragged huts to join in the excitement. The old men clutched at each other as they hobbled across the sand, and their eyes, blue and milky with age, were straining in the darkness. " Loot ! " they shouted to each other. " If we get into the fort there will be loot."

" The younger are stronger and will take it from us," some other shouted. Many of these dried-up and wrinkled old men, with the skin loose and crinkled in folds on their bellies, had once ridden as dervishes of the Mad Mullah, and had killed when and where they wished. They had now to sit in their huts waiting for death, and bearing the sneers of the young ones who begrudged them life, and who waited for them to die. The old, who had camels and goats, knew with agony that they could not take their flocks with them, and sometimes they saw the interested flash in the quick looks of the young who watched them struggle and groan to their

6

feet. Death hung on their backs, his claws dug deep, but now, in the mad scramble to join the crowd at the end of the town, they forgot him.

The deep, terrible hunger for possessions of those who have little was stirring in them, and some held knives in their withered fists.

They screeched to each other when they saw the roaring mass of the people. " Many there are, like herds of camels at a counting," they shouted hoarsely.

Then a bright, white light bathed them all, shining like silver on their black faces and their flashing teeth. They uttered a low, savage roar when they saw that the light came from the headlamps of a truck near the wall of the fort some two hundred yards away. One of the clever young men picked up a rock when he saw an *askari* run from the truck back into the fort. The clever one ran into the darkness, and made his way, unseen, to the bonnet of the big truck. Then swiftly he smashed both headlamps, and the crowd howled and yelled and began to stamp its feet on the sand, and as the hundreds of feet took up the rhythm it became a terrible and frightening sound like soft thunder in the earth.

The women swayed, packed together behind their menfolk, and they sent up a loud crying, banging their hands rapidly against their mouths until their shrieks mingled into a fierce ululation.

The sound excited the men, some of whom began to show their agility by leaping into the air and spinning like ballet dancers, their great shocks of hair flopping and spreading over their eyes. One young woman clenched her thin hand in the air and screeched, " Are you men, or are you women ? " and the men answered that they were men.

Watching the heaving, stamping mob from the shadow of a mud hut was Yussuf, the ex-sergeant-major of the Italians, and he wore an old green army tunic over his brightly-coloured *lungi*. He wore no turban and his shaven head showed a long, white scar where a Senussi sword had cut him many years ago. With him were two sons of one of the imprisoned Omar Bilash chiefs. They carried, like the majority of the howling men nearby, long thick sticks with flattened, club-like ends. These sticks resembled the pestles with which the women pounded grain, but they were weapons peculiar to this people. With these club-like sticks it was customary to pound a fallen enemy to death as though he were clay.

Yussuf was watching the mob which had now worked itself into the state where it was ready to sacrifice itself, for it was screaming, " Kill, kill, kill all ! " An old man with a hennaed beard began to remind them that they were children of Islam, and children of the great and noble warrior Omar Bilash, and that their blood was sick with slavery.

" Once we had a master," the old one shouted, " and we were like a dog, and we had a master. But now we are a dog and we have no master. Kill ! Kill ! "

One of the chief's sons plucked Yussuf's sleeve and said, " There is no firing from the fort. No words. No officer has shown himself. What now ? "

" The crowd is ready to fight," said Yussuf. " Those soldiers within the fort who belong to our tribal group will refuse to fire if ordered to do so. They have told me this, and I have told them that we will stone them to death if they break their word and fire. But there are the flat-nosed ones, many of them, and the two officers. The flat-nosed ones are cowards, and we will take their rifles, but the officer, Turnbull, is hard and he is a real shield carrier, a true warrior. The new officer I do not know. They have machine-guns, and I do not know if they will use them. They are sitting up there in those turrets watching us and we cannot see them."

" Let us rush the gates of the prison," said the younger of the chief's sons. " It is outside the fort and we can rescue our chiefs. Perhaps the English will not fire. They are frightened of us."

" That is the plan, fool, is it not ? " said Yussuf scornfully. " We want the chiefs, but if we could take the fort as well, we could have all the arms and ammunition and take to the bush. Against us then the Yonis Barra could do nothing, and even the English would be careful of us."

"Who will lead the people now?"

"Both of you," said Yussuf. "You are young and brave, and if you rescue our chiefs you will be honoured among us."

They smiled happily, and one said eagerly, "And what will you do, Yussuf?"

"I am like a general," said Yussuf gravely. "I have fought in many wars and I learned a clever thing from the Italians. It is this. The general must never lead his soldiers and get killed, for there is then no brain to watch and advise and direct the fight. But instead I stay here and watch, and if things go wrong I can correct them. That is the way the white men have defeated everybody. Do you understand?"

They said that they understood this, and that Yussuf was their *akil*, their brains and knowledge.

"Then go now and attack the prison. God will help you," said Yussuf. "But one important word. Do not kill the white men or capture them. Leave them, and do not kill the flat-nosed ones unless you have to. If you have to, the English will be much fiercer with us, so try not to kill." He knew that these were stupid words in the ears of the two young men, and he knew that they would kill. But he had learned the value of evidence, in his career with the white men. Those last words of his would be legendary among the people within a few days, and if he were ever captured by the English he could call that evidence on his behalf. His people might be puzzled by those words but they would remember them, and he had learned that it did not matter what the people thought so long as they followed you. They were stupid and a nuisance. But if they rescued the chiefs they would praise Yussuf as a great leader and a chief.

"Go now," he said impatiently. "If the English fire do not waver, but move swiftly to the prison and attack. Smash the door and get the chiefs. If you see a chance of getting into the fort, do so and take rifles. But be careful. I know that the soldiers of our tribes in the fort will join you if they get the chance."

When they had gone Yussuf sat down and wrapped an old army blanket round his shoulders. The crowd was chanting and stamping to the beat of clapping hands, and though Yussuf sat quite close to them he could only see a greyish yellow dust cloud, from which figures reeled and spun for a moment before vanishing again into the dust. He was happy that he was not one of them. The last time he had faced machine-gun fire was in the last stages of the Italian retreat, and he had known then that he was getting old. His once keen sight had deteriorated, his hands on the rifle, once steady, were shaky, and the last climb up the rocks under mortar fire had found him weak and uncertain. The English had held him prisoner for some weeks along with thousands of others, but as the vast numbers of prisoners increased they had released the natives and held only the Italians, allowing Yussuf to return to his people at El Ashang.

He wrapped himself tighter in his blanket as the crowd moved away towards the prison at a slow, shambling trot. A moment later, he heard the clatter of machine-gun fire, and from the wall of the fort which was lit by the flicker from the gun muzzle, he saw a long, red cord of fire which zig-zagged and bounced when it struck the ground, well ahead of the howling mass. The English were using tracer ammunition, probably so that they could observe the direction of their fire, thought Yussuf. He did not move from his cover, but watched the crowd which had come to a heaving standstill. The machine-gun was silent, and from habit Yussuf memorised its position. He wondered if it was a flat-nosed one or a white man who sat there behind the gun, crouched in the darkness. That burst of fire was the warning to disperse. Next time, if the crowd moved forward, Yussuf was sure, the machine-gunner would fire into them. He could hear cries of rage above the roaring of the crowd and the shouts of the leaders, but he could not distinguish what they were saying. He thought they must be exhorting the people to go on with the attack, and as he watched them tensely, he heard the Mullahs calling on Allah to help, and the answering roars of the mob which once more began to stamp its feet on the ground.

The machine-gunner in the turret fired again, one burst striking the ground nearly a hundred paces to the left and in front of the mob, and another burst much nearer. The groups of tracer bullets flew into the sky like burning red cinders, and this time the crowd retreated a few yards, though its animal howling did not cease. Again the darkness closed in over the turret, but Yussuf was certain that the mob would not break now unless the machine-gunner fired into them. He heard the high yells of the women again, like thousands of mad birds, and he saw the flash of upraised spears among the dark and almost indistinguishable mass of surging people. The time for the real test of warriors had come, and Yussuf saw the crowd thinning and heard the roaring grow fainter as they began to rush towards the prison. He gripped a dried twig in his hands tightly until it snapped, his eyes fixed on the turret which he could now faintly recognise. He uttered a cry of pleasure and stood up, for no sound came from the fort. Perhaps the soldiers had mutinied, or the English were afraid to fire. Captain Turnbull was no longer real for him; that formidable figure had receded into the background, lost among the English who did not want to shoot, or would not shoot. Perhaps after all the English Government did not allow its soldiers to fire on the people, and all the drills, the training, the threats and the machine-guns themselves, were bluff and lies. For a moment Yussuf wanted to rush across that open space and lead his people into the gaol, but he thought better of it and stayed where he was. Then he heard thuds—it must be the mob breaking the doors of the prison —and cries and shouts ; then two shots and a gradual diminishing of the crowd's angry voice. He sat down and waited, his eyes staring fixedly at the turret.

Turnbull felt the sweat break out all over him as he watched the mob break back after his two bursts of fire. Sole had not returned from the prison where Sergeant-Major Abduruman was posted with nine riflemen. As the sweat soaked him and became cold, Turnbull breathed heavily, his teeth pressed into his lower lip, while his hands gripped the traversing handles of the machine-gun. Absent-mindedly he rubbed his thumb across the knurled, steel button of the trigger, while his humiliation struggled with his will and his anger. He could not believe that Sole understood the seriousness of his order. Not to open fire, not even an excuse which would allow him to fire under certain conditions ; nothing, only Sole's surprisingly cool order, " I forbid you to open fire." Did Sole really think that he could quell the mob with a speech ? It was not that Sole was drunk. They had both had a few drinks, but Turnbull knew that Sole was in possession of all his faculties. But the important thing was that Sole was the Civil Power, and however much Turnbull might threaten the chiefs, he knew that ultimately, when the situation arose, it was Sole, the Civil Power, who decided on the use of troops ; who tried every political trick he knew to smooth the situation and if all these failed then he called on the troops to act. And when he did that the matter was in Turnbull's hands, for it meant that the political officer could not deal with the situation by threats, speeches, collective fines, or arrests. Turnbull had made the arrests in the certain knowledge that his action would be approved by any political officer. But Sole disagreed with that for a start. So now Sole was going to try politics on this mob of fanatics. He squinted into the darkness where he could see the crowd milling and he could hear the pounding rhythm of their feet. " There must be a couple of thousand of them," he said aloud, " mad for blood." One burst from his gun would break them and send them whimpering to their huts, but no, Sole must play on, like Milton, trying anything but the whip, the blow that would stun and wither that fury which was now about to try itself against the Government in El Ashang.

The troops were quiet in their positions, standing easy and occasionally whispering to each other. " Silence," shouted Turnbull in his parade voice. " Silence. Watch your front and close your mouths. Await orders." There was immediate silence, then the distant voice of the crowd and some excited gabbling from the direction of the prison a couple of hundred yards away. Turnbull was sullen while he chewed his bitter thoughts, trying to make up his mind what to do if Sole's plan went wrong. He shivered in his sweat-soaked shirt, and even his leather wrist-watch strap disgusted him with its soaked coldness about his wrist. He saw the mob moving forward again, and he loosened the gun on its traverse, moving the barrel slowly ahead of the crowd. The soft clink of the loaded cartridge-belt satisfied him. He cursed Sole with words he had not used for years. He felt the great, collective power and venom of the crowd which was now surging like a herd of bellowing animals across the sand. There was soft starlight on them now, and the dust from the thousands of feet rose into the air as the chanting, stamping herd moved towards the prison and away from Turnbull in his turret.

Sole's throat was dry and he swallowed hard, feeling his heart moving in him like an excited hand, its fingers spread, until he almost gasped for breath. The excitement and apprehension caused him to tremble slightly, though to Sergeant-Major Abduruman he appeared perfectly cool and poised.

" *Effendi*," whispered Abduruman in English, " I don't trust the *askaris* with us. They are talking among themselves. They are the same race as these people. Watch them, *Effendi*."

Out of the side of his mouth, Sole said, " Then why the hell did you bring them ? Why ? Why ? "

" They were sent to me by Sergeant Elmi, *Effendi*, and I think Elmi did it purposely. The *askaris* should have been of the river tribes, but it's too late now, unless I hurry and get another section."

" No," thought Sole. " Too late. But maybe he's wrong.

They're all bloody intriguers, anyway, and I can't trust any
of them."

"No," he said excitedly. "You may be wrong. And it's
too late now. Look, here they are." The mob had appeared
out of the dust and darkness some twenty yards away, all
teeth and eyes and blades, and a wild, savage, frightening
voice like that of a beast in loosening chains. Then a ragged
man with eyes rolling and his black face shining with sweat
leapt out from among his companions. He cavorted in front
of them, a dagger in his hand, pointing at the sky, and he
jumped about until he was about ten paces from Sole, when
he began to hop slowly from one foot to the other. He
snarled some guttural words, repeating them like the words
of a song, and he fixed his insane eyes on Sole's as if in an
attempt to hypnotise him.

"He says they have come for the chiefs, *Effendi*," said
Abduruman hoarsely. "*Effendi*, can we fix bayonets now ? "
He was urgent.

"Yes," said Sole. He wiped the sweat from his face, then
he changed his mind. "No," he snapped. "Not yet. Wait.
Translate for me." He tried to moisten his dry mouth again
before speaking. "Perhaps I will win," he thought : "Anyone can kill them." But he did not know now which was the
right path. He wanted to run away from this situation in
which he was now placed, unbelieving in the value and
righteousness of his rifles and machine-guns, in Turnbull and
the troops.

"Tell them they are wrong to do this and if they do not
go now the Government will punish them severely. The
Government will imprison them and fine them. They must
go away now. Tell them."

Abduruman, his heart burning with shame, began to shout
Sole's words in the barbaric tongue of the mob which swayed
and shook its head, its roar almost drowning his voice. Their
answer was a scream of fury and a shower of rocks and sand.
Sole turned quite pale and his face seemed to shut up like a

knife. He turned his dark, straining eyes on Abduruman.

"Fix bayonets," he said, and Abduruman, his voice exultant, shouted the order, only the slightest note of anxiety in it. They heard the quick swish and the ring of the steel as the bayonets were wrenched from the scabbards, the clicking and thudding as they were fixed.

"Load," said Sole, and Abduruman gave the order. There was the uneven clashing as the *askaris* slammed their rifle bolts and stamped their feet into the "on guard" position beyond Sole and Abduruman, who took two paces back into the line of the *askaris*. Sole drew his pistol and pulled tight on its lanyard which hung round his neck. He was suddenly afraid, and this fear caused him to regret having forbidden Turnbull to fire. Was it fear then that kept empires secure, fear on both sides? Now, with the sweat pouring from his body, he was about to send Abduruman running to Turnbull with orders to fire, but he saw that the mob had cut them off from the fort. Rage and fear now took hold of him, the same feeling which had taken him by the brain in that bloody and useless attack on the German Spandau positions in Libya. He let it work in him and tried to feel anger for Turnbull who *must* shoot after all. Sole did not believe in his job or in his Empire, but now, trapped, he lifted the symbol of violence until its short barrel pointed at the dervish in front of him. He shouted the order to fire. The crowd rushed, black and tumultuous, its hands and blades raised, dust and stones flying, teeth bared, wild yelling mouths. As he fired, Sole knew that his *askaris* had gone into the darkness, he could hear them running away towards the village, unmolested by the crowd. As the mob closed on him he heard Abduruman snarling like a dog, all effort and striving as he fought. The pistol was wrenched from Sole's hand, and he gasped as a fierce, hot pain followed in his shoulder. He could feel the blade turning in him as he fell.

Abduruman bayoneted two men as they drove him against the prison door, but the third, with the bayonet up to the

hilt in his chest, seized the muzzle of the rifle and held it
until Abduruman was battered to the ground by blades,
sticks and fists. Then drawing back like a wave, the mob
tensed itself and charged the old wooden doors of the prison.
They fell like a long, wooden flooring into the small courtyard. Two terrified warders holding hurricane lamps were
cowering against the wall of the prison barrack. They cried
out, something of fear or pleading, but they were seized by
the mob and flung like dolls against the grey cement walls
which housed their prisoners. Then the mob seemed to
become frantic, as though possessed of some new, demoniacal
energy, and they began to break in the cell doors, and wrench
at the iron bars covering the small windows. Those who
had been timid, from experience perhaps of the Government's
will in the past, now rushed to the front, and the old men
tottered about on the edges of the crowd, clawing the young,
and begging not to be forgotten when the share-out of the
treasures began. The young men pushed them aside, hardly
knowing they were there, and the men posted on the doorway
stared at the dark shape of the fort which was still silent, and
a rumour ran amongst the leaders that the soldiers in the fort
must have mutinied and even killed their officers.

Sole lay on his face, covered with dust which had caked
on his blood-soaked tunic, his fingers buried in the sand as if
clutching it. Against the wall of the prison Abduruman's
body was bundled into one of the almost impossible
postures of violent death, his head under his shoulder, his
right leg twisted up under his humped body, one arm
broken across his back. His right hand clutched some of
the arid sand of his country as though in death he had
valued it.

In a few minutes the crowd, quiet now, swarmed into the
darkness, the chiefs whom they had released still blinking
and surprised. They made a detour, avoiding the fort, and
streamed into the village, the Mullahs leading them and
mouthing prayers of thanks.

CHAPTER THIRTEEN

SOLE'S servant, Yassin, had spent only a couple of hours exploring Milton's house, which was to be the new home of his master, and Yassin's to look after. He had found two bottles half-full of gin and rum, and after drinking some gin, he not only lost the pains and stiffness of the long journey to this hell of sand and rock, but he began to sing in a thin, reedy voice. He sang the "*Mudundu,*" the fertility song of his country, where it was green and hot, where the soil was rich and the women were fat. As the music excited him he began to sway, slapping his thighs with his palms, his eyes wide and soft. They seemed to be full of unshed tears as he swayed about in Milton's sitting-room among the aged basket-work chairs, the broken bookcases and the dusty occasional-tables. As he passed the table on which stood the two bottles, he snatched one of them and drank absent-mindedly, his thin legs rising and falling to the rhythm beating in his mind. He forgot the commotion of the village which he had watched from the verandah, the mob running into the darkness towards the gaol, and the red flash of the machine-gun fire. He had not joined them for he was not of them. They would kill him, for he knew that a great trouble had arisen this night for the Government. He had been frightened when he saw his enemies flood towards the gaol, the enemies of his people, the haters of the flat-nosed people of the big river. But the white officers had guns and troops, and as the machine-gun fired, faintly illumining the mob, he had run back into the house, his mind closed against disaster, yet conscious that he was alone amongst these bitter and arrogant people who had once ruled the whole of the land and its peoples. The white men would win and would punish them all.

He wandered through the big house which he knew he

should get ready for his master, but he decided to wait, for it might be that his work would be for nothing if they killed the Captains, for Captain Sole would not then need the house, and then the people would come to kill him too. It depended on the white men. There was nowhere for him to go, no escape, and he began peering into cupboards and drawers, assessing the loot they would have if they destroyed the white men. There was much, but they would not know what to do with some of it, these pigs and fools who were so proud of their tribes, their blood, and their accursed empty land. They would foul all these rooms, like cattle, and they would do it exactly in the middle of each room. He had seen them do it in the raids on the houses of the Italians near Korma during the retreat of the Italian army from the British. Like all of his people who worked for the Government officers, he wished to see the British crush all who were not subservient, to rule with an iron hand and to bring safety and well-being to those who loved the Government. Yassin loved the Government, especially when he saw danger as he saw it now. He admired white men because he had grown away from his own tribal ways and his people. When he made his rare visits to his village, he felt lost among his people, cut off from them. They did not know how to use a tin-opener, or a spanner, they did not know that when a man took a woman there was no need to have a child, or that white men were just like black men but with the difference that they enjoyed everything, everything, and nothing was forbidden.

One bottle was empty now and Yassin was drunk. He stopped dancing, swaying slightly, his bright eyes moving aimlessly about the room. His breathing had quickened and he gave little gasps as the strong liquor moved him. Why should those pigs have all the loot which this huge house contained? Why should he not save some of it, and hide it somewhere, so that even if all went well and the white men won over the people of the village, he could tell his master that he had taken and hidden these things so that they would be safe for him? However he looked at it, it was good, it was right. For a moment he was moved by his own goodness and virtue, and he could imagine the gratitude of the Captain for his thoughts of his master's welfare. Then he suddenly remembered the Captain's gold cigarette case, and the disappointment nearly brought tears to his eyes. That cigarette case, thick and heavy, a slab of carved gold, was something which he had always coveted, and he had had arguments with himself over it many times. How often had he reasoned that if he took it and fled, it would be worth it, but the thought always came of the three hundred-odd shillings which he had earned in the Captain's service, and which he had not drawn. The book which registered the money in the Captain's handwriting was in the pocket of his shorts now. He clapped his hand to it and his heart jumped. Tears came from his eyes now, and he tasted them on his thick lips. Not only was the coveted cigarette case in the Captain's possession as usual, probably never to be seen again, but he would never see his three hundred shillings either. He had slaved all these long months for nothing. He began to weep bitterly, and he thought of his home and of how he was lost now, masterless among these people who would kill him. It was the Captain's fault, and sudden hatred for the Captain filled him, baring his teeth, squeezing the tears in a rush on to his face. He picked up one of the tables, and growling like a dog he hurled it against the wall, and the release of violence gave him back some of his power. He took the bunch of keys from his pocket and began opening the Captain's metal trunks. He knew what he would take now, but first he would do something he had always longed to do. He would wear the Captain's uniform, the uniform of the cold country which the officers never wore in this land of sun. When he found the khaki barathea service dress he began to put it on, excitedly, his tears forgotten. It fitted him well, and the smart tunic with its brass buttons and badges thrilled him. Then he found the dark-blue side-cap and crammed it on over his thick, woolly hair, and began running from room to room until he found a mirror. He stood there entranced, almost laughing with pride and pleasure. When the uniform was arranged to his satisfaction he staggered back into the sitting-room and began to take the clothes which he had always thought of as those he would most like to possess. But he could not resist anything now, and the pile of coveted things grew until they were spread across the floor. In his frantic searchings for his favourite clothes, he did not see the figure which came quietly through the door and stood behind him. Some moments later, bent over one of the boxes, he saw a long shadow move across the floor in front of him, and he gasped, stood up and jumped round, and when he saw the young, almost naked stranger before him he uttered a yell of fright.

" Who are you ? " he whispered, bending, ready to escape. The other, his reddish-brown body glistening fiercely in the light of the uncovered electric bulbs, smiled, his big, hard eyes moving slowly from Yassin's feet to the officer's cap on his head.

" I am Fara," he said. " I killed the officer who lived here, the fat one, and I have come for some things for myself." He held out his left arm to show Yassin the gold watch flashing on his left wrist to which it was tied with a thong of camel hide. " Have you one of these ? " he said proudly, and Yassin shook his head, his eyes fixed on the watch.

" It was his ? The dead one's ? " he said, and the other nodded. Then Fara drew his dagger but did not move from his position, and Yassin began to whimper softly, his mouth working while Fara stared into his eyes.

" Why are you taking the things which belong to me, flat nose ? " Fara said in a sharp voice.

" They are mine. I am taking them from my master. Is he dead yet ? " Yassin appealed to him. The heavy uniform and his fear had caused him to break into a deep sweat, and like most of those who had left their tribal ways, he did not wash often, so that his sharp, acrid smell offended Fara, who spat at him.

" You stinking, flat-nosed dog," he said, and Yassin began to cry. " No, no, please, no. I will give you it all. Please do not kill me."

Then there was a sudden noise on the verandah, heavy footsteps, and Captain Turnbull came into the room, followed by four *askaris* carrying the unconscious Sole. Fara ran round the room like a wild animal which has found itself in a strange and frightening situation. He saw the high window and went towards it like an eel, almost bewildering Turnbull, who rushed after him and grabbed him as he climbed on to the sill. Fara squirmed and as Turnbull's hands slipped on the goat-fat which covered the toughly muscled body, Fara stabbed him through the fleshy part of his left forearm, missing the thick neck which had been his target. Turnbull hissed with pain, and he seized Fara's right arm in his two big hands and twisted it with all his strength until he heard it break. Fara uttered no sound, but continued to struggle, his face close to that of the white man which was now contorted into a light-coloured glare and a row of bared teeth.

"Got you, you bastard." Turnbull threw his arms tightly about Fara's ribs. He locked his right hand on his left wrist behind the brown back and squeezed until Fara's eyes were distended and glazed and he gasped and struggled for breath. The rage, the frustration of the months which had ended in the attack on the prison, and the pain of the knife wound, all seethed in Turnbull's eyes, and he wanted the pleasure of killing the man now struggling for breath in his arms. But there were things he must know, and he picked Fara up until he was level with his head, and then threw him against the wall, and the body fell to the floor like a heavy bundle and lay there motionless.

The *askaris* had laid Sole on a rush mat and stood as if paralysed, watching Yassin, who was cowering in a corner, terrified, and Turnbull, who stood groaning softly and holding his wounded left arm, the blood seeping through his fingers.

When he saw Yassin wearing an officer's uniform, he stared unbelievingly, half of his mind on the wound and the prostrate man who had stabbed him, and the other half trying to understand the fantastic picture of the woolly-haired Yassin in a captain's service dress.

Yassin half ran and half staggered towards Turnbull and threw himself at his feet, and he pressed his head against the dusty ammunition boots, kneading them with his forehead. " *Effendi*," he sobbed. " *Effendi*." He embraced the puttee'd legs until Turnbull booted him disgustedly away so that he was forced to place his forehead on the floor and continue his gabbled implorations. A dresser appeared at the doorway carrying bandages and bottles, and Turnbull remembered Sole, who lay moaning faintly in the glaring electric light.

"Well, don't stand there," shouted Turnbull harshly. "Put the officer on the bed in there." He pointed to the bedroom doorway. To the dresser he said, "If you don't make the Captain well again I'll make you regret it," and the dresser, a small black, compassionate man with big, liquid eyes, smiled and shuffled into the bedroom behind the *askaris* who carried Sole.

There were so many events, one after the other, to piece together, that Turnbull's mind, still shaking and nervous from the shocks of the night's happenings, could hardly calm itself for those which he was afraid were still to come. He turned on Yassin and kicked him. "Shut your whining mouth," he shouted. "Who are you?"

"I am Yassin, the Captain's servant. My master is dead and I am alone."

"Your master is not dead." Then Turnbull pointed to the scattered heaps of Sole's clothing. "But you were too quick. You should have waited, you and your friend, before you robbed him. You jackal's dung, you."

"He's not my friend, *Effendi*." Yassin knelt up, still in

tears, his drunken eyes rolling. "He was going to kill me. He told me he had killed the Captain who lived here, and he had come for the Captain's things."

Turnbull bent down and, thrusting his hands into the thick mat of Yassin's hair, he gripped it and pulled the terrified servant to his feet. He bent Yassin's head back and stared intently into his eyes as though searching them for some hidden treasure.

"Say it again," he shouted. "What did you say? Say it again." He began to shake him frenziedly, full of hope, yet ready to find that Yassin was a liar, like all the others in this country of intriguers and plotters. Yassin was shrieking, clawing at Turnbull's belt as those strong and frantic hands tightened in his hair and shook him so that he was unable to see or think in his terror. Through his teeth Turnbull continued to mouth unbelief and curses, all his misery running into his muscles, and the suppressed violence of months eating his will and his distorted sympathies.

"If you lie to me again, I'll break your neck." He screamed the words, dragging Yassin's wet, black face right up to his own until Yassin could look into the white man's peering eyes which were like those of a wild cat, pale and mad and absolutely frightening. Closing his eyes, Yassin whispered that he would swear on the lives of his family and on the book itself that he spoke the truth.

"You swear it?" said Turnbull in a low, coaxing voice. "You swear it? If you lie to me I will kill you at once." He said this as though he were promising him some boon or promised favour, and its conviction caused Yassin to moan and sob again. He said that he swore it. He told Turnbull that his officer had all his wages for the past months, that he was alone in this terrible land and that he worshipped the Government, which was his father and his mother. "I swear it," he cried, opening his eyes. "I swear that this man told me he had killed the fat Captain and had come for his things." Then he remembered the gold watch on Fara's wrist and he began to laugh like an idiot, holding Turnbull's hands which were still gripping his hair.

"The watch," he cried. "The gold watch which he said he took from the officer. He showed it to me. It is on his wrist. It is on his wrist." He laughed hysterically, his voice broken.

Turnbull unlocked his hands and Yassin fell at his feet murmuring his gratitude to God and to the officer and the Government, and Turnbull was dragging the still unconscious Fara on to his back. He took the man's dagger and cut the thong which secured the wristlet watch, and he remembered the gold links which he had found beside Milton's body. He muttered his satisfaction as he stared at the thin, handsome, wolfish face of Fara, who had begun to move his lips. Turnbull walked over to the heaps of Sole's clothing and picked up a pair of puttees with which he tied Fara up, lashing his arms to the legs which he drew up behind the man's body. The incongruity of the broken arm's movements caused Turnbull to scowl with disgust and made him shudder. To Yassin he said sternly, "Take off that uniform, and go across to the fort swiftly and call a corporal and two *askaris*. Run fast." Yassin stripped off Sole's uniform as he made his way to the door, and once free of it, he ran from the house, his heart all glad and happy again, his money and his life safe and assured once more.

The dislike and distrust of these tribesmen which had been sometimes fanned into anger and as quickly cooled again in Turnbull's heart, had now become an almost consuming hatred. The sight of Sole's body in the sand had moved him, even overcoming the angry contempt he felt for him, but the sight of Abduruman's battered and broken body had moved him almost to madness and the hot tears had blinded him. The *askaris* had stood nearby, huddled and silent, watching him as he wandered about near Abduruman's body, his face dead white and anguished in the light of the hurricane lamp which he carried. Turnbull had begun to shout in

English, his face turned to the village, and the *askaris* saw his hatred like a power which he wore on him. They knew that Abduruman had been his friend and his closest follower, that Turnbull was Abduruman's chief as he was theirs, but that Abduruman was like the chief's eldest son and his right hand, and now he was dead. They were sorry for Turnbull, but not for Abduruman, though they understood what his loss meant. For them, life would be much easier without him.

Turnbull knew that there were nine *askaris* in the village with rifles, and that they had joined their people. He wanted to turn Sole over on to his back and shout his rage into his face, to tell him what his policy had done. He had lost his prisoners, the chiefs, and much, if not all, of his prestige, by the freedom which Sole's orders had allowed the mob. Mob law had won, but he knew his men must back him, for like him they were far from home amidst a hostile people, and they relied on him to win against the people and return them to the safe position which they had once occupied in El Ashang. Their faith in him was shaken because he had not let them fire on the people, yet shrewdly the older *askaris* had told the young ones that they must connect this fact with the arrival of the Captain Sole. One who claimed to understand English said that he had heard the officers having words near the machine-gun, and he said he could tell by the tone of the new officer's voice that he was ordering Captain Turnbull not to do something. They therefore were willing to wait and see what Turnbull would now do, for the new officer was unable to give any more orders, perhaps he might even die.

Turnbull brought up the medium machine-gun and set it on the roof of the ration store near Milton's house in a position commanding the town, and he put two light machine-guns in such a position that he could sweep the town with fire. The town was quiet, and as its buildings were closely packed, it covered only a small area, and petered away into huddled buildings and the huts of nomads. He told the troops that he would let them kill if trouble came again, for all reasoning with the mob had failed. And he reminded them that fighting had by now almost certainly broken out in the desert between the Omar Bilash and the Yonis Barra. And he worried about Lieutenant Cuddy and his detachment wandering on their patrols near the wells north of El Ashang.

When troops had taken up their positions on the roofs of the highest buildings on the edges of the town, he called Sergeant Elmi to the fort, where one section of *askaris* was waiting in reserve. There he arrested the sergeant and placed him in the cells, and he was interested to note that the sergeant showed no surprise and asked for no explanation. He was of these people by blood and tribal group, and he had deliberately sent *askaris* of his own tribe to Sole at the gate of the prison as he had agreed to do with the chiefs some hours before. He thought Turnbull knew the details and he was satisfied. He, more than any member of the mob, had ensured by his action the success of the crowd's attempt to rescue their chiefs. The *askaris* had agreed not to fire and to join their people. In the cell the sergeant sat and waited interestedly to see if Turnbull would win against his people.

When his troops were settled, Turnbull had gone into the armoury with an empty haversack, alone, while the dresser had given Sole an injection of one of the Italian drugs which were in his charge. Then they had taken Sole to Milton's house.

When he had finished tying Fara up, exulting in his lucky capture of Milton's murderer, Turnbull picked up the haversack and unbuckled it. From it he took two Italian ground flares. They were long, grey metal tubes with thick rubber tags at the ends. He placed these in the pockets of his tunic, and though they protruded he was satisfied that they would not prevent him from fast movement if that should be required. When he was satisfied, he sat down and watched Fara moan his way to consciousness.

Turnbull was now in the mood to commit himself to

massacre, for his long tradition of military pride as well as his own vanity of personality had been gravely wounded, and the scars of older humiliations at El Ashang were all alive again and raw, like fires which had consumed his judgment. He was ready now to inflict what he considered to be the right answer to the tribal intrigues which had worked for a year like a cancer into Milton, and into the fort amongst his troops, and finally into his own person which he had once considered safe from hysteria and the spirit of revenge. Things had gone wrong, culminating in a victory for a mob of savages, and these savages, who had trampled on his pride and his experience, would pay. If he got the opportunity he would now kill them, not a few as a deterrent, but many, as many as he could, as a lesson which they would never forget, and for which he was satisfied he was prepared to pay with his career. If they forgot the British Government they would not forget Turnbull. He would be the British for them, he wanted to be that, for he believed with all his heart that the British should be respected and feared, and this feeling had increased since he had assumed officer's rank. He had a sympathy for the coloured peoples of the Empire, but this sympathy did not envisage a desire on the part of the coloured peoples to rule themselves. He could not help feeling that because he had no colour bar he was in advance of most of his white comrades and fellows, and this made him certain that he knew what was best for disturbed natives, savages, or tribal peoples. When these people were insolent, ungrateful, dangerous, as they were in El Ashang to-night, he was wounded deeply, for he was their friend if they but knew it. He knew what was best for them and they would not listen. He was wiser than they and they cast his wisdom into his face and would kill him as they had killed Abduruman if they got the chance. Now he wanted them to attack again, and as he imagined the scene he felt a deep emotion, exalted and overpowering, the prelude to the powerfully inflicted pain and death over which he had command in the magazines of his rifles and machine-guns. Though he did not yet know it, he was afraid. This hatred and this exaltation was the same as that which enlivened the hearts of the savages whom he had come to hate.

Turnbull was certain that he could never forgive Sole for what he had done to-night by his orders against firing. He felt hatred for Sole, too, not Sole personally, but for the doubt and the half-baked theories of Sole's kind. Sole was either frightened of his job, or he was one of those new kind of people who would be conscientious objectors if they had the courage. The army had plenty of them, people who did not want to fight, but did so, half-heartedly, because they were too frightened to refuse. And yet, Turnbull was sure they knew that the war was a just war against evil and cruelty, but they were cowards who, when the time of important decision came, behaved like Sole and like Milton. He decided that Sole must be a coward, and yet he *had* faced that mob. That meant that he was one of these " peace at any price " chaps. "Well, there's one thing, anyway," thought Turnbull, " that spear wound in his body will make Sole think a bit."

Yassin came in with a corporal and two *askaris*. They slapped their rifle butts and he greeted them. When he told them that he had captured Milton's assassin they uttered the cries of pleasure which officers expected on these occasions, though Turnbull twisted his mouth irritably and silenced them.

" I want him chained up," he said. " Chained, and with padlocks in a cell, alone. He is to have no food, no water and no sleep. No sleep, do you understand ? " The corporal nodded, but said :

" How can we stop him from sleeping, *Effendi* ? "

" There are several ways," said Turnbull. " But the way I want it done is for an *askari* to sit in front of him with a stick and prod him with it every time he starts to go asleep. The *askari* is to be changed every two hours. The prisoner is to have no sleep, none at all, and no food and water. If that order is disobeyed, I'll break you."

"Yes, *Effendi*," said the corporal, "I will see to it that he gets nothing, nothing. He has killed an officer and death is too good for him. I will see——"

Turnbull silenced him. "Get him into the cell at once, alone, and nobody is to talk to him or to answer a question if he asks one. For your own sake, see I am obeyed." He knew the corporal would not disobey, for already the young corporal was seeking Sergeant Elmi's stripes. The whole company knew that somebody would be made acting-sergeant within a few days, and he could sense the great striving among the N.C.O.s, for the new acting-sergeant would almost certainly act also as sergeant-major in place of the dead Abduruman.

He watched them drag the prisoner to his feet while one of the *askaris* loosened the puttees which bound him. He was gabbling to himself and then he opened his eyes and addressed his gabblings to the *askaris* and to Turnbull. He bared his teeth and tried to free himself, and his eyes opened wide and began to roll as he struggled. Turnbull looked at the contorted mask in which the white teeth glistened, and at the hot, animal eyes which had begun to examine him.

"What is he saying?" said Turnbull to the corporal.

"He is cursing you, *Effendi*," the corporal told him humbly. "He says the Government is ended here and that all men of the land are happy now. They will get justice with their own hands."

"What is his tribe?"

"We do not know, *Effendi*."

"Tell him that he has much information which I am going to get from him. Tell him I know already many things about him."

The corporal spoke these words harshly to the prisoner, who listened gravely, and then smiled contemptuously. Turnbull's cheeks flushed with temper and the *askaris* were interested to see that he was visibly angry, his right fist clenching tightly.

" Take him away and do as I have said," he shouted at the corporal.

When they had gone Turnbull went into the bedroom where Sole lay moaning. The small, black medical dresser sat near the foot of the bed on his haunches, his eyes fixed on the sick white man.

" How's the Captain ? " said Turnbull. It was strange to think that Sole's life lay in the hands of a half-trained native orderly, and the thought made him glad of his own good health.

" The spear went through the top part of the Captain's left shoulder, *Effendi*. It did not go through his lung. I have bathed him in hot water and have bound him up in two of the English field dressings. His temperature is high, and he is sick. I poured some tea down his mouth. He has been saying things."

" What things ? And do something for this knife wound in my arm, it's hurting me."

While the dresser examined his arm, Turnbull said, " Will he die ? Is he going to get well ? "

" He is very strong and young, but his wound may go bad. He should go to Korma soon."

" Soon he will go," said Turnbull. " I have sent signals to Korma about what has happened, and the Government may send an aeroplane for him. We will wait and see. You are to stay here night and day with the Captain, do you hear ? "

" I hear, *Effendi*," said the little man. " The Captain will be safe with me."

Turnbull bent over Sole and examined his face. It was greyish and moist, the flesh drawn tightly, and the eyes sunken in dark sockets. A faint whispering came from his lips and Turnbull laid his hand on Sole's forehead, feeling dry, burning heat there. At the pressure of Turnbull's hand, Sole tried to move, and then spoke aloud, wearily, his eyes still closed.

" All those men with their hands full of sand. Said it was a lie. If you can't, then take me straight to the club. Barbed wire and the riot act. Barbed wire. Barbed——"

Turnbull snatched his hand away. Sole rambled on, his words now indistinguishable, until he suddenly groaned and began to curse aloud. His curses ended in a whimper and the room was silent again, the medical orderly rocking slowly on his heels, hugging his bony knees.

" You thought you were bloody well right, didn't you ? " said Turnbull aloud as he bent over Sole. " But you weren't, you know. You weren't. They fixed you and they killed Abduruman, and they took the chiefs into the bargain. And I carry the baby ! But I've told Korma, I gave them all the griff in the signal, and while I'm carrying the baby I'm going to show these bastards who's boss." He could feel the two flares in his jacket pockets and the thrill of rage ran through him again.

Sole moaned, and said, " Elizabeth, you tart, d'you really think that that's the thing to do ? But this fellow is too much for me. Matter of conscience, I'd say. Ugh ! Remember that legal course I had before the exam. God ! " He moaned again, and Turnbull withdrew.

It was warm outside and the moon was hidden by cloud. There was a faint breeze on his face, pleasing and clean. It was as though El Ashang and its people, the violence and the death, had been a dream, for the soft darkness hid everything. There was no sound, and yet, within the village some few hundred yards away were the chiefs and the deserters with their rifles, probably knowing they were surrounded by machine-guns and rifles—but it was more than likely that they had escaped. Turnbull was fatalistic about the natural talents of law-breakers in a country which they knew. Their feats of endurance, their intuition, their cunning, did not surprise him any more. But the cure for these people was violence, he was sure. He walked quickly towards the machine-gun position which covered the market. Near the market were groups of old huts with thick, straw roofs, dried and tindery from years of the sun.

He reached the huts after a few words with the machine-gunners. He gave them to believe that he was going back to the fort to inspect the prisoner, and when he was well out of sight of the *askaris*, he walked with long, quiet strides through the darkness to the dilapidated huts on the edge of the town. He pulled the rubber tag of the flare and rammed it deep into the grass roof. Then he ran for about fifty yards and placed the second flare in the roof of another hut.

He then made his way towards the fort, until he heard the pop of the flares and saw the great silver flowers of light blossoming, bathing the sand and the buildings, like two enormous moons risen from the earth. Then the flames began as he ran towards the troops who were shouting to each other on his right. By the time he reached them they could hear the voice of the fire rising as it consumed the deserted huts and advanced on the village from which came a rising chorus of shouts and screams.

Turnbull smiled thinly. No one would die, he thought. They never did die in village fires, which were frequent if the women were stupid in the way they laid them in their kitchens. New brides generally caused the village fires, but this one, which would destroy El Ashang, would render the Omar Bilash, who lived there, homeless, as well as many other tribal villagers, but the fire was for the Omar Bilash. The destruction of the village would give them something other than intrigue to think about.

" *Effendi*," cried the *askaris*. " What shall we do ? "

" Do ? " said Turnbull gravely. " Nothing. Nothing at all."

The glare reddened and grew fierce ; the crackling and the roar of the flames drowned the excited hubbub of the village, and against the glow of the burning huts Turnbull could see people running excitedly to and fro. If all else had failed, this calamity he had brought upon them would now crush that insolent spirit which had paralysed the government of this

cursed desert. It was for their own good he had done it.
Turnbull was satisfied that the destruction of the village was
the one weapon which would ensure a return to ordered ways.
He was exultant as he watched the catastrophe he had caused,
but his pride, which these savages had humbled, was alive
again, fierce in his heart, shaking him. Had he been able to
see himself, to examine his face, his voice and his eyes, he
would have known that defeat had come to him, not from
those enemies he knew so well, guns and bored soldiers'
minds, but from the sun, from loneliness and from power. It
was power which shook him now, fear and a kind of ecstasy,
clenching his teeth until his jaws ached.

"Nothing!" he shouted at the troops. "Do nothing!
Nothing! Nothing!"

The troops were pleased, their black faces shining in the
glare of the fire which had now engulfed the village, the home
of their ancient oppressors.

CHAPTER FOURTEEN

SOLE'S fever had gone and his eyes opened to stare into
those of the medical orderly. Then he saw Turnbull
sitting at the foot of his bed. He noticed that Turnbull's
face was thin and very pale, and the eyes burning strangely
in the sockets. Something had gone from that face which
had been so strong.

"Hello," he said weakly. His smile was hardly noticeable.
Turnbull nodded, his face tight, shut up, and his mouth
compressed.

"How am I?" said Sole.

"You're doing all right," said Turnbull in a dull, neutral
voice. "Flesh wound, but right through you. How do you
feel?"

"Weak, but alive. Whose room is this I'm in?"

" You're lying on Milton's bed," said Turnbull. " He was killed on it."

" Ugh, Christ ! " Sole tried to move without realising it, and then it all poured back into his mind. The tribes, the bitter prairies of rock and shale, the mob and the terror of that moment before the stabbing.

" You'd better tell me what happened, Turnbull," he said. " You look all in. Or are you feeling that you've been let down ? You'd better tell me all about it." To the orderly he said, " Tea. Bring me some tea."

The orderly's eyes seemed to melt with pleasure. " At once, *Effendi*," he said, and hurried away. His fame would spread and his heart was full with happiness. He had saved the white man's life, just like a doctor.

" Tell you about it ? " said Turnbull. He examined the wedding ring on his finger without knowing it, turning his hand until the ring shone. " Yes. You shot one man. Got stabbed with a spear, and Abduruman, my sergeant-major, was killed."

Sole's eyes were miserable. " I'm sorry, Turnbull," he said. " I'm really sorry. I liked Abduruman."

" That's kind of you," Turnbull replied, his voice flat, empty of expression. " He was a good sergeant-major."

There was a silence between them as Sole stared at the ceiling and Turnbull watched a miniature of his face reflected in the ring on his short, thick finger.

" I suppose you want to know about the chiefs," said Turnbull. " They're free, in the village. The mob got them away safely, and nine of my *askaris* deserted with their rifles, but I've got them back, the *askaris* that is, chained up, but none of the rifles. They've been sent to the Omar Bilash in the bush. The chiefs have disappeared too. And the town has burned down. Two nights ago it happened. Nearly every hut gone."

" Good God ! " said Sole. " And what about the people ? Where are they if their houses are gone ? "

"They're here, don't worry," said Turnbull, the first hardness coming back into his voice. "But they're very sorry for themselves, very quiet. They want help from the Government. They want sugar, grain, oil and a few other things." Turnbull's voice became a snarl. "They say that the Government is their father."

"God!" said Sole. "How did the fire happen?"

"Don't know," said Turnbull. "Probably a cooking fire in one of the huts. There were a few explosions during the fire. Grenades and ammunition hidden in the huts. Don't tell me you're upset about these bastards, Sole, after what has happened." Turnbull looked at Sole for the first time with a sharp interest, hostile, but still with that queer, broken look in his eyes.

"Listen, Turnbull," said Sole, his voice stronger now. "You look ill to me, and I'm ill too. Do you think it's going to do any good if we quarrel now about who's right to feel what?"

"I've had months of this stuff," cried Turnbull. "Months of it, and between you and Milton I don't know where I am. There'll be an inquiry into this mess, and I'm going to say my piece. I've had enough, I tell you."

"I think you have," said Sole gravely. "You wanted to kill them, didn't you, that night of the attack on the prison?"

"Yes. And I was right. Christ, do you mean to tell me that after what happened to you and Abduruman, let alone the gaol, that you still think you were right to forbid me to fire on that shower of savage bastards?" He was demanding an answer. His eyes were wild and sad, like those of a man who has suffered too much. He could feel his nerves like tightening wires in his body as he looked at Sole and awaited an answer.

"You can't go round killing people these days," said Sole irritably. "For God's sake stop talking about shooting people. I'll admit that when that mob went for me I had a moment when I wished you would shoot, but——"

"Oh, you did, eh?" said Turnbull harshly. "You admit it."

"Wait, wait," said Sole, lifting his hand for the first time. "I say I had that moment, but it was natural to feel that, but not right though. You'd have killed maybe a hundred people if you'd fired. Do you think that's worth keeping a few decrepit chiefs in gaol for, chiefs whom you've arrested on a private suspicion too. A private suspicion, mind you——"

Turnbull shouted him down and there was a sound of hysteria in his voice which alarmed Sole. "Decrepit? A private suspicion? Not on your life, chum. I've got a bloke in the cell who killed Milton. I'm certain he's an Omar Bilash. He admitted he killed Milton, to your own servant who was busy ransacking your boxes when I brought you here unconscious." Sole tried to speak, but Turnbull would not listen. "Yes, your own bloody servant got the story from the prisoner himself, who was going to kill your bloke anyway. A private suspicion, is it? What the hell do you blokes want before you act, a photograph of the murder being committed and a signed confession? I tell you I've had enough. I'm going my own way. I'll get the story and I'll arrest the chiefs if it's the last thing I do."

"I'm still in command here," said Sole. "You're here to do what I tell you. I'm the political officer, and I indicate what I want you and your troops to do, and don't forget it. I think you need leave. You're going out of your mind. You may be right in many ways about who did this or that, but you're too anxious to use your troops, to shoot and kill. I tell you you've got to stop it, Turnbull."

"Going out of my mind?" Turnbull shouted. "Not on your life, Sole. I know what I'm doing. Something's got to be done here and I'll do it." He felt afraid. Was he going out of his mind? He had seen many men crack up, but he could not see himself. It was Sole's spite. He had expected Sole to be apologetic about his mistaken order not to fire,

but Sole was going to brazen it out. He wanted to curse him
to his face.

"You'll do nothing without my orders," continued Sole.
"I'm getting up now, and if you start anything without my
orders, I warn you I'll hold you responsible."

Turnbull stood up. "You're sick," he said in a calmer
voice. "Maybe *you're* going out of your mind, not me. And
remember, there'll be an inquiry anyway. I'm quite confident
about where I stand. Are you?"

"No, not at all," said Sole. "Not at all. But as far as I'm
concerned I'm quite happy. I'll deal with this in my own way
and without massacring the people. The first thing is to start
relief measures for the townspeople."

"Relief measures," shouted Turnbull again, his voice full
of despair. "Haven't we had enough humiliation already?
I trained my troops for months to keep order here, but you
come along and tell me not to open fire, and you allow a mob
of savages to smash their way into the gaol. They kill my
sergeant-major, a bloke who was worth two of you, and they
stab you into the bargain. Well, where do you think government begins, Sole?"

Turnbull had bared his teeth, forgetting Sole's wound, his
sick face, the resentment in the dark eyes. Instead he saw
himself as the soldier, betrayed by the smart alecks with their
bits of paper and their files and their lists of likely approaches
to a problem. And behind all was the humiliation of those
crippling minutes behind the gun in the turret, powerless to
break the animal howl of the mob below. And behind that,
too, was the loss of his vast territory of the will, the territory
stretching over years of hunger for his wife and family.

How often had he pitied those men who gave in to the
need for women, men who should have got over that youthful
snare, but who found a comforting false strength in their
weakness, detailing at some bar, in some dreary mess party,
the list of female nationalities, the physical types, the great
number of those who had fallen in battle in their beds. Behind

his loosely tethered despair, he could see Aurella, who had torn his rank from his pride's shoulders, showing him the sad chimpanzee who had lived in him, uncomforted for years.

And there was something almost right about Sole's point of view, it seemed to Turnbull in his misery now, for Sole had stuck to his mistake, even though he had been afraid and admitted it, wishing Turnbull would fire the machine-gun after all. But his humiliations were too powerful, feeding his frustration like secret fuel, making him appear to Sole as a man about to surrender to hysteria.

"You killed my sergeant-major," Turnbull was shouting. He leaned over Sole, his hands clenching. "My troops think I'm a bloody ninny. And now we've got to be nice to the people who've nearly killed you. I've had enough, enough. I'm a soldier, not a clerk, and I bloody well refuse to do any more creeping to the Omar Bilash and the rest of them. You tell me you're here to give me orders. What orders? To be a nursemaid, after they've killed Milton and Abduruman and attacked you too?" He lowered his voice. Sole looked fixedly at the contorted face and the darting eyes, feeling Turnbull's frantic spirit and measuring those signs of breakdown which are part of all men's concealed equipment, but which are drawn out by the pressures of a situation which defeats the character. He knew his own too. They were working in him now, calling him to shout back at Turnbull, to explain his fear of power and his longing for peace. But he lay still and listened to Turnbull emptying the pigeon-holes of his years; the shut-up, barred, disciplined years of the regular soldier, and he thought he could see Turnbull's crisis, the crisis of one who had prepared for command and who now was crushed under its weight.

"Why don't you try and relax a bit?" said Sole calmly. "The village is burned down, you tell me. Isn't that enough? I agree we've got to get the chiefs back now if only to save face. You say you've got Milton's murderer. That's enough too, isn't it? What do you want? I've told you I don't believe in being tough if it can be avoided. You want to be tough. Why? To show the people who's boss? What do you want to do to them?"

"Get them back in gaol," said Turnbull angrily. "Shut them up so they can't move. But it's too late. You forget that they've got thousands of men out in the bush waiting to fight."

Then Turnbull seemed to give in. He spread his hands and Sole could see the shape of defeat in his eyes. "I don't understand it," Turnbull almost whispered. "I feel mixed up. You seem to think that what's happened here is nothing. I don't understand that, I tell you. I've always been taught that what we have, we hold. But between you and Milton, I don't know where I am any more. I'm tired out, tired out." He rubbed his face with his hands, looking drawn and beaten, his eyes vacant. He was trembling slightly and Sole was sorry for him.

"I've told Korma the situation and I've sent a copy of the signal to Colonel Casey," Turnbull was almost musing. "The Colonel will come here himself and then you can have a great big political talk about everything. I've had enough now."

"Right," said Sole, "then don't do anything else until the Colonel gets here. Keep the curfew on and the patrols, that's all."

"And be nice to the people," mocked Turnbull softly, his eyes wandering over the whitewashed walls of the room. "Well, I've got the bloke who did for Milton anyway. And I'll make him talk too."

"Make him?"

"Oh, don't worry. I won't do anything nasty or brutal to him. I'll be specially nice to him." Turnbull gave Sole a bitter smile. "Now I'm going to have a look at him," he said. "He may clear up a lot of things."

"Look after yourself," said Sole. "You look tired. Will you come over this evening and have a drink?"

Turnbull considered it for a few moments.

"No, thanks," he said. "We've got nothing particularly nice to say to each other——"

"Oh, come on, Turnbull," said Sole irritably, but Turnbull ignored his words.

"No," he went on, "let's drink on our own. I think the less we see of each other the better, and you've got to think up a good story for the Colonel, I should think, haven't you?"

Sole made a gesture of impatience.

"Have it your way," he said, closing his eyes. He heard Turnbull's nailed boot on the stone floor and the slam of the door.

He settled back on to his pillow, daggers of fire moving in his wounded shoulder, and a feeling of Turnbull's despair threatening him, mingling with his own.

Hearing the white men's voices, the orderly had waited outside with the tea. He had wrapped his turban about the teapot to keep it hot, and now he came in, impassive save for his eyes, which began to shine with kindness as he approached the wounded white man.

"Dress me," said Sole.

"*Effendi*, you are sick——" cried the orderly.

"Dress me," snapped Sole. "Do you hear?"

The orderly nodded resignedly. When the white man's voice sounded like that it was simplest to obey.

After calling an *askari* interpreter, Turnbull went straight to the cell where Fara, his most prized possession, was chained to the wall. It was wrong to chain a man, headquarters would say, but headquarters do not see everything, thought Turnbull. It was wrong to torture a prisoner, headquarters would say, but headquarters did not condemn what it did not see. And torture to most people meant beating, flogging, hot cigarette ends, but these left marks on the body. Lack of sleep left no mark on the flesh at all, only a faint hollowness in the face, a glaze in the eyes, a stumbling exhaustion in the mind. Turnbull had once seen a tough, shouting fanatic humbled like a little dog after four days without a wink of sleep, his hands begging, his eyes rolling far back, and his voice whimpering for just one little lie down, just a few minutes free from those prodding hands which kept him awake. A little darkness, a minute without the bright lights that shone into his face.

He could smell Fara as he entered the small, airless cell, and he saw his dark-brown, oily skin glisten and heard his chains as he stared through the light of the two petrol lamps whose glare had filled the cell with an almost oven-like heat. The prisoner shook his chains and lunged at him, snarling, his broken and swollen right arm hanging loosely. One of the *askaris* struck him in the face, and Fara struggled and heaved in his chains, panting and slavering as he stared into the cold, pale eyes of the white man.

The interpreter laughed aloud because he was amused, and because he felt one with the white man who had the power to do this thing, to chain up anyone he wished and to keep him there. The interpreter was a small, fat, black figure in badly cut shorts and shirt, and a pair of Arab sandals. His head was shaved and oiled, and the nostrils of his flat, African nose quivered as he breathed the thick, rank smell of sweat from the naked prisoner and from the *askaris*. He laughed heartily.

" He is feeling like a camel who is tied up too long, *Effendi*," he said in English. " And he smells like a camel too."

" Tell him that I am ready to listen to his talk," said Turn-bull. He kept his eye on the prisoner's face, wanting to punch it, to destroy that handsome, animal mask which jeered at him. And he wanted to close the eyes which shone hate on him, like beams of black light. The prisoner bared his teeth and struggled in his chains as the interpreter began to shout in a monotone, the barbaric words sounding like threats of violence. " The white man is going to cut out your heart unless you speak, you pig, you dog. Do you hear ? "

The man grew still in his chains, his head to one side, and

his lips drawn back mockingly from his beautiful teeth. Then he spat at Turnbull, who dodged it, resuming his stare into the prisoner's eyes. One of the *askaris* stood in front of the prisoner and struck him across the face with a stick, and when Turnbull said nothing, he struck him again, until Turnbull said, " Stop it. I want no marks on him." The prisoner stared like a snake at the *askari* who had struck him, memorising him, reading his face, his flat nose, his slave's eyes, his thick mouth, and the *askari* shrank from him, uncertain of his power. Then the prisoner turned his eyes on Turnbull again, and began to speak, arrogantly, while their eyes held each other, searching behind the face, hate and contempt in conflict. As the harsh voice stopped after each peroration, the now sweating interpreter translated. Because the prisoner was insulting the white man and the Government, the interpreter hesitated in his words, and Turnbull was sharp with him. " No nonsense," he said. " Don't change one word he says."

" He says, *Effendi*, that you are the Government and that the Government has many men and plenty of power, and that you are a white man, and you are strong and you have guns and soldiers." They listened again, and the interpreter went on. " You have a fire in your heart, he says, which burns you and has made you want to destroy the people, but you cannot do it. No one will destroy the people, and even though you make the other lesser tribes fight the bigger ones, and bring all the guns in the world, you will not destroy the people. They will get their own water."

The prisoner began to shout in a high, fierce voice, and he beat his clenched left fist on his chest so that the thud of the fist and the clank of his chains formed a rhythm behind his words.

" ' You can keep me without sleep,' he says. ' You can beat me with iron whips, you can cut out my heart, but I will tell you nothing. You have said that I killed the Captain, and that you will make me admit it, but I will tell you nothing.

Take out your pistol and shoot me now. I swear to you that I will tell you nothing. Many men will die in the desert, men of all tribes, because the Government will not leave them alone to make their life. The Omar Bilash and the Yonis Barra will fight for their water, and the Government is saying that all men are the same. But all men are not the same. The Yonis Barra will drink where they like, if they are strong. The Government cannot kill the people, and the people will not be broken like sticks.' "

The prisoner had gone into an ecstasy. His eyes were full of hot light, and foam was gathering on his lips. He looked like a demon from Turnbull's childhood mind, frightening and full of the savage, pagan strength of his people. He was stamping the soles of his feet on the sandy floor to the same rhythm of his beating fist, his lithe body shining as though varnished with oil.

" He is cursing you and all men who deny justice to the land——" The interpreter was cut short by a wave of Turnbull's hand. In a weary voice, Turnbull said, " Let him rave. He's mad." He knew that this was the moment of his life here which mattered most. Fear had come to him at last, and it would shape his thoughts and actions of the future. He had sworn before the *askaris* and to the prisoner that he would drag the truth from him, but he knew that he would not and could not do it. This savage meant what he had said, Turnbull's experience of men assured him, especially his experience of captured men of unwillingly subject races.

He knew those who would break. This one would not break, he would be like a sheet of steel that bends and returns to its original shape when the pressure is removed. He could kill him, but get no information. He had defeated Turnbull who stood before him, his pale face drawn and grim, and he stared contemptuously into the white man's eyes, as though conscious of what he had done. He could see the sweat on the white man's face, the tremor in his mouth, and he waited for the white man to strike him, to beat him, shoot him ; but the white man turned and walked out of the cell. The prisoner jeered after him, shouting that there was no God but God, and when an *askari* threatened him, he screwed up his face and shook his chains at him. " Flat-nosed one ! " he shouted. " Flat-nosed one ! " and he began to utter long, piercing howls, laughing in between them. The tired *askaris* who were there to break him began to beat him, but he had grown clever in the use of his chains, warding off their blows. And when they stood back tired, he laughed at them and began to howl again.

CHAPTER FIFTEEN

COLONEL CASEY was in the leading armoured car as the convoy skirted the fort and drove past the blackened heaps of ashes that had been El Ashang. He told Captain Rimmer, who was driving, to stop.

" They've certainly had a party here ! Look at the people. Sitting about like vultures on a kill."

They watched them, hundreds of them, sitting about in the ashes, and it was as though all the huts had suddenly been blown away into the air, revealing the people as they had been sitting within their walls. There was an air of apathy, an apathy which the Colonel had seen among villagers in that other war in France, when a bombardment had destroyed their homes.

" So these are the indomitable warriors of the Omar Bilash and the Yonis Barra ? " said the young captain.

" Don't be misled," said the Colonel humorously. " They haven't had a fire in the bush, and they'll be up to form out there, don't worry ! Let's go on to Milton's house—that's it, over there. I must find out what the devil has happened."

When Turnbull's signals had begun to arrive, Colonel Casey had been deep in a new book about China.

First Milton killed, then Sole wounded, warnings of tribal warfare and God knows what, all from that fellow, Turnbull, and all in a couple of days. He was upset about Sole being wounded. Nice chap, and it had been quite a nice party they had had when Sole had passed through on his way to El Ashang. As for Milton, well, he was not really surprised. Black crumpet and El Ashang was a bad mixture, really, but apart from Milton's being a British officer, there was also the question of his own, the Colonel's reputation. El Ashang in a few days had produced a difficult situation. He had not wanted to come, and anyway he had no troops, so he had awaited the arrival of troops from Korma bound for El Ashang, and had joined them.

There was going to be a hell of a row down in Korma over this, and a row further afield if he knew anything about Government service. It had been a wrench leaving his comfortable house. True the station was godforsaken, but he had made it home. A good supply of brandy and books, peace in the bush, and life had been happy enough. But no, these bloody wogs could not rest. They had to start something, but unfortunately had started by killing an officer. And now he would have to clear up the mess and write as satisfying a report as possible to Korma. Not that it would stop there, but it was always a good thing to paint as clear and smooth a background as possible at first, and then let the ugly bits stick themselves on to the picture until they formed the pattern. A little guidance here and there helped the pattern to form. It was a pity that Milton had not shot himself as many better chaps had done in the Colonel's experience. To get killed implied that the one killed was a good, innocent chap cut down in his prime, and the hunt had to start. Someone had to pay. Many people deserved to be killed, and the picture was better without them, but still, the murder of a British officer was a serious thing, and someone was going to pay for it. This murder of an officer would give the wogs ideas. He wondered who had burned the village. He was pleased about it, and the people looked as if they'd had enough of it. But headquarters could not take that view. Headquarters had to mix its own bitter knowledge with the gluey fiction of liberal ideas and tolerance, understanding and tact. Most men would want to shoot these bloody wogs who would not live quietly in their desert, but while the junior officers could curse the wogs among themselves, the senior officers had to look grave and speak of responsibilities and the people's rights, save in the mess, when they could get it off their chests over a few gins.

It was the freedom bug that was at the bottom of the world's troubles. All the wogs on earth were after freedom now, and it was just no use, a chap could not govern any more. The polite fantasies of schemes for uplifting these savages would eventually cause revolt. Milton's death, thought Colonel Casey, was a symptom of what was going to happen to the Empire.

The armoured car stopped and the Colonel opened the thick steel door and clambered out into the glare.

" You'd better go and quarter yourselves in the fort," he said to Captain Rimmer. " Tell Turnbull I'll see him in an hour. Tell him to come over here to the house."

" Right, sir," said Rimmer. The long, dusty convoy of trucks moved off to the fort, the troops staring curiously at the field of ashes which had been the village.

Sole was sitting up in bed when the Colonel came into his bedroom.

He smiled and the Colonel said :

" Well, I see they took a poke at you. Hurt badly ? "

" No, not badly, sir, thanks. But it hurts. A spear wound."

" H'm," said the Colonel. " Not many of those about these days. Who burned the village ? " He sat down on the edge of Sole's bed and lit a cigarette. There was red dust in his grey hair, and a fine powder of it almost hid his tanned face. The blue eyes were the same, Sole noted ; clearer, if anything. The Colonel could not have had much to drink on that bone-wearying journey across the rocks and sand. His anxiety was soothed by the Colonel's friendliness.

" The village ? Well, it just burned as far as I know, sir," said Sole. " Turnbull was in a little while ago to tell me about it. Is it very bad ? "

The Colonel could not decide if it was bad or not. Bad meant if it was bad for the people *and* for the Colonel's reputation. Good could mean good for the people and good for the Colonel, good for the Government because there was peace.

" It's not too bad," said the Colonel. " The village has disappeared, just ashes. And yet, I suppose they've asked for it. Do you mean, Sole, that the village just went on fire of its own accord ? It's strange that it should happen when it would do the most good. The burning down of El Ashang is the best distraction the people could have had, and I think it's worked. But who did it, eh ? " He laughed softly, cocking one eyebrow at Sole.

" He's off again," thought Sole. " How he enjoys everything," and yet underneath all the malicious banter he knew there was the old, experienced administrator who never was quite good enough, never ambitious enough, who had fallen back on to his failure in a kind of bitter amusement.

" Why do you think someone did it deliberately, sir ? "

" Because it's too neat, too nicely timed, that's why. And I've also got a suspicious mind, and I'm nearly always right. Intuition, I agree, is a bad thing to work on, especially in Government, but it's there inside me, like an old woman, I suppose." He laughed again and was pleased to see Sole smiling. Then he was serious and said :

" Now look here, Sole, I want your honest opinions on things round here in general. What exactly has gone wrong ? "

Sole looked away and his eyes were sombre. " This is the beginning of my real trouble at last," he was thinking. " This is where I lay myself open at last, with all my bloody chaos and confusion." He rasped the blue stubble on his jaw and turned his eyes again to the Colonel, who was watching him closely, dropping his usual mask of cynical amusement.

"I can only give you a half-formed opinion, sir," said Sole. "I was in the middle of a riot about an hour or two after I got here, and I've been in bed since. The village people began to form a mob near the fort and Turnbull's machine-gunner fired over their heads. That was the first warning we got. Then I took over. Turnbull had arrested the chiefs of the Omar Bilash following Milton's murder, and the mob was heading for the gaol. I ordered Turnbull not to open fire and left him on a machine-gun in one of the fort turrets. I went down to the gaol with Turnbull's sergeant-major, and a section of *askaris* came out of the fort and stood behind me. I warned the mob to break up, but they attacked. I fired my pistol twice, and that's all I remember. I was stabbed, the sergeant-major was killed and the mob broke into the gaol and got their chiefs out. The *askaris* left me in the lurch. They ran away." He did not mention his frightened shout to the *askaris* to open fire. It was his secret.

"Did the chiefs go voluntarily from the gaol, or were they forced to go by the mob?" the Colonel cut in, his eyes sharp now, as he entered the atmosphere of intrigue which he knew so well. Embittered chiefs, blood rituals, lion men, leopard men, old men with visions, all the Africas he had known, the Africas which had changed so much in his lifetime, but in whose secret darkness were these same forces in conflict with the Government ways—to-day, as in the past—with the brains of the white men who did not draw upon darkness for their force, but on books and papers, on history.

"I don't know how they went, sir," said Sole. "I've only just come round."

"Well, hasn't Turnbull given you a report on it?" The Colonel was prepared to be angry.

"Yes, he came in to see me, but we weren't in a fit state to do much. And I think Turnbull is feeling the strain of the last few months. I think he feels he's been let down."

" Let down ? What do you mean ? " The Colonel curbed his temper. Sole was very pale. He must remember that Sole was a sick man.

" Oh, I don't know, quite, sir. But he's all worked up. I think he's going to have a breakdown if he doesn't get out of here soon. It's a pretty horrible station at the best of times, but just lately I think it's been too much even for Turnbull."

" Why ? Do you think Turnbull is really any good ? " said the Colonel.

" Definitely," said Sole. " But not quite up to this situation. After all, what could he do ? The Omar Bilash waiting to start raiding, Milton murdered, and then waiting for me to arrive. He's played out."

" He's got no right to be played out," the Colonel said in a hardening voice. " Officers are not kept here to deal with peaceful situations, but to be ready to deal with bad ones. If Turnbull's not up to his job, I want you to say so."

" It's not as simple as all that," said Sole. The Colonel watched Sole's dark eyes beginning to smoulder. He had omitted to say " sir," the Colonel was quick to note.

" Do you think I was correct in ordering Turnbull not to open fire on the crowd, sir ? " said Sole. There was no anxiety in his voice, no call for help. Because the Colonel was angry he wanted to punish Sole with some enigmatic remark, to worry him. But he was worried about his own reputation too, and the more he thought of the happenings in El Ashang, the more he struggled to find the happiest solution of his worries. This caused him to say, " Of course, my remarks about setting fire to the village are made in fun, Sole, you understand that. Now you ask me if I think you were right about your order to Turnbull. My answer is, do *you* ? Do *you* feel you were right ? "

" Most definitely I do," said Sole. Again he had omitted the " sir," but that might mean nothing. The Colonel thought that perhaps he was too sensitive about it anyway, yet the

lack of " sir " could make a junior officer's statement sound
quite different.   An ordinary reply could sound insolent
without it.

" Right," the Colonel's mouth grew firmer.   " As long as
you feel you can explain yourself when asked.   There'll be a
stink about this, I suppose you know that, Sole ? "

" Of course," said Sole wearily.   " Beggar my neighbour
and trump cards and all that."   He was angry when he thought
of Korma.   The Colonel grunted as he digested Sole's remarks.
He gave Sole a swift, keen look.

" It won't be very amusing," he said.

" I know, sir.   I'll be in it.   Right in it."

" You're bitter, Sole.   What's the matter ? "

" Not bitter, sir.   Just sick and tired of it all.   I wasn't cut
out for the Colonial Service, I'm afraid."

" Why do you say that ? "

" I can't explain just now, sir.   But to get back to Turnbull.
I think he's going round the bend."

" You mean going—a little mad ? "

" Well, yes.   You know how it goes.   All wound up.
Wanting to hurt people.   Misunderstood.   Nervy.   The usual
signs."

The Colonel was silent.   Yes, he knew the signs.   There
was a set of signs for every type of human being who had too
much of a station for which he was not equipped.   One chap
would get slack about his meals, would give up the ritual of
the soup, the main dish and the sweet, for no matter how vile
the food and how hellish the station, it was good to keep
the rituals.   He would eat only one meal in the day, or perhaps
two, and gradually would descend to eating bully beef straight
from the tin.   Old biscuit crumbs littering the table, a book
propped up against a jam tin.   Another would start suspecting
his servants of some evil design and would end by ridding
himself of them, suspecting all about him of a share in the
evil design.   Another talked to himself and acted little plays
aloud, thinking he was unobserved.   Another wrote fantastic

to headquarters, saying he had seen a mysterious figure
fort and had received a curious communication. Every
er had a pistol, the small death-carrier which could end
tyranny of his days. Yes, he knew it all. But Turnbull
d seemed to be of tougher stuff.

" I wouldn't have thought a type like Turnbull would
get softened up," said the Colonel. " Even though he's a
ranker."

" Turnbull's type go crazy faster than anyone else when
they can't get a cut and dried solution," said Sole. " They
care far more than other people. Turnbull feels that he should
be allowed to shoot up the Omar Bilash. He hates them. He
thinks they insult the Government and everything it stands
for. He feels he knows the situation inside out and is not
allowed to settle anything. He's very worn out. I think
he's had his ration of this place."

" He should be along to see me soon," the Colonel sighed.
" I'll go and start sending signals and see if I can unravel
things. I'll be in Milton's office. Do you want any tea ?
I'll send your chap along."

" Oh, by the way," said Sole. " Turnbull claims he's got
the man who killed Milton. He says that my servant knows
the whole story and that this prisoner of his admitted to
Yassin, that's my chap, that he'd killed Milton."

" Oh, he does ? Sounds fishy to me. Don't usually catch
chaps who murder officers in their beds. But we'll see. That
could be very interesting."

The Colonel put on his dusty cap and hurried away to the
office.

" They'll want a victim urgently," thought Sole. " He
was very cagey about giving his opinion on my order to
Turnbull. Clever old chap. No commitments if possible. Of
course, they'll nail his skin on the wall, too, if they can, but
he's smart. A really smart old boy." It was always interesting
to see each man who had been involved in a trouble drawing
a curtain of defence about himself, making remarks which he

wished remembered and getting up to scratch where there had once been slackness.

Sole wanted to prepare himself, too, but he could not decide who was right. The problem was difficult, involving the spirit and the heart, not just the book of regulations. To restore order by killing? Or to do everything to avoid killing? And yet he had killed one of the mob with his pistol. That dead man became suddenly more important than Sole's regret for his death. He saw for the first time that he had denied his own order to Turnbull, had killed, and still had lost the chiefs, had caused the Government to be defeated and humiliated. Yet he had only killed one. Turnbull would have killed a hundred. But still it was a matter of principle, not numbers of dead.

" Oh, Christ," he said aloud. " Where does it start, and where does it end ? "

Had it all begun that day before the war when he had sat on his first murder trial, hungrily watching the accused African's bewildered face, and wishing he could depart from the burden, the duty which would claim him when he must write his decision, guilty or not guilty ? Was it then, or was it in bed in the dark, silent night beside his sleeping wife, nursing the wounds of a deeper defeat, the burning wound, the gulf between this woman and himself ? Habit, kindness, pleasure, not even time could bridge that gulf, for beyond the flesh there was nothing, only silence. But he could not end their sullen marriage because someone else would have her again, so he must win, over himself and over her, crush himself. Was that when this sickness began, this inability to use the power of government in achieving obedience and order ? " They," as yet unknown, officers drinking gins in Korma, officers not yet briefed for the task, " they " would descend on him like vultures. " What time was it when he heard that ? " " What time was it when Turnbull said that ? " " What was the man's name ? " " Had he ever seen him before ? " " I suggest that you meant this when you said

Sole sucked his lip. "Oh, Christ," he said again. ... won't rest until they've got a victim."

...ng in Milton's office, Colonel Casey called for the ...reter, the clerks, the messengers, the tribal retainers, the ...I gaol warder, and for Sole's servant, Yassin. When they ...he salaaming, some pious and grave, some, to the Colonel's ...nd, over-familiar and careless, he sent the head warder to ...t alone in another office, and the tribal retainers he instructed to sit under a tree outside the office. It was some time before the Colonel's tall and restless interpreter found Yassin. He looked ill, and he was restrained from throwing himself at this stern-looking Colonel's feet.

"I am alone," he cried, "alone. My master is dead and I am alone."

The Colonel laughed to discomfit him. "I am alone, too," he said, "and yet my master is alive."

The assembled staff heard it keenly, read it and laughed heartily until the Colonel frowned. He had created the atmosphere in which he was to work. The word ran quickly from this office to those sitting under the tree, who passed it to the village. The Colonel was a clever one. He laughed when he said hard things. In the office the staff hushed as they watched Yassin twisting himself like a snake under the Colonel's words. Milton's interpreter, a small copper-skinned Arab, pointed covertly to the damp footmarks which Yassin's movements revealed on the polished stone floor of the office. To those about him the interpreter whispered, "He is afraid. He is going to tell lies. That is why he is afraid."

"Shut up, you," said the Colonel in English. "You are an interpreter, not an interrupter." The Arab laughed and dropped his eyes. Regretfully, the Colonel knew that his sally would not translate. It had to be told in English.

"Well," he said to Yassin. "What of this man who killed the officer? What did he say?"

"I do not understand," whimpered Yassin. He wiped his sweating palms on his dirty, khaki shirt. "No man said anything to me. Which officer is dead? My officer is dead too."

"Your officer is not dead," said the Colonel calmly. "A man told you he killed the Captain who used to sit in this office. What did the man say to you?"

"I do not know who worked in this office, *Effendi*. I am a stranger here. I am sick."

"A man told you he had killed a British officer. What did he say to you?"

"I do not know any men here, *Effendi*. I am a stranger. Someone is trying to injure me with words."

"Oh, Jesus," said the Colonel aloud, "give me strength." His voice was quiet, but his eyes were beginning to sharpen and light up.

"You told Captain Turnbull that this man admitted he had killed an officer."

Yassin burst into tears. "No, no," he shouted. "No. It is a lie that men have said to injure me."

The Colonel could imagine the slim, hard tribesmen, their hands on Yassin in the darkness, their voices saying, "One word from you, pig, and we will cut you into pieces. Silence or we will cut you up."

"You are frightened," he said to Yassin.

"Yes, *Effendi*," sobbed Yassin. "I am frightened. I am frightened."

"Lock him up," said the Colonel to the interpreter. "Lock him in the gaol." Yassin began to bawl like a camel as he was dragged from the office. "No, *Effendi*," he shouted, "no. Men have injured my name."

"Turnbull was on the right track," thought the Colonel, "but up a gum-tree. Shut mouths and careful lies. All the old stuff. Oh, Jesus, give me strength." He began to question the clerks. The office grew cooler as the sun fell slowly beyond the fort, and the Colonel went on with his inquiries. He knew that by now a definite impression of him and his ways with men must have passed to the people of the village. They would now be discussing the best kinds of approach to him, for they would want help. Well, it would be fifty-fifty. No information—no shelter and no grain. No chiefs surrendered —no salt, no tea, no release from the threat of communal fines. He would show them who was who and what was what. The destruction of the village was a gift from God. He would make use of it. When he decided he was ready, he said to his interpreter :

" Go among the people and say that I want the chiefs who left the gaol to come to my office. I have many words for them. Good words and bad words. Tell them to come now."

" Shall I take soldiers with me, *Effendi* ? "

" Take no one. Take yourself only. And use your brain." The interpreter was pleased. He too knew the value of a destroyed village, of grain stores and shops reduced to ashes. He represented the Government which had grain and salt, now suddenly more powerful than guns and prisons. It was a joke after his own heart. The Colonel was a cunning one.

" Good, *Effendi*," he said, and, hitching up his snow-white robe, he hastened to the ashes of the village, practising his words on his tongue.

" Hungry ones," he would begin, " Hungry and homeless ones, I have words for you——"

" That fellow Turnbull, he hasn't turned up." As he looked at his watch, the Colonel was annoyed. He told Milton's interpreter to call the Captain from the fort, and when the interpreter had gone he opened Milton's diaries and read idly here and there. Then he reached for a book marked " Chiefs and Notables." This was the dossier of all the chiefs, paid and unpaid, hangers-on, the hopeful and the disappointed, those whose grandfathers had been chiefs under the Sultan, and those who had a following and a message but no power. The notables were those men with influence, either with Government, and in the Government's pay, or who had influence within their tribes and were unpaid. There were

Mullahs and those the people called learned men, alleged saints, and those who had given up everything to work for Italian money and medals, and who still had influence among a people who could not yet take to the British. Beside each name were Milton's written comments. "Very willing, anxious to help the Government. Has a grievance because the British will not let him carry the sword awarded to him by the Italians. Continually requests permission to carry his sword." Another, "Very intelligent and untrustworthy. When he comes to see me always wears the medal of the Star of Italy, despite my orders against doing so. Led a large number of Italian troops (*askaris*) during the last Italian campaign. Does not like the British. Says we have cold hearts." And another, "Claims he studied at Al Azar in Alexandria. Sent there by the Italians. Lived in Italy five years. Very pro-Italian. Difficult type. Will not obey orders."

After nearly an hour the Colonel's interpreter returned and said that the chiefs were ready. He implied that they feared the Colonel.

"Tell them to sit under the tree," said the Colonel.

He came to the page he sought. "Kalil Abukir, Chief of the Omar Bilash. Age about sixty. Translation of Italian record inserted here. 'In 1940 offered the Italian Government his tribe against the English despite his long resistance to our Government in the past and despite certain difficulties the Government experienced in the past in recruiting soldiers from his tribe. Said he would fight the English because he wanted " *Onore* " with the Italian Government. Later accepted English Secret Service money for information which he gave to informers. No proof. No action taken beyond careful watch and promotion in pay. Cavagliero of the Star of Italy for services rendered during the campaign against the Negus.' " Milton's notes followed. "One of the Mad Mullah's leaders, wounded in the legs in action against British forces between 1910-1916. Hates the British. Feeling towards Italians warm. Absolutely unreliable. Difficult to understand. Powerful personality. I think he hates all white men. Intriguer. Continually stirring up feeling against the Yonis Barra."

The Colonel sighed and turned to Milton's notes on the Chief of the Yonis Barra.

"Very willing. Trustworthy. Surrendered all his tribe's arms after Italian withdrawal. Likes the British. Needs help against the Omar Bilash. Dislikes the Italians."

"Well, well, well," said the Colonel aloud. Milton feared Kalil Abukir who was a personality, and his bit of stuff had been a Yonis Barra woman. Putty! Like all men when there was a bint involved, Milton was putty. "Well, well." He lit a cigarette and tried to remember the name of a Chinese general who had once surrendered his army on condition that he could keep his favourite concubine. And what did it matter now? It did not matter at all. Only the specialist knew of the Chinese general and of all the others throughout history. But Milton mattered despite all that, because his little dreary lusts had now involved a colonel and two captains, and the Colonel's peace had been destroyed and his future threatened.

"If only we had a few commissioned eunuchs we could use up here," said the Colonel in English to the tall, black *askari* who stood at ease by the door. "What a difference it would make, wouldn't it?" The *askari* came to attention, not understanding a word of the Colonel's question. "*Effendi*!" he said.

"Go and tell my servant to bring me some brandy and glasses and water," said the Colonel in a mixture of three dialects.

"*Effendi*," said the *askari*, and went off to obey.

When it was dusk the thin, sad breeze sprang up, spattering sand against the doors and windows. The Colonel sent for a lamp. "*Effendi*," said the interpreter, "the chiefs are still under the tree."

"I know," said the Colonel, smiling. "I will call them when I am ready." He poured some brandy, smiling to himself. The chiefs would wait under the tree for as long as he wished.

He knew what it was like for the chiefs when catastrophe had come upon their people. The people plagued their chiefs to approach the Government for help. These Omar Bilash chiefs were in a difficult position. Having escaped from gaol they did not wish to rush to the Government for help, though eventually they would have to humble themselves, or defy their angry and homeless people. Rather than await their voluntary approach, the Colonel knew he had been clever to send for them so that they came at the Government's bidding. The brandy heightened the warm feeling of pleasure he experienced as he pictured Chief Kalil Abukir, sitting hunched under the thorn tree, drawing his robe tighter as the keen breeze found his ageing bones.

The Colonel was raising his glass to his lips as Turnbull entered the office. He was hatless, so he did not salute the Colonel but half stood to attention. His face was drawn and greyish white, and his eyes reminded the Colonel of high fever and hysteria.

" Turnbull ? " he said. " Why have you been all afternoon coming to see me ? " His expression was severe, the thick, grey brows drawn down over his eyes.

Turnbull took some time to answer. He appeared as if he had just woken from a deep sleep.

" I didn't know you were here, sir," he said in a low voice. " I've been having trouble with myself lately."

" Trouble with yourself ? How do you mean ? And sit down over here." The Colonel pointed to a chair on his right behind the desk. Turnbull walked across and sat down so close to the Colonel that he could see the red dust on the older man's face.

" By God ! You look done up, Turnbull. Do you feel all right ? "

Turnbull did not reply to this question. Instead he said, " Well, have you heard Sole's story ? " He stared defiantly at the Colonel and then half smiled. The Colonel was annoyed, but fought against it.

" Did Sole tell you I was going mad ? " Turnbull's smile had gone.

" Will you have a drop of brandy with me ? " said the Colonel, seeking time to think. The fellow was definitely a bit touched.

" Thanks, I will."

" And will you add ' sir ' occasionally when you speak to me ? " The Colonel's voice was soft, conversational.

" Yes, I will."

" Thanks," said the Colonel. He poured the brandy. He felt certain that Turnbull was hardly listening to what was said to him. He saw the Captain's thick fingers squeezing and unsqueezing. H'm. The chap might really have gone starko, ready for the strait-jacket.

" I didn't know you were here," said Turnbull. " I wouldn't see anybody because of what happened in the cell." He sat forward and leaned one arm on the desk. " You know that bloke's pretty tough. Tougher than me, anyway. I had to pack up but I know he's the chap all right."

" Is he ? " said the Colonel pleasantly. " What did you do to him ? Did you ask him the right questions ? " He was guessing but confident that Turnbull was speaking of Milton's suspected murderer.

" That's just it," said Turnbull. " I've got the wind up at last. This bloke's the worst I've ever seen. But I know he did it. But what can I do ? Can't raise a finger round here, anyway. You ask Sole, he'll tell you." He laughed, looking into the Colonel's eyes. " But they stuck a bloody spear into him *and* he still thinks he's right. ' Don't hurt them,' he says. ' No violence.' But he shot fast enough when they came to do him, did he tell you that ? No ? Oh, yes, he shot fast and killed one too, right through the face. And what about Sergeant-Major Abduruman ? Got to bury him to-morrow and I only planted Milton just before they did for Abduruman.

Sole's all right, though, that's the main thing, isn't it ? " He took the brandy from the Colonel, who wanted to pour water into the glass. " Yes, please. Not too much though." The Colonel watched him from under his brows as he poured the water. " Quite starko," he said to himself. " Quite starko."

" What was I saying ? Oh, yes. Abduruman. Two of them he bayoneted before they got him. But no firing by order. Did Sole tell you about my deserters ? Oh, yes. But I got them back—without rifles. Just a detail, a mere detail. And then there was me sitting on a gun I could not fire. I demand to be placed under arrest." He finished the sentence calmly and looked straight into the Colonel's eyes before raising his glass to drink. He seemed to have forgotten what he said for he smiled and said :

" Did you have a good trip up ? "

" Splendid, thank you," said the Colonel. Yes, this chap was what Sole called " round the bend." He gave the impression that he might scream at any moment, or do something violent. But Turnbull seemed to grow calmer, though more off-hand towards the Colonel.

" Yes," he said thoughtfully. " We've had quite a nice time here all told. I'm the only one untouched. Milton, Sole and Abduruman have all had a bashing, but not me, yet."

" No," said the Colonel. " You've managed to stay in one piece, haven't you ? "

Turnbull laughed pleasantly. He looked much older than his forty years now.

" Yes. All in one piece," he said.

" One piece my foot," said the Colonel to himself. " You're quite, quite barmy, son." Aloud he said :

" Anything particular on your mind, Turnbull ? "

Turnbull thought about that for half a minute. " I've had plenty on my mind, but I've chucked it all up now. I worried a lot, you know, sir." The Colonel wondered why he had put a " sir " in just there. " I worried a great deal, but for nothing. When it came to the push I found rotten officers, rotten troops and rotten, bloody people who took their rotten chiefs from under my nose. The only one worth anything was Abduruman, and I wonder how the poor sod stuck it so long. I simply had to pack up, especially after the village burned down." He laughed for a few seconds, as if to himself. " Poor chaps, no homes, no food. They've only got rifles and royal blood." He drained his glass and put it on the table.

He could not tell the Colonel of the strange forces which he could feel shaking him inside, as though they would leap from him and reveal themselves to the world, shaking their fear and failure like flags. He had a pain in his mind and he knew that if he let it, his body would shake as if in the clutch of a virulent fever.

He wanted to go away because he could not do what he still knew was his duty despite the seeds of doubt which Sole had scattered in his mind, but mostly because the savages had won. They had won, outside the gaol, and in his bed where his own savage had lived his surrender for him.

Looking at the Colonel, he envied him. He knew he could never look like this man, and the Colonel's look was a reflection of the things he thought and did, part of an affectionate contempt for the people he ruled. He felt the weight of the badges of Captain on his own shoulders but false, making him look what he was not. It was this suave knowledge which even Sole had that counted, the right to rank and the background that goes with it. Turnbull felt shut out by the Colonel's friendliness, which resembled that of a battalion commander's attitude to his regimental sergeant-major.

Then his mind rambled away again, following its own worries, fears and secrets. He wanted to tell the Colonel about Aurella, to confess, to report his lapse, but why ? For the Colonel it would just be a funny story, he knew, proving that men were only human. But for Turnbull, Aurella stood at the back of his mind, like a dark accusing figure, the plunderer of his pride.

The Colonel saw him trembling, but ignored it, and Turnbull stared vacantly at the cigarette burns on the desk.

" Have another ? " said the Colonel. Turnbull refused politely as he took the bottle and poured another drink for himself. " I don't really think I will," he said in a serious voice, looking at the Colonel directly. He drank, and the Colonel burst into a roar of laughter, unable to control himself, and Turnbull laughed with him. He had taken a liking to the Colonel. A human sort of chap, and he looked reliable too.

He did not ask the Colonel what amused him. He seemed to forget things quickly, and the Colonel looked serious again when Turnbull said, " When are you going to show these blokes the flag ? Don't you think we've had enough humiliation already ? " He bared his teeth for a moment, and the Colonel stared back at him thoughtfully. He heard Turnbull's soft, nervous sob and it worried him.

" How did you burn the village, Turnbull ? " he said in a warm, friendly voice. Turnbull looked at him for several moments and then smiled.

" Me burn the village, sir ? " he said. " Good God, no. Not me. Why should I do that to all those harmless people who are our best friends ? Why ? I ask you that, sir ? Why should I do a thing like that ? " He did not blink under the Colonel's assumed kindliness.

" An old sweat you may be," the Colonel was thinking. " But can you refuse praise ? We'll see, eh ? "

" Because it's solved the whole situation, that's why," the Colonel told him. " It's perfect. I thought it could only be you who'd done it. It's broken the trouble in the town for us. They will now do what they're told. They need the Government, and I imagined you'd done it to bring them to heel."

Turnbull did not reply at once, and the Colonel searched his face, waiting for Turnbull's admittance. " I only wish I had now," said Turnbull at last. " When you put it like that, I see the value of it. But if an officer did a thing like that off his own bat, surely the Government wouldn't back him over it ? " His eyes, deep set and cold now, were innocent as they looked into the intrigue in the Colonel's face.

" Naturally, the Government doesn't hear everything, Turnbull. A fire like this is just a fortunate accident, that's all, and is reported as such. If you had fired the village and quietened the town as *well* as punished it at the same time, as has happened here, naturally I wouldn't tell the Government that—unless it was necessary." " Now will you bite, you bastard ? " he wondered.

" I wish I *had* when you put it like that," Turnbull replied. He smiled as the Colonel smiled.

" You mean you didn't set fire to the village ? "

" No, I didn't." Turnbull sipped his brandy.

" This is not a Court of Inquiry, you know," said the Colonel, having one last try.

" Oh, no. I realise that, sir."

" I see." The Colonel could hardly control his irritation. Seldom was he wrong about men. And this one was barmy, but he had a mind like an adding-machine. He poured another brandy and called for the chiefs.

CHAPTER SIXTEEN

A LITTLE ageing Arab came to the door of Sole's bedroom and asked for permission to enter. He spoke good English.

" Who are you ? " said Sole warily.

" I am Hashim, Captain Milton's interpreter, and now you are my officer, *Effendi*," said the little man, advancing to Sole's bedside. "I know you have been wounded. Are you feeling well, *Effendi*?"

"Yes, thank you, Hashim." Sole examined the Arab's face. It was sad and resigned, and his large and intelligent eyes inspected his new master quickly, before they dropped again. He knew he had worked for a master who was discredited and corrupt, and he had shared in that corruption, but he had hope for a new life under this new master. It was something he could not discuss with Sole. His future was in Sole's hands.

"I have brought the chief of the Omar Bilash to see you. He has not stopped all afternoon asking me to bring him to you. His name is Kalil Abukir. He says there is much trouble. The Colonel has sent for all the chiefs of the Omar Bilash but is not ready yet to see them. Kalil Abukir wishes to see you before he sees the Colonel." Hashim folded his arms inside his robes and looked down at Sole's bandaged chest. "He says he knows you are a man of peace, *Effendi*. You will understand the trouble here."

"I cannot see a chief if the Colonel wishes to see him. It's not right. You know that, Hashim. What does he want to say?"

"He wants your advice, *Effendi*."

"My advice?" Sole showed his surprise. "But I thought this Kalil Abukir was a man of war and asked no man's advice?"

"The town is in ruins, *Effendi*," said Hashim, and a faint smile passed over his brown face. "Kalil Abukir's plans are all changed by the fire, but it is too late. It is said that the Omar Bilash are moving in thousands and have already attacked the Yonis Barra at the wells. El Ashang is burned down, the Government does not like the Omar Bilash, the people of the town are angry with their chiefs because of the fire, and the chiefs do not know what to do. And now the Colonel is here. He may send the chiefs into exile and the Omar Bilash will have all their camels taken by the Government."

" But what does Kalil Abukir want me to do ? " Sole forced himself up on to his elbow and Hashim helped him tenderly.

" If you see him, *Effendi*, you will find out."

" Then bring him quickly, I will see him."

" He's outside, *Effendi*. I will bring him."

When Sole saw the tall, thin, turbaned chief approaching his bed, he felt pity for Milton. " God, what a face ! " he thought. Kalil's black, emaciated face was set in lines of terrible gloom, ravaged as if by a hunger for death, and Sole could see through to the mind which moved behind the chief's hooded eyes.

" *Salaam*," said the chief, his lips moving his mask for a second so that Sole could see the white teeth, big and moist like those of a young man. Kalil wore a white turban and a white robe, and the blackness of his face seemed to be lit by his eyes which reminded Sole of an eagle he had once seen watching him from the branch of a tree.

" *Salaam*," he said. He fought hard against the power of this man's presence. He could understand why Milton had wished to please him.

" If you wish to speak you must be quick," said Sole coolly, " for the Colonel awaits you." Hashim translated this.

" Let us speak in Italian," said Kalil in that language.

" How do you know I speak Italian ? " said Sole, forgetting to hide his surprise. The chief squatted on the floor, his back to the wall.

" There are men here who know you," said Kalil. " Traders who have known you in the South."

" Did they tell you I have a soft heart ? " Sole smiled, enough bitterness in his smile for the chief to see. " Did they tell you I am easy to deal with ? "

The chief said nothing but looked gravely into his eyes and waited. This disturbed Sole and made him feel foolish. He saved himself quickly.

" What do you want ? " he said crisply.

" This is a land of blood," said Kalil. " I have come to
you for words. I have come to offer you the rifles which
my people have if you will help to bring peace. Fire has
destroyed the town. The people are homeless and hungry.
And in the desert the tribes have begun to fight. The Government has been against us always and the people are bitter."
He waited for Sole to speak, but Sole was lost in his examination of the chief's sad and cruel face. He was thinking how
unfortunate it was that no painter had ever captured this
finely cut, ageing and devilish face, cast in disappointment
and death.

" You are defeated, Kalil. Is that it ? " he coaxed the
words until they were kindly. The chief took a long time to
reply, and he flexed the long, crooked fingers of his right
hand, listening to the crack of the bones, brooding on the
white man's words. Then he gave Sole a terrible smile, the
fine lips curving back slowly until they revealed the mouthful
of perfect teeth, and his eyes lit up lazily and then died again
as he contemplated Sole.

" It is interesting that you should say that, lying defeated
in bed," he said in his best Italian, " while I am able to walk
about." Then he moved rapidly away from jest, giving Sole
no time for shame or annoyance. " I am old," he continued.
" The Government will punish me, but I wish to arrange
justice before I am imprisoned."

" You were glad to be in gaol, were you not ? " said Sole.
" You had arranged all. Your people would defeat the Yonis
Barra, and your job was done. You wanted peace. When a
man is old, exile is peaceful if he is too old to fight."

The chief's eyes were mocking and Sole could see that he
had struck home.

" You have the murderer of the Captain in your gaol,"
said Kalil. " He is a Yonis Barra. The village is destroyed
——" Sole interrupted him and the chief seemed amused.

" You say the murderer is a Yonis Barra. We will find out
his tribe in good time. But you must not try and confuse me

by playing me against the Colonel. It will not succeed. If there had been no fire you would have taken the chiefs into the desert among your people and led the raiding. Is that not true? But the people would not let you, would they? Because they were like beggars among the ruins of the town. And remember, we got the Captain's murderer without your help."

"There are a hundred things that could have been," said Kalil. "But if you will call a conference of all the chiefs now, of the Omar Bilash and the Yonis Barra, and give us justice, then we will surrender the rifles. You will find also that the Yonis Barra killed the officer."

"You mean that the Government must feed and support your people. That you be given the wells, and the Yonis Barra driven from them? Is that it?"

"If you will help the people, we may let the Yonis Barra share the wells. We think that the Colonel is a hard man. He will be hard on us. If you speak to him for us, there will be peace and justice."

"A hard man and a soft man could give you justice, do you think? The Colonel is hard, as hard as yourselves. You fear that, don't you?" Sole's heart quickened as he surveyed the opportunity Kalil's offer gave the Government. But he knew what obstacles lay in the path of the Government's acceptance. What was a Government? A Government was men, all kinds of men, some more powerful than others, and a policy had always to be considered in the light of the Government's dignity, its face, its reputation.

"If you offered me your rifles, Kalil Abukir," said Sole, "what would you want in return?"

The chief replied at once. "A conference of the Government and the chiefs to decide about the use of the water-holes, and help for the people of El Ashang who are in misfortune."

"And what do you want for yourself?"

Kalil moved his eyes up from Sole's chest to his face and stared into the officer's eyes.

" The removal of Captain Turnbull," he said.

" Ah," said Sole, feigning a surprise greater than he felt.
" Ah." Kalil closed his eyes with pleasure while he cracked
his fingers. Then he lifted the hooded lids again and looked
at Sole.

" No," said Sole. " You have gone too far. You cannot
gamble with Government officers as if they were here to
please you." In his heart he knew that Kalil was right, but
in any case, when Turnbull and Sole went, as go they must,
in the very near future, the people who knew Kalil's plans
would see the hand of their chief in it. Kalil was right about
Turnbull, just as Turnbull had been right about Kalil. God,
the mess of it all. The answer to all this, Sole thought, was
evacuation of the country so that the people could rule themselves, even if they killed each other for ten years before their
blood-lust was exhausted. But no, the game must go on. He
took up the cards again and dealt one which he was sure Kalil
could not trump.

" You are defeated, Kalil. Is that not so ? "

" There is one thing you have forgotten," said Kalil, and
his voice betrayed pride and triumph. " The Omar Bilash
have begun to drive the Yonis Barra from the water-holes.
They can be stopped. By the Government troops, who will
take months to end the trouble, or by my word now."

Hashim, who understood Italian too, was shocked. He had
never heard a chief speak in this way to an officer, Italian or
British. He waited for Sole's anger. But Sole smiled and
said :

" The time is not right for these words. You are speaking
too strongly. Our conversation must end. That which I have
said and *salaams*." Kalil did not move.

" Will you not ask the Colonel to call the conference ? "
he said.

" You have just told me that the Omar Bilash have begun
to attack the Yonis Barra. The Government does not yet
know of this and yet you know of it. That means that you

gave the order for the attack. It is out of your own mouth. You are defeated, Kalil. You caused the killing, not the Government."

Sole knew that the Government machine would go its way, trucks, troops, rations, punishments, denial of the use of wells, fines and proclamations. It could not and would not bargain with Kalil Abukir. Because he, Sole, would like to bargain with Kalil Abukir and save all the waste and bitterness and misery which operations against the Omar Bilash would entail, he was not fit to govern, he knew. It was necessary to work with power to keep power, and he no longer knew his own mind. He must escape from this kind of work. He must find work which would save him from these decisions which involved the lives and fortunes of people whose minds and hearts he did not understand. The Colonels and the Turnbulls were right. It was their world. Their kind had made it, and their kind must defend it in the way they knew best.

While he watched Kalil's face closing up into its mask of hate and disappointment, he said to himself, " I am weak, I am not able to decide what is right. I am like so many others to-day, anxious to give justice to all but unable to say what justice is." He felt sick and humiliated as the chief got to his feet.

" I will go and listen to the Colonel's words," Kalil told him insolently. " I will know what he is thinking and what he is saying."

" You will understand him," countered Sole with a look of scorn which he did not really feel, "because he understands you and he knows how to punish you. He is a clever Colonel."

Kalil sneered and walked slowly from the room, leaving Hashim to gape at his new officer, an officer whom he could not understand. To be insulted and say nothing showed breeding, and it showed cowardice too. To say things which meant many things showed cleverness, but it showed vanity too. There were many things which a man could not under-

stand, but this new officer was more difficult than them all.
" You can go," said Sole.

Hashim could smell a good story in all this. If his favourite
coffee shop had not burned down he would have recounted
it to those always incredulous ones this very night. But it
would wait. He bowed and left.

" I will not interfere," thought Sole. He would say nothing,
but let the Colonel apply the ancient methods. The strong
hand and the sincere eye. What was it the Colonel had said ?
" The Empire is a filing system ! " It was the Colonel's
Empire. It belonged to people like the Colonel, who loved
it, believed in it, fought for it, and who had begun to destroy
it by staying as they had always been, by being unable to
change. He remembered one elderly administrator from India
whom he had met on leave in London. He said, " We've
made India a place fit for white men to live in, and—for those
Indians who like to live as gentlemen, the chaps who work
with us. We've brought peace to India."

Sole was impressed by their sincerity and was sorry for
their bewilderment in a world which did not want them any
more. They would be pensioned off eventually, and the
world they loved would fade and turn brown in their snapshot
albums. In the ashes of El Ashang was a picture of the world
of those *Sahibs*, those *Effendis*, *Bwanas*, *Thakins* and *Tuans* who
had eaten and lived well in a time when they were powerful ;
but like ghosts of resentment the uneducated masses whom
they had ruled were now screaming on the horizon.

CHAPTER SEVENTEEN

WHEN the clerk had gone to call the chiefs, Turnbull raised his eyebrows.

" The chiefs, sir ? " he said. " I think you'll have a job getting them to-day. They'll hardly come after escaping from gaol."

" My dear chap," said the Colonel patiently, and with a look of pain in his eyes. " I've had the bastards sitting out there for hours under a tree. They're cold now, and miserable. They've had hours to think it over, and they're worried. You don't think, do you, that I'm going to sit here and drink brandy and wonder if I can get hold of our own bloody chiefs who are here to obey our orders. I am the chief in these parts and the people know it, and if I don't get obedience when I send for them, then they know that I will not rest until I have broken every manjack of them, and have them sieving sand for a pastime far from their beloved country." The Colonel said the last sentence to himself again, savouring it, and he saw interest in Turnbull's eyes.

" I wish we'd had a bit of that around here before," he told the Colonel. " But it's too late now."

" It's too late for *you*, you mean, Turnbull," said the Colonel brutally. " Much too late. But you're not a political officer anyway, and it's not your job to carry out policy. Your job is to do what the political officer wants, but any ideas you may have had about policy you can now forget."

" My ideas were the same as yours," said Turnbull indignantly. " But I had to listen to Milton and Sole, and I've had to watch everything I believed in spat on by bloody savages. But I've had enough." Turnbull's voice broke and he went on speaking although no words came from his mouth.

" You need a good holiday," said the Colonel in a fatherly

way. " You're run down. You've done your best. But you'll have your chance to talk down in Korma. There'll be an inquiry into everything that's happened up here, and you'd better have the answers ready."

" I'll be ready," cried Turnbull. " I'll be ready all right."

" That'll do now, Turnbull." The Colonel was firm and kind, like a father caring for his wayward son's welfare. " That's quite enough. Quiet now. Go and lie down until I come and see you. Do nothing. Just remember that I will be doing everything you have so long wanted to see done. Everything."

Turnbull got to his feet and held the edge of the desk to steady himself. There were some unshed tears in his eyes as he thanked the Colonel.

" Quite all right," said the Colonel. " I'll be across to see you later." As Turnbull left the office, the Colonel tried to decide what to do. Turnbull was in the state he had seen many men in before, and he might shoot himself. Should he let it happen ? God no, Turnbull had done nothing to be ashamed of. If Turnbull's ideas had been too big they were now shrunk and he was having a breakdown into the bargain.

" Call my driver," he said to the *askari* near the door. The driver, who had been absorbed in a clerk's stories of the day's doings, came in from the courtyard.

" Tell Captain Turnbull's servant that his officer is very sick, and that he is to stay near him until I come. Do you understand ? "

" Yes, *Effendi*." They all understood, his look implied. Everybody knew that Captain Turnbull was no longer himself. He had a *djinn* in him, the *djinn* which makes men do strange things.

" Then hurry off and do as I said." The Colonel dismissed him and took the batch of signals from an Arab corporal, who introduced himself as the man in charge of the signallers in the fort.

The Colonel signed the receipt and asked the corporal how

he found life in the fort. The corporal said it was good, and it was safe too. The Colonel smiled.

" You don't tell men in the village what you read in the signals, do you, Corporal ? "

" No, *Effendi*," the corporal lied with an expression of serious concern on his face. " And these I have given you are all in code."

" I know," the Colonel told him. " They will all be in code from now on. Thank you."

The Colonel knew what would be in one of the signals. It would almost certainly contain Korma's agreement to his suggestion that he send Turnbull and Sole to Korma, for " rest " and for the inquiry. Also it would request his earliest report. Well, he would leave Sole and Turnbull to the wolves if that was what they wanted, though they could quite easily blame everything on the dead Milton. All save the attack on the gaol and the rescue of the chiefs. That was Sole's pigeon and Sole did not seem very upset about it. Not yet anyway. He was probably still enjoying the sensation of finding himself alive.

Korma would now have received his signal written in the afternoon informing them that Turnbull showed signs of a nervous breakdown. That would be one in the eye for the army, always so certain that the political officers could not manage situations or handle people. He did not know what to say about Sole. Burning the town had been a better idea than firing on the mob, but then again if they had fired on the mob there would have been no attack on the gaol, no wounding of Sole, no killing of the sergeant-major. The Colonel tried to imagine the panic in the Headquarters Messes in Korma. Up here where violence of some kind occurred every day, one got used to it and it took something like the killing of an officer or the storming of a gaol to arouse a real state of apprehension. The killing of tribesmen by tribesmen did not really matter. In many ways it was a good thing and it made the people dependent on the Government, and it rid the world of people who were a nuisance. The killing must never get too big, though, or out of hand. And the officer had to show concern when he heard that a tribe had killed ten men of another. The chiefs thought that the Government was really worried by tribal killings, but they did not realise perhaps, that the Government's main worry was to get hold of the rifles which might be turned on the Government when the tribal killing was over. That was the real problem, the rifles. And the Colonel had decided he would solve that problem now.

"The chiefs are still waiting, *Effendi*," said the interpreter from the doorway. "They are here by the door, ready."

"You can bring them in now," said the Colonel. He hid the bottle of brandy and the glasses in a drawer of the desk. Then he waited until he heard the sound of the chiefs' sandals entering the office and he began to light a cigarette, slowly and with care. By the time he had finished and was puffing at it they were lined up in front of him. He could almost feel their anger in the air. The Government power could make itself felt in many ways. By being kept waiting under a tree at the Government's pleasure when it was certain of victory, men felt its power. Chiefs who had defied the Government and had escaped from its gaol, and then awaited the Government's pleasure, were admitting defeat by waiting. The flames which had burned the town had burned the power of the chiefs too. "What a cunning old soldier you are, Turnbull," the Colonel mused as he coolly surveyed the chiefs, "and able to resist admitting it, too. They'll have a hard time breaking you at the Court of Inquiry, nervous breakdown or not."

The chiefs offered no *salaams*. They glowered and shifted their feet. One or two rolled their eyes fearfully in the lamplight, but the majority tried to look belligerent, and the Colonel waited until the silence was almost unbearable. Then he spoke.

"You have brought me a long way," he said, " but now

that I have come I shall stay until there is no more trouble here. Do you understand that ? " He blew smoke into a swirling blue cloud and waited for effect. They were silent. They wanted him to show his hand. This one was an old one with grey hair and he was cunning. Many young officers in his position would make long, angry speeches, full of threats and words about the Government's power. Or they would say that the people could have one more chance to show their willingness to obey the Government. But old ones were usually different. They had survived many years of Government and were all the more cunning for it. That was what age meant, survival where others had gone in the battle. Like chiefs they were, and the older they grew the more they knew that people were children who must obey their fathers. This one had a tight mouth and eyes like an old hawk.

The Colonel studied Kalil Abukir's face.

" Who are you ? " he said.

The interpreter hastened to explain.

" Shut up," said the Colonel without looking at him. " Let him explain himself."

The interpreter said, " Who are you ? " and Kalil turned his big, hungry bird's eyes on the interpreter, trying to dominate him.

" I wish to speak to the Colonel alone," he said sharply, and the interpreter translated.

" No," said the Colonel " No, he will speak here, before the others. There will be no more private talks. No more honour. No more pride. No more threats. There will be only the Government's word and obedience. Tell them that. Tell all of them, not just this one." He nodded at Kalil Abukir, who scowled at him, but the Colonel was watching the slight hint of concern in Kalil's hot eyes.

The chiefs coughed and moved their feet as the interpreter almost shouted the hard words. They began to look like men who were hoping for the best.

" You have killed an officer," the Colonel told them calmly.
" You have killed a sergeant-major. You have escaped from
custody. You have wounded another officer, and you have
defied the Government. You have also stirred up trouble
between your tribe and the Yonis Barra."

" There is a man in the prison now, in the army prison, who
killed the officer," said Kalil Abukir. " He is of the Yonis
Barra. He killed the officer because he was ordered to do so
by his chiefs."

" We have the word of a servant that this man killed the
officer. And the servant will not talk. It is not enough. Nor
is it enough to say that the Yonis Barra killed the officer.
That may be another lie to confuse the Government, but the
Government will not be confused." The Colonel banged his
hand softly on the table to drive home his words. Kalil
screwed up his eyes in scorn.

" Are we to be blamed for everything? Are the Omar
Bilash to suffer for everything? "

" Yes," said the Colonel, " for everything."

The chief turned to the others and began snarling words
at them in great excitement. The Colonel brought his hand
down with a crash on to the table. " Silence ! " he shouted.
They obeyed him, but they were still excited and Kalil Abukir
stabbed his black finger in the air.

" Justice is for all men," he rasped. " For all——"

" Silence," the Colonel shouted in feigned anger, and the
chief sank back into himself, drawing in his rage until it had
been absorbed again behind the narrowed eyes and the
hollow, black cheeks.

" I am tired of lies and trickery," the Colonel told them.
" I will listen no more. Instead I will tell you, and you will
listen. I give you one week from to-day to surrender the
rifles of your tribe. One week only and no more."

" And if we have no rifles ? " said Kalil angrily. " What
then ? "

" You'd better buy some and give them to me in that case."

Kalil did not like being called a liar in that way and he bared his teeth when he saw the interpreter shaking with laughter.

"It is no use lying to me," said the Colonel. "If you do not bring me the rifles, the village will starve. You will be kept here with them and not sent away as you hope. That makes you think, doesn't it?" He knew that his last remark had shaken them. To be left among their homeless and hungry people, to be forbidden to leave what was left of the town, harassed by the people and cursed for their failure to get Government assistance—to be left there was far worse than exile. Especially after the promises of tribal glory which they must have made daily during the last month. The Colonel lit another cigarette and watched them.

"What will you do when you find that it was the Yonis Barra who killed the officer?" said Kalil.

"That case will be investigated separately. If we find that the Yonis Barra killed the officer we will punish the Yonis Barra. But I want you to understand that the days of lies are over. I will find the truth if I have to question every man in El Ashang. For that is why I am here." He smiled at Kalil, who wore an expression of contempt which could not quite conceal his worry.

"So you will give us nothing until we bring rifles?" said Kalil.

"Nothing. And I am now going to work out the size of a fine I will put on your tribe. There are many things I have to work out."

"Do you know that fighting has started near the wells?" said Kalil, bringing out his surprise weapon. "Many have been killed yesterday and the fighting continues."

"Really?" said the Colonel contemptuously. "And what do you want *me* to do? Send soldiers to stop it?"

"Do you not care that men are killing each other?" the chief asked him sharply. He remembered the imploring eyes of the fat one, the dead officer, trying to bring peace to the people. The fat one had spoken of nothing else every time he had called the chiefs to this same office.

" If men wish to kill each other despite our warnings, it is their affair. I will take one hundred camels from the Omar Bilash for every Yonis Barra man they kill. But I will send no soldiers. Instead I will let the soldiers eat the sheep of the tribe who started the trouble. I am comfortable here and you are not. Remember that. I know you ordered the fighting to start. Now you can order the fighting to stop. It is on you, not me. Do you understand ? "

He could see the hate and misery in the chiefs' faces. If the people of the town did not receive help soon from the Government they would stone these chiefs, and the chiefs knew it. He enjoyed their misery, for it was seldom that the Government had such a victory over arrogance and lies. But he would still have to be careful, for these chiefs had lived through years of trickery and subterfuge in order to stay themselves under foreign Governments. He was certain he had won but he would not be careless.

" Every afternoon at three o'clock you will visit me," he said to Kalil. " You alone. And you will report progress. Every one of these other chiefs will carry the news to your tribe that they have one week to surrender their rifles. The chiefs will be taken in an army truck to the wells and the truck will wait there until they return to it with the news that surrender of rifles has begun. And do not twist my words, not one word, when you carry my orders to your people. If you make a mistake the consequences are on you and on your people. You will all suffer. Now go."

There was no way out for Kalil Abukir but to accept defeat. It choked him.

" Tell the head warder he can go now. I won't need him," the Colonel told the interpreter. As the warder came into the office from the adjoining room the chiefs were filing out, and when they saw him they began to chatter to each other. The Colonel laughed and Kalil Abukir noticed it. He frowned and hurried from the office, consumed by his shame and humbled pride. He was beaten this time, but he would see to it that the Yonis Barra suffered too, if not in dead men even at the cost of one hundred camels each to the Omar Bilash, then in the future, when all this was forgotten and the English were gone from the land. There was plenty of time. The first thing was to get peace, not so much between his tribe and the accursed Yonis Barra, but from the grumbling people of the town, already making threats about what they would do to the chiefs if they did not get help for them.

In silence they made their way to the remains of the village. Hundreds of small fires twinkled there, and about these the people were huddled for warmth. Some of the women were lamenting, their sorrow moving on the wind like the howling of far jackals.

The first news of the Omar Bilash raids had reached the village and the men of that tribe tried to exult over the reported numbers of Yonis Barra dead. But their women and the elders spoke of food and shelter, and the men cursed them and then began to blame their troubles on the chiefs who had been too hasty.

It would be another day before the Colonel heard the news officially, and one or two more before he got a proper report, which he would expect to receive from Lieutenant Cuddy. But it was now common gossip in the village that Cuddy's platoon had not made contact with the raiders. Cuddy had been dead for days, but the desert, and those who lived in it, did not care.

CHAPTER EIGHTEEN

ON the third day the first rifles came in. Some sulking warriors carried them to the office through a lane of women who clamoured for food. The Colonel had food ready in the store but would hold it back until the first fifty rifles had been surrendered. He knew that none would die of starvation, but there would be hunger and want, the pinch of which even these hard and frugal people would feel. He sent a gift of money to the miserable beggars who congregated at the gate of the mosque. Its aloofness from the town had saved it from the fire, and the beggars and orphans who had had nothing to lose in the fire sent their leaders to thank him and to wish him many sons.

" *You* are my sons," the Colonel told them. " I am past having sons and I am too busy with other men's wickedness to create sons of my own seed." They laughed and said that they would eat the money he had given them.

" Poverty is hard," he told them. " I am sorry your life is hard. But it is the bitterness of war and killing and lies which afflicts you here. The poor who must beg at the door of the mosque are God's children and the Government's children. You Moslems and we Christians are all sons of Adam and people of The Book."

A chief of an obscure tribe who had come with the beggars looked cross at the Colonel's words.

" It is no disgrace to be poor," he said with dignity. " I begged at the mosque when I was a boy, for I was poor. It was not war and killing which made me poor. It was the will of God."

" Ah," said the Colonel in English to the wall. " The bloody voice of the warrior." He closed his lips tight and then said that the interview was over. It was stupid of him to have relaxed his defences. One slight waver and they were in through the chink, waving their pride like a flag of defiance.

" I want to speak with you," the old chief complained. " In a time of honour I was given none. When all were rewarded I was friendless. I have kept silence until——"

" Go," said the Colonel, pointing to the door.

" When the Government needed its children I was there. It was I——"

" Get out." The Colonel stood up, towering above his desk. The heat and his own irritation brought the sweat to his forehead. " Who's this bumbling fool ? " he demanded of the interpreter.

" He is an old chief who wishes to help you in the punishment of the Omar Bilash, *Effendi*. His tribe is even more noble than that of the Omar Bilash, but they have few men. They are holy too, and because of this no man ever kills them."

" Write his name down. If I need him I will send for him." When the interpreter translated this the old man's eyes lit up. He wagged his hands and walked back to the Colonel's table, selling himself, one eye feverishly beckoning the interpreter.

" Get out," the Colonel shouted. " Out of my sight." The interpreter pushed the protesting chief through the office door. When he returned he said :

" There are many small tribes who wish to help in the punishment of the Omar Bilash, *Effendi*. They wish to offer their help."

" Let them wait." He knew that the almost overpowering camel-hunger had come upon the smaller tribes. If the Government seized the great camel herds of the Omar Bilash there would be opportunities for all. The price of their help would be so many camels for each guide, spy, or scout supplied. The great tribe was to be humbled and the small could spit on the warrior of yesterday. " Vultures," said the Colonel to the interpreter. " Vultures."

" They are hungry, *Effendi*. They have children but no

camels. If a man could make camels they would make them instead of children. That is what men have said."

Then Sole came into the office, a loose jacket buttoned across his bandaged shoulder. He was still pale, and the curious, furtive expression which the Colonel had noticed before was still present in his dark eyes.

"Up and about at last? Good!" The Colonel smiled and rearranged the pen-tray on his desk. "How do you feel?" Then, without waiting for a reply, he told Sole that the Omar Bilash had begun to raid the Yonis Barra near the water-holes. He seemed pleased about it. "We'll get a report from Cuddy soon," he said.

"Many dead, sir?"

"Don't know. And how's Turnbull to-day? I haven't seen him since yesterday morning when he seemed very quiet, but quite mad, if you ask me."

"I think he's had it, sir," Sole told him gravely.

"Had it? Sole, I don't like these expressions. Just what does 'had it' mean?" He gave Sole a quick glance of annoyance and then sat back to listen.

"Sorry. I mean he's going mad. He's sacked his servant and his cook. He thinks they want to do him some harm. When I went in to see him about a quarter of an hour ago he was in bed, and he hasn't shaved for a couple of days. He thinks he's going to be put into a strait-jacket, and he told me that the prisoner, the chap who's supposed to have told my servant he killed Milton, he thinks the prisoner is the fellow who killed the sergeant-major. He talks about Sergeant-Major Abduruman more than anything else, and he's developed a pet phrase about it. 'The humiliation of the soldier' is the phrase. 'Everything is aimed at the humiliation of the soldier,' is how he puts it. He's in a pretty bad way, sir."

The Colonel made a sound of impatience with his tongue. "Always the same with these chaps when they have a strain put on them. They go to bloody pieces. It's sad, I agree with you, but it proves what I've always said. This is a job for gentlemen, people with background and breeding. It comes out, I tell you. The wog has spotted the flaw in Turnbull and he knows it." The Colonel sucked his teeth thoughtfully and then rapped a question at Sole.

"And what about you, Sole? What was that stuff you talked to me about not being cut out for the Colonial Service? And you also asked me if you were right to forbid opening fire on the crowd. What does it mean, Sole? Have you got the wind up?" His gaze was keen and frank as he asked the question.

"*You'd* call it wind up, I expect, sir." Sole looked away, sighing as if weary. "I'd call it doubt. I can't do this stuff any more, that's all. I can't believe in it. Can you understand that, sir?"

"No." The Colonel snapped the word through his teeth, looking at Sole as he would look at a traitor to some cause he prized.

"We've made such a mess of the world that I can't preach to these people any more. I mean people we call savages, primitives, any of the people in our bloody Colonies. It's impossible to wave the flag and read the Bible to them any more."

"Who asked you to read the Bible to them?" The Colonel spoke to his subordinate impatiently, demanding an answer.

"Oh, I mean the Christian messages and the light for the heathen stuff. The idea that we've got it all solved. I can't believe in my job any more, I mean as an official. I can't get near the people. I'm either the big, kindly father to them, or I must punish them, often when I don't wish to. When I consider how we are beginning to appear now to the people we've always treated as stupid children, I just can't do it any more. Look at Europe to-day! Do you understand what I am trying to say, sir?"

"Quite well, thank you, Sole. The sooner you leave the Colonial Service after the war, and this job as soon as possible, the better for everybody, if you feel the way you speak. You sound a bit *bolshy* to me. *Are* you a bolshy ? "

Sole smiled and said, " No, I don't think so. I just can't stand preaching a lot of stuff of which I have become ashamed, that's all, sir."

" And if we all felt as you do what would happen to all these people who depend on us for protection and help ? "

Sole thought about it. What *would* happen to them, he wondered.

" I don't know, sir. Probably they'd kill each other for a bit. Starve a bit. Do stupid things in plenty. But we'd feel better. *We'd* be free, too."

" Oh, for Christ's sake," said the Colonel heatedly. " You sound like one of these Oxford Group fellows, like that fellow we had in Korma last year. Wanted to morally rearm the Italian Army to fight the beastly Germans. What you're saying, Sole, is that you've lost your nerve, and if you ask me, you've got bolshy ideas too. Was that why you forbade Turnbull to fire ? Because you had the wind up or because you didn't want to hurt our poor black brethren ? I ask that apart from whether you were right or wrong."

" I find I am unable to open fire on civilians, sir," said Sole. His face was flushed, and he felt foolish before the hard soldierliness of the Colonel, for whom the world was simple, for whom the Empire was a sacred thing, a sacred club of which he was an elderly member.

" You'd better tell them this in Korma," the Colonel said, his eyebrows cocked. " They'll be interested, I'm sure. You may need a good rest. It may even be that your wound has upset you."

" No," Sole told him patiently, " it's nothing like that. I began to hate this job in 1938 when I'd only been a year or two at it. I hate the Empire and I don't seem to think as a good European should about the niggers, about the dagos and all the rest of it. It's very difficult to explain this. What

I'm telling you, sir, is that I'm a failure. But it doesn't distress me. Not at all."

"That's very nice for you," said the Colonel innocently. "It saves you a lot of worry as to whether you're right or wrong, doesn't it?"

Sole sighed and did not answer.

"There'll be a plane, probably to-morrow." The Colonel spoke as though their conversation had not taken place. "There'll probably be a doctor on it. He can look at Turnbull and at your shoulder. And he'll take you both to Korma. I'll give you all the mail. You and Turnbull will have to report to headquarters on arrival, and I'll be here to finish the job." He said the last words grimly, and for a moment Sole wanted to quarrel with him, but he held his tongue.

As far as the world of power was concerned, as far as the broad outline of policy was concerned, and as far as the savages in the desert outside knew, the Colonel was in the right. He was a man conscious of certain responsibilities to the backward peoples, as long as these people did not annoy him too much. To kill men of another tribe did not condemn the savages in the eyes of the Colonel. But to work against the Government, to want the fantastic new toy, freedom, that was treason and merited distrust and the badge of enmity.

"What time do you think the plane will come, sir?"

"Don't know. Do you think Turnbull's well enough to have a drink this evening?" Pleasantly, the Colonel put his hand on Sole's shoulder as he rose from behind his desk.

"We might go across to him later and see, sir." Sole was touched.

"All right," said the Colonel, removing his arm suddenly, embarrassed with himself. "I don't like your ideas at all, Sole. You've shocked me, but I've found that most young men of your age seem to feel the same as you do, more or less. They are ready to fling aside the work British officers have done for centuries. They are ashamed to have an Empire. Why is that? Can you tell me why you feel as you do, Sole?

What is it that makes you unashamed to admit these things ? Remember, I'm not dealing with you over what has taken place here, but what you've told me has given me a lot to think about. They are terrible things you've said."

" It's impossible to explain it to you, sir. You look on the Empire as a religion. I can't. Not many of us can nowadays. And I can't believe that British officers have done their work for hundreds of years because they looked upon it as a vocation. It was a good job with plenty of freedom and decent rewards, and it still is. The officers liked their jobs. Nobody objected to them. And they either believed in the Christian religion or pretended they did. But those days have gone, sir. I have no sense of mission, I only have a sense of feeling ridiculous in trying to pretend I represent something splendid and good."

" Christ, I never thought I'd hear this stuff from an officer," said the Colonel. He was upset, not angry, but concerned and somewhat sad. " If it's not splendid and good, then what is it you feel you should represent ? "

Sole looked into the older man's thoughtful eyes and said, " Something useful, if we really want to use it, as a means of uniting Europeans, Africans, Indians and all the others. But as it is, it's something stupid and untrue. It tells the natives with one voice that we are all the same, and with another that all the rooms are engaged, all the tables are full. The South African guests might object and we'd lose customers. To really rule the Africans, the Indians and the others, you have to despise them, or if they get too clever you have to try and make them think that they can be just like Englishmen, the finest thing there is as far as the English in Africa and India are concerned. It is people like you, sir, sincere and sure of yourselves, who have destroyed the Empire you built, because you never tried to identify yourselves with the people. They have to come up to our level, by loving the Government, before they really meet us. We can't go to them. It's not done. Turnbull believes in your kind of Empire, sir. He has to. It's a matter——"

The Colonel cut him short. " I'm going to report these views of yours, Sole. I must. They are seditious." His voice was cold and full of contempt. " I will not stand here and listen to any more. I wonder if I shouldn't put you under arrest. But I asked for your views, and now I've got them. Having heard them I must say I sympathise with Turnbull and what he must have felt while trying to work with you. What you have said makes a lot of things clear to me now. We'll say no more now. I'll see you in Turnbull's room at six-thirty. Have you got a bottle of whisky or brandy you can bring ? I'll bring one too." Then he turned away and began searching for a file, his straight back seeming to express his indignation.

Sole knew that the Colonel's report could almost certainly secure him a release from the Colonial Service, a career he had so idly chosen. The war had eaten his half-formed ideas, had chewed his mind, leaving him like a cud in the sand. He saw himself as someone who could not explain his fears and doubts because his colleagues would be hostile, either because they violently disagreed with him, or because the holder of such views was not good to know, was an embarrassment, causing silences by his presence in the mess and the club. And he had no plan. He could only say that he hated the Empire in which he was supposed to work in peace, and fight for valiantly in war.

He saw it in the future as a huge slum on the edge of the West, negroes in torn trousers leaning against tin shacks, the whites of their eyes gone yellow, hands miserably in their pockets, tired of vice, sullen with boredom, and gone in the teeth. And the white women twittering with excited anxiety as they imagined the dark, powerful river of African seed outside the window, the flat throb of the drums like the savage heartbeat of the new Africa, the ruined beast. The savages of El Ashang had no place in that frightened empire, for their desert would not change. But they had shown him his weakness, as he knew they had shown Turnbull his. He could

not go back to the Africa he had briefly known. Better to
be some kind of craftsman who could teach the Africans how
to lay bricks, or a doctor, an expert on soil erosion, but not a
white man with a message. His message had died when he
first felt the slow, almost indistinguishable resentment in the
eyes of the detribalised Africans who had come before his
court. They had begun to hate the white men and had begun
to worry about skin, woolly hair, thick lips, feeling like comic
apes before the white man. They could not part their hair
like other men, it was too woolly, so they cut the partings
into the hair with razor blades. Remembering it all, he knew
he could not go back when the war was finished, and he
could not do any job which entailed the ruling of primitive
peoples.

The Colonel would report his words direct to the General
and he would be asked to explain. He did not know what he
would tell them, but the Colonel knew what to explain and
he would pen it with great feeling.

" I'll go, sir, if you don't need me," he said, half standing
to attention.

Without turning round from his perusal of a file, the Colonel
said, " Oh, Sole. One other thing. You shot one man, didn't
you, during the affair at the prison gate ? "

" Yes, sir," Sole replied in a low voice.

" Can you explain that ? I'll have to mention it, of course."

Sole took some time before replying, and the Colonel half
turned, one eyebrow quizzical, mocking.

" I lost my nerve, sir," said Sole defiantly. " I was unable
to do anything else at the time. I did it before I realised it."

" Interesting. And if you had been able, would you have
changed your mind and ordered machine-gun fire on to the
crowd when you lost your nerve and fired your pistol ?
Think, Sole. I want your honest opinion."

It was the most formidable question he had ever been
asked. There were two answers. One was " Yes, I would
not then have been harmed," and the other was " No, I

would stand by my first decision," and the second answer was untrue, for he had fired his pistol and killed a man. His hand had raised the pistol, informing his brain of what it had done just after the jolt of the pressed trigger. The Colonel would laugh at him. He did not know what to say without sounding like the Colonel's Oxford Grouper, all sincerity and bared breast and long hair.

" You would have fired, wouldn't you, Sole ? " The Colonel pressed him gently for the answer.

" Maybe I would," he said. " Maybe I wouldn't, sir. I can't say."

" No," the Colonel agreed. " You can't say. That's what's wrong with you, Sole. You talk like one of our jumped-up plumber-politicians frothing about exploitation in the Colonies, but when it comes to the push you don't know what to do. Well, we'll talk no more about it now. I'll see you at Turnbull's place at half-past six. We'll crack a bottle of brandy." He smiled sadly and turned away, like a father whose son has admitted to evil.

Sole walked back to the house across the hot, yellow shale, screwing his eyes up against the sun glare, feeling miserable, and a faint longing for his wife awoke in him, an angry need of her. He began to visualise the Court of Inquiry, the Court Martial. No matter what form official displeasure took, he was certain that he would find himself with a platoon of infantry again in some desert or jungle, alone in himself and free of policy and of the civil power. Turnbull would understand that, Turnbull with his broken dream of power.

The smell of camels was strong in the hot air and Sole watched them ambling across the sand to the wells on the edge of the town. The camel-drivers cursed them or cooed to them as the mood came, driving the herd in a half-circle before them. The women, wet and glistening, pulled on the long, hide ropes with the men, drawing up the hide bags full of water and pouring them into the troughs. This was their life, camels and water, from birth to death. It seemed a pointless life when viewed against the teeming ideas of Europe, the concrete and the steel and the rubber, that surge of life and death which sucked hundreds of millions of people into it, but this life of camels and water was something for which these nomads would fight and die. The white men were in their way, enforcing a peace upon them which tried to destroy their economy which was based on the spear. The spear, used properly, could multiply a man's camels, but the white men hanged a man who used a spear, if he caught him.

Sole greeted the camel herders but they did not reply. Instead they regarded him quietly as he went by. He meant nothing to them and they knew he had nothing to give them. One blew his nose into the sand and coughed, and another made his wife cover her baby's face, for the white man had the evil eye. Sole looked hard at them, wishing he could be their friend, but the barriers were too great. He could be like the Colonel, a ruler with definite ideas and therefore a force among them, but he could not be their friend. They did not need him. They knew what they wanted, and he could not give it to them.

CHAPTER NINETEEN

THAT night they drank until the Colonel's servant, Abdi, went to the kitchen and gloomily told the cook that the Colonel would not eat. The Colonel would get drunk and the two Captains would be drunk before him. He announced this to the silent kitchen, where Belai rolled his eyes in the flickering light of the stove. Belai had said little all the evening, even when Abdi had told him:

" Your Captain is sick in his head. It is said that he has lost his way. Do you do all for him that he deserves ? "

" I do all," Belai had said, " but he is not as he was. He is sick in his head and his heart."

When Belai found out that Aurella had slept with his master he had closed himself in a grim silence, especially when the *askaris* had joked with him about it. The blow to his pride had hurt him as if Turnbull had beaten him. His master had handed himself over to the tongues of the people, and Belai suffered their taunts in a kind of half-understood grief. Now he wished to go from here, and when he heard the news that the two Captains were to fly to Korma, taking him with them, he was glad. His problem now was whether he would stay in Turnbull's service or not. Turnbull's aloofness from these savage people had been his pride, and he had shared in the fear and respect his master had inspired. Now it was gone and the Captain was changed, even becoming slovenly and careless. He smoked more often now, and sat in his armchair as though asleep, though his eyes were open, staring before him.

Now Belai watched the old servant, Abdi, who, when he had made his announcement to the cook, turned to Belai and said :

" You will be in the aeroplane to-morrow with the two Captains, and they will be sick, like all white men who have taken too much of their Christian drink. Take with you two or three bottles of cold beer in the aeroplane if they have any left, for it is cold beer which white men desire when they are sick of drink. Do you hear me ? "

" I hear," said Belai.

" Have you packed all for your master ? "

" I have."

" I have packed for Captain Sole," said Abdi, " for his idle thief, Yassin, will rot here in the gaol for many weeks. Let them drink and talk to-night, and when it is cold and nearly dawn, they will call for food. It is often so when the Colonel drinks with other white men. He kills his stomach."

In the living-room where Aurella had so often played the gramophone for Milton the Colonel was animated, his blue eyes glittering in the cruel white light of the pressure lamp.

He was telling Sole and Turnbull of incidents in the sun-beaten, lonely, official life he had lived in the deserts and jungles of Britain's empire.

Turnbull had drunk enough to half close his willing eyes, and Sole lay back on a couch, holding his glass on his chest. He, too, had drunk enough, enough to forget the ache of his wound.

"I won't think about her," he was saying to himself, "I have enough on my mind."

The Colonel did not care any more whether they listened or not, until Turnbull sighed loudly.

"Anything wrong?" said the Colonel. "Are you falling asleep?" His voice sharpened as when he spoke to a sulky chief. "If you're bored, go to bed."

Turnbull slowly focused his eyes on the Colonel, who could almost see into the worry and the apathy behind the Captain's haggard face.

"Well, it's *your* empire, sir," said Turnbull earnestly, but with a difficulty that might have been due to the brandy, or to the soft rain of failure which had been falling on his mind for several days.

There was a tense silence and Sole rolled his dark eyes until they could see the Colonel's mouth twitching and the searching look with which he seemed to be reading Turnbull's face. The only sound was a sucking noise as Sole drank some brandy.

"What do you mean, Turnbull?" There was an urgent demand in the old man's voice and there was suspicion too.

"Can't we talk about something else except the bloody empire?" said Turnbull petulantly. He turned to Sole. "Hey, Sole, what do you say? Haven't said a word all evening, you haven't." Then he looked at the Colonel again. "I feel sick," he said. "Terribly sick all of a sudden." They gazed at each other, the Colonel nibbling the end of his still trim moustache.

"You can't carry your liquor, Turnbull," he said quietly.

" You're tight. Can't carry your liquor, that's what it is."

Then Turnbull began to cry, silently, his eyes wide open, and large tears spilling slowly from the grey eyes on to his cheeks. The Colonel did not turn his eyes away from this sight. He gripped his knees and squinted at Sole, who was staring at the ceiling, idly swilling the brandy about in his glass.

" What's the matter with you ? " the Colonel asked Turnbull crossly. Turnbull shook his head from side to side, saying nothing, and the tears flowed on. The Colonel became embarrassed and called angrily to Sole, " Sole, what's the matter with this chap ? He's blubbing here in front of me."

Sole sat up and saw Turnbull's wet eyes turned to him. He got up and laid his arm round Turnbull's shoulder.

" He's had his chips, sir," said Sole in an icy voice to the Colonel.

" His chips ? " The Colonel raised his eyebrows and made a motion with his head, telling Sole to take Turnbull away.

" Yes, his chips," said Sole. " He was very fond of the Empire, you know. Talking about it must have upset him."

Turnbull bent his head and began to shake softly, no sound coming from him in his quiet grief.

" Are you trying to be funny, Sole ? " said the Colonel interestedly ; he cocked one eyebrow in the way which Sole knew so well.

" No, sir. But your exploits which you have been describing have upset old Turnbull here, and there's the booze and the Omar Bilash and the rest." He spoke into Turnbull's ear now. " Come on, Turnbull, let's go. The plane comes for us to-morrow morning. Let's get some sleep."

He led him from the room, saying good night and thanks. The Colonel mumbled a reply. When they had gone, the Colonel poured himself another large brandy, extra large this time.

" Just enough to flatten me," he said aloud to the empty room. He heard Abdi coughing in his sleep on the verandah.

Then he drank the brandy at one gulp, gasping with pleasure, and he leaned back in his chair, hardly seeing the debris of ash-trays filled with cigarette ends, the ash spilled in patches among the spilled brandy on the tables.

" Fancy Turnbull blubbing," he said. " There's nothing like a good blub when you're out of your depth, I suppose." He fell asleep, slumping in the chair, unable to feel the cold of approaching dawn. He growled in his sleep, and settled down like a man on an uncomfortable railway journey. The fierce light beat on him and a rat came out of its hole, followed by others. They began to play in the shadows and the sleeper did not disturb them.

CHAPTER TWENTY

FROM the door of the office the Colonel watched the big plane disappear into the sky. He felt ill and stiff, and he had been short with Sole and Turnbull. Turnbull had almost forgotten to salute him as they turned to climb into the plane and Sole had nudged him.

" I wish you luck," the Colonel had shouted over the roar of the engines. " You'll need it." He gave them a savage smile.

Now they were gone and he would stay here until some other idiot was sent to make another mess. He made a mental promise to himself that he would arrange things so that El Ashang would trouble him no more during the remainder of his service in the country.

He would go back to his quiet fort, far from El Ashang, back to his books and to Abdi's smooth routines, but not until he had clamped a lid of peace on the Omar Bilash and the Yonis Barra that they would never shake off again.

He settled down at the desk, soon forgetting the ache in the back of his head. It would be a long time before he had

another binge, he reflected, and next time there would be no
one to cry in that horrible silent way which he had seen last
night. It had been quite revolting.

After reading Milton's files and diaries, the Colonel sent
for the chiefs of the Yonis Barra and went straight to the
point. He could only make guesses, but he saw at once that
he was right. He pretended that he knew the tribal identity
of Turnbull's prisoner, Fara, but that he was puzzled as to
why he should have killed Captain Milton.

They wished to speak about the Omar Bilash raids at the
water-holes, but he would not let them.

" Would one of your tribe kill an officer just to steal his
watch ? " he said incredulously, his eyes full of friendly surprise. They looked hard at him like old hunting-birds at
their master, and while they thought about that, he went on :
" Captain Turnbull thought the prisoner was an Omar Bilash,
but as soon as I knew he was one of your men, a Yonis
Barra, I sent for you, for I know how this news will hurt your
hearts."

They nodded approvingly. The oldest chief, who resembled
a mummy in a green turban, said :

" Yes, *Effendi*. He is a famous thief and he must have
done this for the watch. Did he take the officer's watch ? "
The others strained their ears for the reply, and the Colonel
took the watch from a drawer of his desk and held it up for
them to see. They were relieved, but showed only slight
interest. They had had many secret meetings since the
Colonel's arrival, and had discussed agonisingly the arrest of
Fara. They had sent Aurella back to her clan, over a hundred
miles away, with orders not to return to El Ashang until
they sent for her. Furiously she had fought them, but she
knew, when she looked at the circle of their old, silent faces,
that they would kill her if she did not go. Their plan had
worked. The Government had blamed everything on the
Omar Bilash, and this interview, while it showed them that the
Colonel knew the tribe of Milton's murderer, did not indicate

that he was going to punish their tribe for what he obviously considered to be one man's personal crime. But they were wrong.

" You only knew for certain during the last two or three days that this man had killed the officer, I know," he said regretfully, " and it must have worried you greatly, for I know you are faithful to the Government. I know you handed your rifles in to the Government when we conquered the Italians. If you had known earlier about this man's crime I know you would have come to me, wouldn't you ? "

They stared at him, grateful, yet each waiting for another to speak. The Colonel turned his innocent, kindly eyes to the old chief in the green turban, encouraging him with lifted eyebrows.

" That is so," said the chief. " We have kept the law, and that one of our men should do this is shame upon us. But he is a madman and a thief. The Government must shoot him."

" How did you know for certain that this man had killed the officer ? " the Colonel asked in a soft voice. " Did you make certain of his guilt so that you could inform me, knowing that the Government might punish the whole tribe if you did not ? You are wise men and I think you wished to save your tribe from the Government's anger." He gave them a friendly smile as if he were one cunning old man praising the cunning of another. They were struck dumb, regarding him suspiciously, and though he waited they gave him no reply. He had gone in too deep there for a moment, he knew at once, and he raced back to the friendliness and trust of the first sentences.

" Well, he is a bad man and he will be punished." He picked up one of Milton's diaries, and when he had bent his head to read they exchanged swift looks, one eye on the interpreter, who, knowing his master's ways, had forced himself to look away so that he should not disturb the Colonel's game.

The chief in the green turban was anxious about the prisoner.

Almost certainly the prisoner would not talk ; the fool ought never to have been caught, but torture by a determined officer might drag words from him. The old chief had twice suggested introducing poison into the prisoner's food by bribing an *askari* to do it, but the other chiefs were afraid of the plan. And now, while it seemed certain that the Government would hang Fara as a thief and murderer, there would be a trial, and the Government, in its curious way, might find some evidence that would incriminate the chiefs. The old man did not know what to do. Silently, he called a curse on to the grey head of the Colonel, who was idly reading as though he had forgotten them.

The Colonel was in no hurry. After a day and a night in gaol listening to the big rats gnawing his sandals, Yassin had sent a message to the Colonel indicating that he would tell the truth. He told the Colonel of how Fara had come to steal clothes, and had boasted of how he had killed the fat Captain. He put his thumbprint on the typed statement, and on the advice of the Colonel returned to the gaol until, joy of joys, he could return to Korma with Captain Sole in a few days.

Yes, the Colonel had plenty of time. The tribal retainers brought him plenty of news and one of them had attended a Yonis Barra meeting about the arrest of Fara. The Yonis Barra were very worried. The Colonel knew that Aurella had been sent away, and he knew also that it was common talk in the town that she had deserted Milton and had spent a night in Turnbull's house.

" Captain Turnbull had been too long without women," the town said, " and Aurella is a white man's toy."

The Colonel wondered how far he should probe, whether he should not be satisfied with what he had. A burned and cowed village. Frightened chiefs, Milton's murderer in gaol and rifles beginning to come in. It was greedy to want more, but because Milton had been stupid about the Yonis Barra he was tempted to hurt them in order to show his impartiality.

He decided that he should be satisfied, but he could not resist frightening them. It would worry them for days, this thought thrown from the brain of the Government.

" Next," he said, " I want the woman brought to me. The woman Aurella whom you sent back to her people. She has offended the Government."

The faces of the old chiefs slowly froze as they took in the words and tasted the soft bite in the Colonel's tone. Then the Colonel rose, and they followed suit, hushed, apprehensive. Everything seemed to be perfect. The Omar Bilash had enraged the Government and the use of the water-holes by the Yonis Barra had been all but condoned, but now across the pleasure of this had fallen the shadows of " the fat one " and Aurella. They said nothing, but the chief in the green turban bowed his head slowly to the Colonel and led his colleagues from the office.

The Colonel radiated happiness as he watched them go. It was as if he had squeezed their hearts for one brief moment and he savoured again the sensation of triumph, like a man who has tamed a group of savage animals who have defied all but him. He felt the thirst for the long drinking he had promised himself. The machine of official revenge was in motion and smoothly it would absorb the fears and doubts, the jealousies and ambitions of the chiefs of the two tribes, who were not sure how much he knew and what he would do next. Impartiality, even apparent impartiality, was the most cruel weapon of all in the white man's armoury, for it implied that all men were evil and probably had motives which did not please the Government. Impartiality killed pride before the desk and poured freezing water on to the fire of intriguing certainty. The Colonel rubbed his hands together when he thought of the crushing power his frown could now wield, the trepidation his stare might arouse or his smile dispel. He was only a failure as far as the gazettes and the decorations were concerned. He did not require the praise of men, for there was satisfaction enough in being able to spit in the face of savage arrogance or to force obedience where it had not been known before.

Without Turnbull's fire, though, it would have been harder, it might not have been possible. The killing in the bush had begun, and Captain Rimmer with his armoured cars should soon report contact with the chap no one had seen for months, Lieutenant Cuddy. The killing could go on for a while as far as the Colonel was concerned. Useless to burn petrol in fruitless chase in an effort to show Governmental displeasure. The satisfaction of memory warmed him again when he relived the blow he had struck Kalil Abukir, those words about one hundred camels' fine for every Yonis Barra tribesman killed by the Omar Bilash. Frantically Kalil Abukir was seeking to stop what he had begun. He would end as the butt of his tribe's hatred. " Kill," he had told them, " and fear nothing." Now he cried, " Stop, each one you kill costs us one hundred camels."

The Colonel chuckled. He could kill their women, abduct their children, arrest their warriors and they would cry out, but to take their camels drove them into a grief which those who had not seen it would never believe. He heard the bugler blowing the sad notes of *Tamaam* parade and he went out into the sandy courtyard and looked across the low wall at the flag, beyond which the sun was sinking. It fluttered slowly down as the bugle notes resounded on the bitter desert. The sun was never allowed to set on the Union Jack, and the Colonel stood to attention, bareheaded, pride and loneliness stirring in him. The sun did not set on the flag, he reflected sadly. But it had begun to set in the hearts of those who saluted it and the Empire it had represented, and he could not understand that terrible sunset.